Grilled Cheese

AND

Goblins

NICOLE KIMBERLING

BLIND
EYE
BOOKS

Grilled Cheese and Goblins
By Nicole Kimberling

Published by: **Blind Eye Books**
1141 Grant Street
Bellingham, WA. 98225

Cover Art by Dawn Kimberling

First Edition October 2018

ISBN: 978-1-935560-56-2

This book is dedicated to Tommy Jordan.
(Yeah, that checks out.)

Contents

Author's Note

Special Agent Keith Curry of NIAD is only one of many, many characters in the shared-universe property of the Irregulars.

Several other wonderful creators have expanded and enriched the world. Ginn Hale, Josh Lanyon and Astrid Amara have all contributed novellas to the original volume (*Irregulars*, Blind Eye Books, 2012).

Tommy Jordan produced an audio-drama podcast featuring Special Agent Keith Curry's daily case files—as explored by his twelve-year old cat sitter—called *Lauren Proves Magic Is Real!* (available for free on iTunes and SoundCloud). Jordan is also writing and producing a forthcoming podcast set in the Irregulars world called *Silver-Tongued Cypher*.

If you like what you read here then please check out my fellow creators' amazing works.

CHERRIES WORTH GETTING

"We must not look at goblin men,
We must not buy their fruits:
Who knows upon what soil they fed
Their hungry thirsty roots?"
—Christina Rossetti, "The Goblin Market"

For reasons unknown to Agent Keith Curry, food carts proliferated on the mostly rainy streets of Portland, Oregon, like they did in no other city in North America. Their awnings sprang up like the chanterelles in the Pacific Northwest forest, sometimes filling an entire parking lot.

Keith preferred visiting these eateries because many had permanently rented parking spaces and settled down like oysters cementing themselves in place. The parking lot near his hotel supported one of these colonies, so he thought it might be as good a place as any to begin his investigation, though he didn't expect to find much.

Rarely did venues like these serve human flesh.

Hidden places, places with concealed entrances, front businesses with makeshift kitchens, art galleries—he found contraband in places like these, but the average health-department-certified cart?

Probably clean as a whistle.

Keith stepped up to the cart—a converted Airstream that sold nothing but grilled cheese sandwiches—and ordered a "Kindergartner"—American cheese on white bread. A slight vibration came from his wrist and he glanced down at his watch. It was a prototype designed to alert a human wearer of the presence of extra-human beings. Now the numeral seven shone blue, which indicated that a faerie had come within fifty feet of him, setting off his proximity alarm. Briefly, he scanned the people queueing up to the food carts, wondering which customer hid a fae nature. Business heels lady? Sparkly hippie juggler, busking? Little blond kid eating a snow cone? It could be any of them—or maybe all of them. Probably more than one faerie was abroad, actually, this close to the upscale condos in the Pearl District. Faeries didn't concern him this time around. What he needed to watch for was the red three that indicated the presence of goblins.

He returned his attention to the amiable, bearded guy currently buttering the bread that would shortly become his sandwich.

"You mind if I ask you a question?" Keith asked.

"Go right ahead." The bearded guy slapped the bread down on the food cart's small but impeccably clean flatiron and applied the cheese.

"Do you know where a guy can find any flesh joints around here?"

The cook laughed. "There're too many strip joints to count, man. Just google 'stripper.' You can get any kind you want."

"I don't mean naked ladies. I mean bloody protein."

The cook looked up at him in mild disdain. "Not really my style."

"Not that into meat?" Keith asked casually.

"Not into performance art shit," the cook replied. "I believe in cooking food, not eating it raw in front of a smoke machine while some pretentious dick plays lame beats."

"So you've never been to the Theater of Blood Carnivore Circus?"

"One of my buddies went to it, but I don't really remember where he said it was. Like I said, it's not my thing."

"Do you think I could convince you to call him and ask? I'm only in town for a few days and I want to experience the entire Portland food scene before I put up my report."

At this the bearded guy perked up.

"You a food critic or blogger or something?" He handed Keith the sandwich. It smelled amazing—like something his mom would have served alongside a bowl of canned tomato soup.

"Or something." Keith winked. Generally speaking, restaurant reviewers did not reveal themselves to people whom they were to review. The grilled cheese guy understood this and nodded sagely.

"If I call him, he might remember."

"I'd appreciate it." Keith took a bite of his sandwich, made a show of savoring it before pronouncing, "Delicious."

"You should try it with our spiced turkey." The cook tilted a pan to show him half of a roasted bird, concave rib bones visible. "Just roasted it with harissa and preserved lemon. Want a sample?"

Keith's stomach lurched slightly, as it always did these days when he saw a carcass.

He held up a hand in refusal. "None for me, thanks. I'm a vegetarian."

Keith ate his sandwich and the grilled cheese guy phoned his friend, who came up blank. Too drunk, he said, to remember where he'd been. But he'd seen the poster for the show when he'd been clubbing downtown. Maybe, he said, it was still there. Keith thanked the cook and headed east, walking the length of the central business district to reach the Willamette River. Huge clubs of every persuasion, including gay clubs like CC Slaughters and Silverado, dominated the streets. Since it was lunchtime, few were open.

Portland's old town, like every other urban center in the midst of being gentrified, was a perfect combination of swank and sleazy. Genuine homeless alcoholics loitered on sidewalks next to trust fund students merely posing as alcoholics. Wingtips mingled with Converse.

The combination of Portland's art, music and food scenes made it the perfect place to hide a blood orgy. Even when civilians happened upon the carnage, they often simply believed it had to be some kind of performance. Keith had investigated orgy sites where there had been twenty or more witnesses all standing and watching some victim being dismembered just because a cameraman was filming it. The presence of a camera implied fiction and a sense that some authority was in control.

That was right, at least. But few spectators ever asked themselves who that authority might be.

Keith didn't blame them—the spectators. They couldn't know how many monsters existed in the world. Hell, his own agency, NIAD, went out of the way to make sure they didn't know. The NATO Irregular Affairs Division, often simply called the Irregulars, had been tasked with the duty of policing other-realm traffic, beings and artifacts.

NIAD policed NATO territories, providing justice for the wronged and infrastructure for the hundreds of thousands of unearthly refugees, members of the diaspora and émigrés who now lived hidden within NATO borders.

The array of agents employed by the department included rumpled old magicians, witches in business suits and faerie lawyers as well as a wide variety of extra-human consultants. But the people who did most of the work were regular old human agents, like him.

Keith turned onto SW Stark Street and walked slowly, scanning the brick facades for arcane symbols hidden in the graffiti. He pulled his NIAD-issue glasses from their case and put them on. Through the enchanted lenses, he could now see that a few faint faerie signs marked the first building he passed. They were remarkably like hobo signs: circles, slashes and arrows indicating what a passing extra-human might encounter. The building directly in front of him was marked with symbols indicating that cream was left out.

Not surprising. It was an ice cream parlor. But Keith noted it all the same. If the owners left product out intentionally to feed passing extra-humans, they might have some other-realm connections. If this had been New York or Boston, the whole bottom six inches of the building would have been scribbled with vulgar Gaelic epithets left by leprechaun gangs. Here only a couple of marks had been left at ankle level, and they looked like elf work. Apparently one could find work with a shoemaker nearby. He walked up and down the street. Here and there other spirits had left their mark. He found some ancient Japanese cursive left by displaced *yokai* that had been overwritten in English by a local Native American salmon spirit.

At last he came to a telephone pole plastered with flyers and handbills for various shows, crudely taped and staple-gunned over one another. One caught Keith's eye. Carefully, he peeled aside a flyer advertising a Dykes-n-Dogs singles meetup (canine companions welcome) to reveal the words:

Theater of Blood
Carnivore Circus
One Night Only!
Lulu's Flapjack Shack

A quick map search revealed that the restaurant was located on the city's east side. The sun was setting now. As Keith predicted, his proximity alarm started to gently flash as more and more extra-humans emerged from their lairs, homes and office buildings. Blinking green nine: vampires. Yellow two: pixies. Red three: goblins.

Across the water, the city's east side, with its hipster bars and award-winning restaurants, beckoned, but Keith's days of gourmandizing were long gone. Besides, the east side of Portland was known to contain the largest naturalized goblin population in the world. If he was going to go asking questions there, he'd need backup. Preferably backup that both spoke the language and understood the treaties that existed between humans and goblins.

Because of the necessity for human flesh for certain historic goblin rituals, NIAD, in conjunction with other human governments, had struck a bargain: ten death row inmates sent to the goblin realm every year, no questions asked. In return for this, the goblins had agreed to an extradition treaty that had curbed the ability of goblin human-hunters to disappear on the wild white mountainsides of their snowy kingdom. Keith could see how, when the deal was made a century prior, it would have seemed like poetic justice to render up a sinner to the tortures of hell.

The program had been largely effective, but not completely. Certain goblins still chose to hunt human beings. The only time Keith had ever used his mage pistol against a hostile was when he'd neutralized a pair of goblin butchers in an abattoir in Chicago. He wasn't excited about the prospect of using it again. Avoiding direct conflict, through use of the greater communication skills provided by a translator or community liaison, would provide the most desirable outcome.

At least that's what the NIAD field operations manual assured him, and he was willing to give it a try, if only to sidestep filing the mountain of paperwork required by investigating agents who discharged even a single laser-etched incantation bullet.

He phoned the field office for backup, then returned to his hotel, stopping only briefly at a supermarket to purchase bread and cheese.

◆◆◆

Keith's room at the Mark Spencer Hotel was small and not at all hip, but it had the two things Keith needed most—a bed and a tiny kitchenette. He laid his mage pistol on the small square of counter next to the range and started dinner. He heated the warped nonstick skillet that had come with the room and laid one piece of buttered bread down in it, hearing an appealing sizzle. He added a couple of slices of Havarti and another slice of buttered bread and waited. He didn't really watch his food so much as he listened to it—

smelled it. Behind him the television let him know about events currently taking place in the Willamette Valley. There was a brewer's festival and a triathlon, perfectly representing Portland's twin obsessions: the culinary arts and outdoor recreation. The open window let in a pleasant summer breeze.

Keith was pondering his chances of still being in town for the brewer's festival when he felt a slight vibration from his wrist. He glanced at his watch. The numeral three glowed red—goblins close by.

There was a knock at his door. Out of habit, Keith switched off the range and shifted his skillet off the electric element. Mage pistol in hand, he moved to peer through the fish-eye lens. Outside his door he saw a tall, well-muscled man wearing the standard black trench coat favored by their department, despite the fact that it was nearly eighty degrees outside. He had lustrous black hair and blue eyes and a jawline perfect enough to get him a job selling any men's cologne on earth. The man smiled and held up his NIAD badge. The circular insignia of the Irregular Affairs Division gleamed dully in the yellow hallway light.

Gunther Heartman. Keith cracked his knuckles. It was a bad habit and also a tell, since he did it only when extremely irritated, but he found he couldn't stop. Gunther worked in the San Francisco office as a field agent and member of the strike force. He also did do-gooder double duty as a community volunteer, coordinating the annual human returnee Christmas party. Held in San Francisco, this party was arranged for the benefit of humans who for whatever reason had been away from Earth for too long to be normal. Some had been hostages, others lost in amateur magic-using accidents only to be retrieved years later, addled and hopelessly out of sync with everyday human life. Still others had never lived on Earth at all and were dealing with the problem of having been repatriated against their will. It was a mixed bag of scratched and dented individuals who needed further socialization before being allowed to roam free in the general population.

Gunther had convinced Keith to come in from HQ to participate the previous year. And because Gunther was a good-looking man, Keith had been happy to oblige, on the notion that he might find opportunity to seduce him. He'd taken the red-eye from DC and six hours after landing he stood alongside Gunther, running a little table where he helped the human race's long-lost weirdos create, decorate and ultimately eat the most disturbing Christmas cookies imaginable.

Still covered in sprinkles and colored sugar, they'd had sex for the first time. Keith had thought he was in love at the first taste of Gunther's mouth, but he'd played it cool, returning to DC on the next flight.

Gunther had phoned him about a week later. He'd been in DC for some meeting. They'd met, screwed and parted that very night.

This pattern repeated itself a few times as the two of them casually entered each other's orbits, only to be pulled away again the next day. That suited Keith fine for a while.

Then, just like that, Heartman had ended it.

He'd ended it just as Keith had been about to suggest that they try to see more of each other.

Keith pulled the door open, but not far enough to let Heartman enter. "What are you doing here?"

"You called for me."

"I called for a goblin linguist."

"And here I am," Gunther replied. "There was no one else available, so they sent me."

Keith gave a resigned sigh and pulled his NIAD-issue utility knife from his pocket. He folded the identification light out and focused the beam. "Light verification please, Agent Heartman?"

"I suppose it's too much to hope that you'd feel comfortable calling me Gunther." He offered his ID again.

"Let's just keep it professional." Keith shone his light across the plastic surface. Text previously invisible revealed itself, including Agent Heartman's species: naturalized goblin.

Keith's breath caught in his throat. He hadn't known that, though he could see how Gunther would have failed to mention it.

Oddly, Gunther's photograph didn't shift under the light to show any other image. It looked just like he looked—like an actor who would have been cast to play a hot federal agent in some action film. The lean planes of his face would have photographed well from any angle. Probably even upside down.

"There's no secondary ID photo here," Keith remarked.

"There wouldn't be. I'm transmogrified." Gunther took a pack of Lucky Strike filterless from his inside pocket, folded one into his mouth, and began to chew.

"It says naturalized here." Keith stared hard at the ID and then at Gunther. Was this some sort of trick? Another creature casting a masking spell to look like Gunther? Keith surreptitiously adjusted the light to pierce illusions and, without warning, flashed the light into the other agent's face.

Gunther winced and held up a hand against the harsh white light, but his countenance remained exactly the same.

"Although I am fully of snow goblin descent, I was transformed to be compatible with this world while still in utero." Gunther kept his voice low and glanced around the empty hallway as he spoke. "This isn't a glamour or masking spell or any other kind of illusion. My real body has been irrevocably reconfigured."

"Right," Keith muttered. "I've heard of that."

Gunther said, "Do you think we could continue this conversation in private?"

"Oh, of course." Keith stepped aside.

Gunther sauntered through the doorway, sidestepped the bed and seated himself in a high-backed chair by the television. His eyes immediately homed in on the skillet.

"Are you cooking grilled cheese?"

"I was." As Keith returned to the range and flipped his sandwich over, his deeply ingrained sense of hospitality took over and he found himself asking, "Want one?"

"Sure." Gunther gave him a brilliant smile, showing his perfectly white teeth. "I'm always hungry."

Chapter Two

Snow goblins were, for Keith's money, the scariest looking of the species. Their pure white bodies seemed to be constructed entirely of bones, talons and teeth. Only red slits marked their eyes and nostrils. They spoke in growls. They drank pure kerosene on the rocks and called it moonshine.

Insofar as Keith knew, Gunther Heartman had never scared anyone. Not even accidentally. He was polite, well meaning and easygoing to a fault. Even when Gunther had ended his relationship with Keith—if you could describe a disjointed series of one-night stands a relationship—he'd been nice about it. "I think you might still be struggling with some issues," Gunther had said, "and I don't think being with me is necessarily helping you. I don't think I'm the right man for you. And I know you're not the right man for me."

At the time, Keith had consoled himself by thinking that at least Gunther had had the guts to give him a real reason, instead of the old "it's not you, it's me" line. Keith had always wondered why Gunther thought he wasn't the right man for Keith. Now he thought he knew. Not only was he not human, he was exactly the sort of extra-human American who had destroyed Keith's previous life.

But that didn't bear thinking about. Keith turned his attention fully back to cooking. Almost casually, he remarked, "I didn't realize that you were of goblin descent."

"There's no reason you should have."

Except that we've slept together at least a dozen times, Keith thought. Aloud he said, "I suppose there are quite a few of you on the West Coast."

Gunther nodded. "About six thousand. More than half of them were reengineered while they were still in the womb, like myself."

"It's odd that you never brought that up before," Keith said.

"Is it?" Gunther gave him a meaningful look, though what meaning he intended Keith to take away was not clear.

"Yes, it is." Keith flipped Gunther's sandwich. "So, you've always looked human?"

"I haven't just looked human, I've been human. I went to public school, ran track and got my first job washing dishes at Kentucky Fried Chicken just like everybody else." Gunther popped another cigarette into his mouth and chewed slowly. He fished in his pocket for his slim, yellow tin of lighter fluid, popped open the red safety cap, and took a swig—something he'd never done in Keith's presence before. Thin, flammable vapor floated from his breath as he said, "I enjoy being human."

"I bet you do," Keith said dryly.

The other man gazed at him with a mild, pleasant smile and then said, "Correct me if I'm wrong, but you seem slightly uncomfortable. Is it because you just found out I'm a goblin?"

"No," Keith said.

"Is it because of our previous relationship?"

"Yes." Keith took his sandwich, cut it in half and offered one plate to Gunther, who accepted it with a strange half bow. Keith took his own plate and sat on the edge of the bed.

"I really didn't mean for you to feel awkward—" Gunther began.

"Let's just focus on the task at hand." Keith cut him off before he could launch into another well-meaning speech. While they'd been seeing one another, Gunther's reflexive urge toward humane action had been one of the qualities Keith admired. Now that same quality not only irked but confused him. "Did you get much of a debriefing?"

"Not much," Gunther said, puffing around his first mouthful of hot, gooey cheese and bread.

"We've had three dead, butchered human carcasses here in Portland in the last six months."

"Any evidence of serial killing?"

Keith shook his head. "FBI says you can never rule that out completely, but our informants say that human protein has appeared in a couple of different goblin venues in the city. The summer holy days are coming up. I think some members of Portland's extra-human American community might be stocking up their pantries."

"For the goblin solstice feast, you mean?"

"That's right," Keith said.

"And so you're thinking that this is the work of some reactionary cadre of old-time religion goblin butchers, therefore you requested a native speaker to assist when you go talk to the community?"

"In a nutshell." Keith thought he sensed a certain reluctance to comply emanating from Gunther but chose not to address it. Not yet, anyway. Clearly the two of them made for a less than ideal team. But if they could get through the next couple of days, they could both go back to their respective offices on opposite sides of the continent, no harm done.

"What about other known predators of humans?" Gunther asked.

"There are three registered vampires in the area. I'm planning to interview them as well, because there was some exsanguination present, but there's nothing to connect them to the crimes at this moment."

"So what do you have to link this to goblins?" Gunther asked.

"The timing and the state of the bodies. It's circumstantial, I know, but these really look like goblin killings," Keith said, and from Gunther's brief expression of distaste he guessed Gunther understood what he meant.

"I might have something more solid soon," Keith added.

"Such as?"

"Maybe a venue. Lulu's Flapjack Shack hosted a show recently that has all the hallmarks of a hide-in-plain-sight blood orgy. I'm heading over there in a few minutes and I'd like you to come along."

"Yes, certainly." Gunther took his remaining sandwich triangle, folded it in half, and, despite the magma-like cheese, ate it in three bites. He then said, "Do you mind if we stop to get another pack of cigarettes on the way? I'm out."

◆◆◆

Lulu's Flapjack Shack inhabited a space that had certainly been continuously used as a hospitality venue since linoleum had been invented. Mismatched vinyl booths lined the dining room walls and small tables filled the center space, creating the feeling of being in a pastiche of all diners that had ever existed anywhere. Keith couldn't tell if this was sophisticated and subtle interior design or the result of buying fixtures piecemeal.

According to the sign, Lulu's was open twenty-three hours a day—the one hour closure occurring between four and five a.m.

Presumably, this was when they mopped.

At nine thirty p.m. the dining room was at about half capacity. Mostly the patrons seemed to be in the prelegal phase of adolescence. Groups of five or six shared plates of french fries and pretended to be adults. At the diner counter, intermittently spaced single older males competed for the lone waitress's conversational attention in between bites of all-day breakfast.

"Where do the bands play, do you think?" Keith asked Gunther, mostly to make conversation. The notion that the goblin currently setting off his proximity alert was standing right next to him disturbed him more than he wanted to admit, even to himself.

"Banquet room." Gunther pointed down the long counter to a lighted sign at the back.

Gunther turned out to be correct.

"I don't like the fact that it's called the Banquet Room." Keith's watch buzzed gently, number three still glowing red.

Gunther glanced at it. "Is that some sort of prototype?"

"It's a sensor. It's coded to alert agents to the presence of extra-humans." Keith gave Gunther the brief rundown on the prototype and its codes. "It's meant to be subtler than other types of sensors. The downside is having to memorize the codes."

Gunther nodded and said, "So what's it say now?"

"At least one goblin within fifty feet. But that is most likely you."

"You know, R&D really needs to get on developing a way for agents of other-realm origin to avoid triggering those things before they take it out of the prototype phase. I could see how that could go really wrong in a strike force situation with limited visibility."

"I'll make sure to include that in my report on how it functions in the field," Keith remarked. Strike force was never an assignment that Keith had coveted, but there was a certain inevitable comparison of masculinity that occurred between agents when one was a member and the other wasn't.

"I'd appreciate that, thanks."

The Banquet Room had been designed when restaurants still routinely catered banquets, sometime way back in the early imitation-wood-paneling era. Like most banquet rooms of this ilk, it offered no windows and only one emergency exit in the back.

Essentially, a perfect space to hold a blood orgy.

Whoever had converted the Banquet Room into a bar had kept the basic fixtures and furnishings. The room seemed largely set up like a banquet room as well, with long tables lined by inexpensive, wipeable pine-green dining chairs. Large mass-produced nautical-themed paintings dotted the wall. Toward the front of the room, where head tables would have been, was a small stage, a ten-seat wet bar and a tiny dance floor.

Few patrons were in evidence—just a pair of young guys at the bar watching cartoons on a closed-captioned television and a couple who seemed to be hiding in the corner table. Keith gave them the once-over. But upon closer inspection, the reason for their furtive behavior became clear. He wore a wedding band and she did not.

He seated himself at the bar next to Gunther. Catching sight of himself in the mirror behind the bar, Keith had the unfortunate experience of comparing himself with Agent Heartman physically. There was no contest whatsoever. Gunther was taller, broader and somehow looked good slouching beneath dank, yellow light. Whereas Keith, sitting in shirtsleeves, tie slightly loosened, resembled nothing more than an off-duty county health inspector. Only the tattoos on his arms revealed that there might be any aspect of his personality that an average person could find interest in.

The bartender set a bowl of popcorn down between them. The man resembled Gunther in the powerful proportions of his body, but his coloring differed notably. He had red hair, small, narrow eyes and a mouth that stretched too wide to be attractive, especially when he smiled.

"What can I get for you?"

Gunther ordered pink vodka on the rocks. Keith stuck with beer—microbrew. The bartender stepped aside to pour their drinks. Gunther began to amiably munch the popcorn. After a few bites he remarked, "This would be a good venue."

"Yeah, that's what I thought. No windows. Drain in the floor."

"I was thinking more for seeing a band," Gunther said. "The decor seems dank and lowbrow for a real goblin feast."

"Have you ever been to one?"

"Do I not have a mother who would be disappointed if I failed to attend?" Gunther tossed a yellow kernel into the air and caught it in his mouth, then slid his gaze slyly around. "I feast every year. Not how you're imagining it, though. My family's feasts take the form of barbecues generally conducted in the garden. The most unsavory item typically present is my godfather's fifth of substandard rye."

"What protein do you cook?"

"You know, a less polite man might find that question, and its implicit assumption, somewhat offensive." His tone shifted slightly, lowering to a near growl.

Keith bristled. "Maybe a less polite man hasn't seen the same kinds of things that I have seen conducted in places much like this."

Gunther folded. His easy manner returned. "I suppose not. I imagine that as the primary investigator for cases like these you've grown naturally suspicious of individuals of my heritage."

Keith lowered his voice to a near whisper. "Look, last year, in Dallas, we busted a group of upper-crust gourmandizing sickos who were human right down to their Manolo Blahniks. Before that we collared a real, live child-eating Russian Baba-fucking-Yaga. But in this particular case, I happen to suspect goblins, all right? If you can't deal with that maybe you should request reassignment."

The bartender turned back and plunked their drinks in front of them. Keith slid the tattered flyer out toward him and said, "I was wondering, did you happen to be working on the night of this show?"

The bartender glanced down and grimaced. "Yeah, I was. Hell of a mess they made." Then, with a bartender's eerie prescience, he inquired, "You two cops?"

"I'm Agent Keith Curry. This is Agent Heartman." He briefly opened his NIAD ID, then closed it again. For most people, just seeing a badge—any badge—was enough to get them to talk. The bartender was no exception. He nodded, stiffening only slightly. Keith continued, "And you are?"

"Jordan Lucky Greenbacks. What is this about?"

"Just a routine inquiry." Gunther gave the bartender an easy smile. "Are the owners in?"

"No, they don't work nights."

Keith took over again. "How long have you worked here, Mr. Greenbacks?"

"Three years," Jordan said.

"Tell me, does the management ever close this room for private parties?"

"Sometimes."

"When was the last time?" Keith removed a black notebook from his pocket and flipped it open.

"Around Christmas last year there was a private party," Jordan said.

"So around the winter solstice?"

"It didn't have anything to do with any solstice, winter or summer." Jordan's tone sharpened. His expression snapped instantly into defensive hostility. He stared straight at Gunther. "It had nothing to do with . . . our community. It was a fund-raiser for the fire department."

Keith raised his eyebrows fractionally. Jordan could have been referring to the gay community, but Keith seriously doubted that.

He wondered if Gunther had already perceived that Mr. Greenbacks was trans-goblin as well. And if so, how did the two of them recognize each other? Psychic power? Smell?

"So, are the owners of this club part of you and Agent Heartman's community?"

"No, they aren't," Jordan said in an insistent whisper. "And they don't know anything about it or about me. I haven't broken the Secrecy Act—"

"Of course you haven't," Gunther said. "The reason we came here was to ask about this particular show. We want to know what you can tell us about these bands."

"Nothing except, you know, the obvious." He looked directly at Gunther as he spoke.

"Define obvious for me." Keith took a sip of his beer.

"Some of the musicians were"—he gave another slight gesture in Gunther's direction—"also part of our community. Obviously you know that already or you wouldn't be here."

Keith allowed himself a tight smile, then said, "Did you happen to get any names?"

The bartender shook his head. "It was a popular show, I was running the whole time. I didn't even have time for a smoke break. You could ask our booker, Samantha. She'd probably have some contact information for them."

"Is Samantha here?"

"No, Monday's her day off."

"Let's get back to the band. Did you notice anything special about any of them?" Gunther asked. "Physical characteristics? Anything?"

Jordan shrugged again. "It was just a metal show. They drank cheap beer and played really heavy, brick-in-your-face metal but didn't do anything"—he leaned forward, whispering to Gunther—"anything magical. They sang in goblin during the refrain, but that was all. Hardly anybody even recognized it."

"That and made a hell of a mess." Keith circled back around to the front of the conversation.

Jordan paled slightly. His fingers tightened imperceptibly around the white bar towel.

There it is, Keith thought, that telling expression of information that has been omitted. "What was so messy about the band?"

The bartender swallowed. "They did some theatrical stuff on stage."

"Such as?" Gunther prompted.

"They drank some stuff that looked like blood. Poured some of it over the crowd." The bartender busied himself with wiping the already clean bar. "A lot of metal bands do things like that."

"Did it look like blood or was it blood?" Keith pressed.

"I don't know." The bartender refused to look at him. "I'm not some kind of expert."

"You cleaned it up, right?" Keith folded his hands, prepared to wait all night for the answer. "Blood has a fairly distinct odor, color and texture."

"I—" Jordan looked to Gunther.

"It's all right," Gunther assured him. "We just need to know about this band. We don't have any reason to believe you are connected with them. Are you?"

"I'm not," the bartender said quickly. "They said it was cow's blood. They poured it out of these gallon jugs that said USDA on them."

Keith nodded. Though strange from the standpoint of an average white-bread American, beef and pork blood were standard ingredients in everything from the Filipino blood stew called *dinuguan* to *verivorst*, the blood sausages Estonians considered crucial for any Christmas feast. It was entirely plausible that the blood had its origin in livestock. It was also possible that they had simply refilled empty containers with human blood. Without a DNA sample and test, it would be impossible to tell.

"How long ago was this show?"

"Last week."

"Has the mop head been changed since then?" Keith asked.

"I don't think so. The laundry service hasn't been here yet. Do you want to see it?"

Keith followed the bartender back into a dank supply cupboard. As predicted, the mop head was still attached to the mop handle, sitting in a yellow plastic bucket.

Keith detached the moist, stinking thing and crammed it into an evidence bag.

"We're going to have to take this with us." He wrote Jordan a receipt, returned to the bar and sat down next to Gunther, who observed the bagged mop head with silent curiosity.

"I'm going to find out exactly what kind of blood the band was pouring out at the show," Keith explained.

Gunther nodded. "That's what I thought."

"Then at least we'll know something about this case," Keith said.

Gunther nodded again. Jordan returned to ask them if they needed another round.

"Not right at the moment," Gunther said. "So, you don't remember anything else about the band? Any detail at all?"

Jordan paused thoughtfully, seeming to come to some painful decision before finally speaking. "The bassist had a Portland Saturday Market sticker on his guitar case. He said he worked there. I remember it because I wanted to know if he knew my friend Spartacus, who sells hard cider in the beer garden."

"Did he?" Keith asked. The Portland Saturday Market was one of many markets heavily run by goblins—an Earth-based offshoot of the Grand Goblin Bazaar.

"He did," Jordan said. "Everybody knows everybody there." A man at the end of the bar suddenly hoisted his empty aloft and began, rudely, to clack his ice as a way of indicating that he'd like additional service. Jordan gave him a professional smile and a nod before saying, "Is there anything else?"

"Tables at the market here are hereditary, aren't they?" Gunther asked.

"Of course. There's a waiting list you can get on, but my friend Spartacus told me it's years long. He only got in because he took over for his mother. He's been studying with cider makers in England for the last few years. He's really a genius. I have it on tap here. I'll pour you one. You'll be blown away."

Gunther accepted Jordan's largesse with grace and some formal-sounding word in goblin that Keith didn't understand.

Keith eyed the cider sparkling in Gunther's pint glass. Apart from their ritualistic taste for human flesh, goblins were well known for the astonishing quality of their fruits. Doubtless this particular cider would be the best he'd ever had. More than that, he wouldn't be able to stop thinking of it. Tasting goblin fruits ruined the flavor of all lesser fruits forever. Eating goblin fruit and then returning to mundane varieties was like having the opportunity to make love to your soul mate for one night, then forever more being relegated to meaningless one-night stands.

He'd once eaten a few slices of a goblin peach. Those soft crescents had been the most amazing flesh he'd ever put in his mouth.

Barring Gunther's flesh, that is.

But again, that didn't bear thinking about.

Now before them sat a glass of goblin cider. If he drank it, no other cider would be enough ever again. Disappointment would be frequent, and yet the temptation of goblin fruits pulled at him. The desire to have the best in the world, even just one time, was one of the very personality traits that had attracted Keith to cooking in the first place.

And somehow, even though his suspicion about food had grown to what could rightfully be called paranoia since he'd joined NIAD, alcohol remained the chink in his armor—especially when he'd just had other alcohol.

Temptation won.

Keith asked, "Mind if I try your cider?"

"Not at all. It's really good, but I'm not much of a hard cider man." Gunther slid the pint over. Keith wondered if the taste of goblin fruits actually affected goblins.

As he suspected, the cider was amazing. Better than amazing. A feeling very much like orgasm zinged over his tongue, electrifying every taste bud with tangy, juicy sweetness. He laughed for no reason. Tears filled his eyes. He closed his eyes and gave an involuntary groan of pleasure.

"If I'd known you were going to like it that much I'd have brought one with me to the hotel," Gunther remarked.

Keith opened his eyes to find Gunther gazing at him with the sort of openly homosexual public appreciation that Keith found nerve-racking, even though he'd been out since he was twenty. Reluctantly, almost involuntarily, Keith found himself returning Gunther's smile.

CHAPTER THREE

The Portland Saturday Market was part beer garden and part DIY art fair. Rows of white eight-by-eight tent canopies inhabited Ankeny Plaza—a brick-paved space in Waterfront Park on the bank of the Willamette River.

Gunther walked with a spring in his step. His black trench coat was draped across one arm in the fine, sunny morning.

Since Keith and Gunther had parted the previous evening, conflicting thoughts and feelings had been twisting through Keith's brain like a dough hook working relentlessly at a fifty-pound batch.

On the one hand, he wanted Gunther. That had never changed. On the other hand, Gunther no longer wanted him. That had also not changed. And yet, the intractability of the situation did nothing to dissuade either of them from smiling at each other when they had met in the elevator that morning. Or from flirting mildly with each other in the car on the way over. Keith found himself alternating between admiring Gunther openly and peering ahead at the market like a child approaching an amusement park.

"My parents used to bring me to this market every weekend," Gunther said.

"You grew up in Portland?"

"No, Oakland. My parents still work as translators for the San Francisco field office, but there's a portal at Fisherman's Wharf. There were always a lot of other trans-goblin kids to play with here and my parents could visit with their fellow dissident diaspora members. Usually people brought sandwiches. Sometimes potato salad. And every now and then one of the men would surreptitiously share his flask of naphtha."

"Replace the naphtha with vodka and it would be exactly like going to a picnic at my grandma's church," Keith said, smiling.

"I've never been to a church picnic, but there was a feeling of community here that we didn't always have in Oakland. Coming to the earthly realm was quite the sacrifice for my parents."

Keith glanced at Gunther sideways. "How do you mean?"

"Well, to make a decision to leave behind the shape of a Luminous One and condemn their only child to wearing the flesh of a homely little human, of course. I retain some goblin characteristics, but there's really no chance of me finding a nice goblin boy to settle down with while I've got this meaty body." Gunther shook his head. "Just too unappealing."

"So that's what you're looking for? A nice trans-goblin boy?" As soon as the words were out of his mouth, Keith regretted them. Why was he showing all his cards and behaving like he had no game whatsoever?

Gunther stopped, standing as if affixed to the green grass by tent pegs, regarding Keith with a slight, sardonic smile.

"I thought you said you wanted to keep it professional between us," he said.

"You're right. That was cheap of me," Keith conceded. "Let's just get to work."

Like many places used for congregation by the extra-human American community, the goblin markets were linked through a series of portals. One could walk into a portal in Portland, step through a door and emerge in Brooklyn or London or Mexico City. In Keith's experience, in markets that were open to the human public, like this one, the portals were generally disguised as out-of-order toilet stalls. Any human brave enough to open the stall door would be treated to an illusion so unappealing as to dissuade casual entry.

Keith knew some Irregular agents who were so comfortable with magic that they used goblin market portals to avoid airport security lines when traveling between the coasts. But being neither a magician nor a mythical creature, Keith had never felt too secure with that sort of travel.

As they walked across the damp grass toward the rows of small, white pavilions, they passed a line of blue portable toilet stalls. Two displayed signs expressing that they were out of order.

Keith put on his glasses and noted, with interest, that Gunther did as well. Immediately hidden text all around him was revealed. One portapotty was marked Fisherman's Wharf while another read Grand Goblin.

Hidden signage on stalls sprang into view as well. One table, selling handcrafted glass, advertised that their product was fair trade—made by elves who received a decent living wage.

"What do elves consider a living wage?" Keith whispered to Gunther.

Gunther just shrugged. "Their own pair of pants?"

They moved through the rows of canopies. Keith followed Gunther's lead, stopping when he stopped, simply listening as his fellow agent softly inquired about the weather and other knuckle-poppingly irrelevant subjects.

Gunther bought a basket of Rainier cherries from a girl named Jeannie, then stood there, munching them in front of her, chatting about rain and the phases of the moon and gardening. Just when Keith thought that Gunther had given up investigating altogether he noticed Jeannie's bike—or more specifically, the Carnivore Circus sticker adhered to it. Even without the glasses he'd have been able to see it.

Jeannie seemed to know and have an opinion about everyone in the city.

"If you need some help with your garden, I can put you in touch with some gnomes," she told Gunther. "They're really great guys and work for peanuts."

Keith's patience thinned.

"Look, we aren't here looking for discount day labor. We need to know where to find meat." Keith flipped out his wallet, flashing his badge. "You know what I'm talking about."

Jeannie's lip curled. Her silver septum piercing glinted. "I know what you mean, and I think it's disgusting. You agents are all the same. You think we goblins are all just waiting around to become cannibals."

"Hey now, that's not true—" Gunther began.

"You're worst of all—standing there with juice from my produce on your lips while taking the man's coin to continue the unfair profiling of your own people."

Vendors in the booths around them started to take notice. The lanky man selling recycled sweaters in the stall next door drifted over. Keith suppressed the urge to reach for his mage pistol. It would only escalate the situation. Besides, Gunther didn't seem ruffled. He munched cherry after cherry, an affable smile on his face. Keith guessed that he was accustomed to dealing with this sort of aggressive reaction.

"We're not here to bother you, miss. I'm sure nobody here has anything to do with the murders that have taken place in the last year," Gunther said. "But we have to check up on every possible lead, you see? We need to speak with everyone who might have heard something about these crimes. Sometimes people aren't even aware that they know important information."

"But why come here first? Why not ask the bloodsuckers? They eat people all the time," Jeannie said.

"We will be following multiple lines of inquiry," Keith said. Then following Gunther's lead, even though it went against his personal grain, he said, "I apologize for being abrupt earlier, miss. But three people are dead. Butchered right down to their bones. Imagine what that must be like for their families to see when they come to claim the bodies."

"But it's not goblins," she insisted.

"How do you know for sure?" Gunther cocked his head slightly. "Have you heard anything about the murders? Anything at all, gossip or speculation? People talking in bars?"

"Have you ever seen this before?" Keith pulled the Theater of Blood Carnivore Circus flyer out of his pocket, unfolded it and showed it to her.

"Never," she said.

"Are you sure?" Gunther asked.

Jeannie clamped her mouth shut and shook her head. She covered her face with her hands and said again, "It's not goblins. It can't be goblins."

"You have a Carnivore Circus bumper sticker on your bike, miss. Now I'm going to ask you again: what do you know about this flyer?" Keith persisted.

"Nothing," she said, from behind her hands.

Guilty, Keith thought. Or at least not entirely innocent. She knew something. Keith wondered how hard it would be to drag her to the Irregulars field office.

"The Carnivore Circus isn't involved," the lanky man suddenly said. "We're just a band, that's all."

Keith's attention snapped immediately to the lanky man. "I take it that you're in this band?"

"Yeah, I play bass."

"And your name is?" Gunther flipped out his notebook.

"Lancelot Paddington, but my band name is the Lancer."

Jeannie laid a hand on his arm. "You shouldn't talk to them without a lawyer."

Lancelot shrugged. "I've got nothing to hide."

"So tell us about your band," Gunther said.

"We're a three-piece metal band. All goblin. Our influences include the Stooges and Three Inches of Blood. We've got an EP out right now. Last week we made a date to talk with a local label—"

Keith cut him off. "Tell us about why someone would think your band has to do with these murders."

"This flyer"—Lancelot pointed at the grimy paper—"it's for two different acts. The first one was Theater of Blood. They sucked."

"Sucked blood?" Gunther prompted.

"No," Lancelot said. "They drank it out of these cheap plastic goblets that looked like they came from the dollar store. They had no style, couldn't wear makeup and didn't know how to play."

"Do you know what kind of blood it was?" Gunther glanced up from his notes.

"They said it was human."

"Why didn't you report this to our agency?" Keith asked.

"They were humans. All of them," Lancelot said. "And they were such poseurs I figured that they had to be lying about the blood. I thought they were trying to impress us because we eat raw meat in our act. A lot of guys get intimidated by that. They think they have to be more macho than us."

Gunther's eyebrows shot up. "You eat live meat on stage?"

"No, nothing like that." Lancelot backpedaled. "We just get really hungry when we're shredding and sometimes snack."

"So you eat raw but not live meat?" Keith clarified.

"Right. Beef mostly. Sometimes, if it's a really big venue, we eat goat because the bones look more, like, human."

"Don't tell them that," Jeannie said.

"No, it's okay, Jeannie. The first time we did it—ate raw meat, I mean—it was just what we brought for lunch. We were in the green room at a club snacking on frozen hamburger patties and chewing butts between sets and the bartender came back and caught us. We claimed to be from Ethiopia."

Keith wondered how that had gone over. Lancelot was white as vanilla ice milk.

"Ethiopia . . . nice one," Gunther murmured, a hint of a smile curving his lips.

"Yeah, well, the bartender—his name is Jordan—Jordan said that he liked our sound but our stage show was boring. It was his idea to incorporate eating raw meat into the act because it would seem hard-core. He came up with the new name too. He's a good guy. He works at Lulu's Flapjack Shack. See Spartacus over there? The guy with the cider? Jordan is his first cousin."

"Yes, we've met Mr. Greenbacks," Keith said sourly. "So he came up with your new name?"

"Carnivore Circus. Before that we were called Grand Coulee Mayhem Tennis Project," Lancelot said sheepishly. "I guess I was drunk when I came up with that."

"So did Jordan set up the gig with Theater of Blood?" Keith asked.

"No, that was our manager, Milton. I can give you his phone number, only . . ." Lancelot shot a sideways glance at Jeannie. She was on the phone with someone. Perhaps Jordan, but most likely a lawyer.

"Only . . . ," Gunther prompted.

"Milton doesn't know we're trans-goblins and I'm worried that if he found out, your guys would put some forgetting mojo on him and then he'd forget he's supposed to be getting us a record deal."

"We will make every effort to conceal both your and our identities," Gunther said.

"Thanks, man." Lancelot nodded absently, his attention distracted by a pair of yuppies perusing his recycled knitwear with some interest. "Would you mind if I get back to my stall now?"

After they released Lancelot, Keith was ready to go, but Gunther insisted on seeing the rest of the market. He bought a dozen light bulbs from one table and three bottles of hot sauce from another. A few vendors gave them nervous smiles as they passed by, but most stared stonily or looked away. Before leaving, Gunther stopped by and bought a Carnivore Circus CD from Lancelot, which seemed to smooth things over somewhat. Lancelot shortchanged Gunther three bucks. Keith wondered if that was malice, nervousness or bad math. There was no real way to tell.

Their last pass was through a row of food vendors. Keith was hungry but at the same time deeply distrustful of food—any food—prepared by goblins. Fortunately, there was Spartacus and his cider. He bought one and found a place at a picnic table.

"It seems like it's getting to be lunchtime," Gunther remarked.

"I'd have thought you already filled up on cherries."

"Merely an appetizer," Gunther said. "Can I buy you lunch?"

"Nothing here looks that great to me," Keith said.

A smile twitched at the corner of Gunther's lips. "Let me take you to lunch in my neighborhood."

"You mean to San Francisco?"

"Home of some very famous vegetarian restaurants, including one little five-star hole in the wall called Verdant. We could be there in half an hour."

"It takes that long to get through the portal?"

"No, but traffic between Fisherman's Wharf and Fort Mason isn't that great at this time of year. What do you say?"

"Portaling to San Francisco for five-star lunch sounds less like a business arrangement and more like a date."

"So what if it is?"

"Now who's not keeping it professional?"

Gunther stuffed his hands in his pockets and shrugged. "Neither of us seem to want to, so why should I adhere to some pretense?"

Keith shook his head. "We've already done this, Gunther. It didn't work the first time and it won't work now."

"We never had a proper date before, just a series of booty calls," Gunther said. "So let me make it up to you the old-fashioned way."

Keith had to admit the temptation. And not just the temptation of going on a date with Gunther. Verdant was legendary. While he'd worked as a chef, he'd never given much credit to the vegetarians in his field, nor had he been any great star. The chef at Verdant was both. And he did want Gunther to make it up to him. Hell, he might even be able to figure out what Gunther found so inadequate about that series of disconnected sexual events that he'd wanted to call them off.

"Wouldn't we need reservations?"

"The chef owes me." Gunther leaned forward and whispered, "Pixie trouble. You know how capricious they can be. One little misunderstanding and they're curdling your cream and luring you off Land's End in the dark. But it's all sorted out now. So how about it? We can be down there, done and back again before this place closes."

Keith was about to refuse. Then the alcohol kicked in, relaxing him enough to say yes.

◆◆◆

Verdant was located in an airy space alongside the marina in Fort Mason. From its wide windows, Keith could survey both the marina and the Golden Gate Bridge beyond.

The chef, a friendly-faced brunette with close-cropped hair, greeted Gunther as a VIP and seated him immediately.

The menu was elegant, filled with heirloom vegetables, local wine and artisanal cheese.

The price tag was breathtaking. Keith, in fact, had to take a deep breath as he automatically calculated price-point-to-food cost.

It actually wasn't that bad, for the location and for what they were getting.

And besides, he wasn't paying.

Like every fine dining establishment that Keith had ever been to, the tables were small and relatively close together. But no one was seated alongside them, so once the appetizer had been delivered, their conversation could continue unimpeded by the presence of civilians.

"So, who do you like for the murders?"

Gunther glanced up, a look of slight confusion on his face. He set his fork down and said, "I don't know. I wasn't thinking about it."

"What were you thinking about?"

"My lunch. My companion." He gave a warm smile, as though it was only right and natural that all knowledge of his current mission should be put on hold just because someone set a radicchio, apple and pomegranate-seed salad down in front of him. "I was wondering, was being an agent your first career choice?"

"No, not at all," Keith said, laughing. "I was a chef with no aspirations at law enforcement and no knowledge of the other realms."

"I wondered," Gunther remarked.

"Why?"

"When we—" Gunther seemed to struggle a moment before finding the words he wanted. "When we were seeing each other before, you seemed to be uncomfortable with extra-human Americans."

Keith shrugged. "I hadn't been with NIAD that long. And the few experiences I'd had—especially with goblins— had been extremely negative and personally painful."

"I imagine they were." Gunther poked at his salad, seeming to consider and then discard some worrying thought before saying, "So when you cooked, did you work in other people's restaurants or did you have your own?"

"Other people's at first. I followed the tourists from place to place. Finally I managed to get the capital to open my own place—a former diner with twenty seats and the ugliest gray linoleum ever manufactured."

"I sense this is when you had your first other-realm encounter," Gunther said.

"It wasn't for about a year. I busted my ass making that place. I was surprised that all my teeth didn't fall out from grinding. I got this gray streak during the opening." Keith touched his temple self-consciously. "I'm thinking of dyeing it. I'm only thirty-four."

Gunther shrugged. "Premature gray is standard in our line of work, I think."

Keith nodded. "Very true."

"You were telling me about how you joined NIAD," Gunther prompted.

"One day one of my customers came by with this special request. He had this family obligation. Some kind of religious feast he wanted me to cater. He'd provide the meat and all I had to do was cook it for this special summer banquet. I asked, 'what's the meat?' He told me it was special pork from Sweden."

Gunther nodded grimly. He took a forkful of salad.

"Right away I knew it wasn't pork. The bones were all wrong, but I needed the money and I just didn't think about it that hard."

"What did you think it was?"

"I honestly didn't know. Some endangered creature, I suppose. I figured if it was already dead it shouldn't go to waste, right?" Keith shook his head. "I was an idiot."

"You weren't an idiot. You just didn't know what you were dealing with."

"Even without the extra-human angle I knew there was something sketchy about that meat and I went ahead and cooked it anyway. Each time I catered for them, I would try and figure out what it had been. I ran down all those endangered Chinese delicacies, trying to figure it out—looking at the bones of sun bears—seeing if they matched. And I knew for a goddamn fact it had to be illegal, but the money was too good to say no. I kept thinking, 'At least I'm not dealing coke, right?' It never occurred to me to look at the bones of one of the most widely dispersed animals on the planet."

"How did you figure it out?"

"I got a piece of protein that had some skin attached and found a tattoo. No caribou, cow or sun bear tattoos Mom on their arm." Keith wiped his lips with his napkin.

"Had you eaten the flesh?"

"Of course I'd eaten it. How was I supposed to tell how it tasted without eating it? I'd eaten a lot of it."

Gunther sat in silence. An unspoken question within him. Since Keith knew exactly what the question was, he said, "It's okay. You can ask me. Everybody asks me."

"How did it taste?"

"Really delicious." Keith pushed his soup plate away. The spinach, chard and escarole soup had gone down easier than he expected, considering the conversation. "The best meat I ever ate. The last meat I ever ate, as it turns out."

Gunther, too, finished his first course and set his fork aside. "That doesn't explain how you got involved with the Irregulars."

"No." Keith waited politely for the slim, pleasant-seeming waitress to take his plate before continuing. "I reported what I'd found to the police and a couple of agents contacted me. They wanted to set up a sting operation and I agreed. That's how I found out that my customers were goblins."

"That must have been a shock."

"Finding out that everything I'd previously believed to be a myth actually existed was a pretty big shock, yeah. During that time, the agents assigned to the case communicated with me extensively. They and I both realized that there wasn't anyone at NIAD who had specific knowledge of cooking or restaurants, while at the same time, there was still this problem with human-sourced protein. I suppose the agents who contacted me had planned to recruit me from the moment that they introduced themselves, but I'm not disappointed. I do good work. Important work."

"Don't you miss cooking?"

Keith found himself smiling. Melancholy drifted through him. "I do miss it. I miss the companionship of the kitchen, the creative aspect . . . I suppose what I miss most is the solvability of all problems."

"How do you mean?"

"Well, when you're cooking during a dinner service, it's a pass-fail situation. Either you get the food out right and on time or you don't. Problems don't linger. At the end of the night you've done all you could and tomorrow is another day where you get a fresh chance at success, no matter how big the fail might have been on the previous day."

"I see," Gunther said, nodding. "Our job is not like that at all."

"No, it isn't." Keith folded his hands, observing the sunset across the bay. "It's not so bad though. I'm the first and only specialist in the detection of contraband food items. I like the idea that I can make a difference."

They spent the rest of the meal engaging in the sort of harmless chat that they'd never bothered to make before. He found out that Gunther's high school track specialty had been hurdles and that he had majored in sociology with a minor in anthropology before signing up with NIAD.

Finally, during coffee and dessert, Keith got the courage to ask the one question he wanted answered.

"So why exactly did you call off our previous arrangement?"

"You made a few offhand comments about goblins that I didn't care for," Gunther said simply. "At the time, I was offended. I couldn't say I was offended because I hadn't told you about myself, so I just called it off."

"Why invite me to lunch today then?"

"I guess I just remembered how sexy you are. And I felt like I'd been unfair."

Keith drained the last of his coffee. He tried to remember what he might have said that could have been offensive. With no small degree of horror, he realized that he'd said plenty. Shame verging on mortification churned through his chest.

"I don't want to sound like I'm making excuses for myself, but I wasn't all that stable at the time. I was still in the humans-versus-monsters mindset."

"Yes, I remember." Gunther's expression remained neutral, even somewhat blank.

"I guess what I'm trying to say is that I'm sorry if what I said hurt you. I'm not all that smart and it takes me a while to adjust sometimes," Keith said. "But I do know it's not all cut-and-dried. I do now anyway."

"That's good to hear." Gunther glanced at his phone. "We should probably be getting back to the market if we want to use the portal."

◆◆◆

Back in Portland, the market was just wrapping up. Their rental had a parking ticket tucked lovingly under the windshield wiper. Keith stuffed it into his pocket to commune with the other three already crammed in there.

"Anything else on the agenda for this evening?" Gunther asked.

"On demand and a shower for me. Unless you feel up to interrogating vampires after nightfall. In which case you're free to take the rental." Keith wiggled the key fob at Gunther.

"Actually, I was hoping to borrow the car to pick up a box of legendary Bauer & Bullock feijoa jam *alfajores*. Apparently, they're the most addictive cookie ever made. I need to bring back a farewell gift for another agent."

"Someone retiring?" Keith had often wondered where old agents went to retire once their crime-fighting days were over.

"No, just moving. Promoted to directing the Vancouver field office. You might remember him from last year's Cookie Jamboree? His name was Rake? Great big fellow?"

Keith had a sharp recollection of an enormous hulk of a man hanging around near the cookie decorations eating sprinkles and silver dragées when he thought no one was looking.

"The mountain with the sweet tooth."

Gunther chuckled. "Right. He was my first partner when I was a rookie. He loves these cookies with a profane passion."

"I've never heard of them, but I'm not really a big bakery guy."

"They're actually sold at a steakhouse. It's supposed to have an excellent bar as well. If you'd like to come along, I'll buy you a drink for keeping me company."

Keith hesitated. Although he'd have never admitted it to anyone, Gunther scared him. And not just because he had turned out to be a goblin. Keith wanted Gunther and that desire had led him to break two cardinal rules he'd long held sacred—never date anybody twice and never stay friends with a guy who dumps you. Keith didn't want to be a chump all over again.

Apparently sensing his reluctance, Gunther said, "Or I could drop you off at the hotel if you'd like."

"Hotel sounds good. I'm beat." Keith tossed him the keys and headed to the passenger side.

As he pulled up to the curb in front of the hotel Gunther said, "I'll be having a drink there anyway. You could come by if you change your mind."

Keith gave a noncommittal nod and left.

Once he'd made it back to his hotel room and gotten through a dicey, but necessary, cold shower, he had time to regret his decision. He decided that, on closer reflection, he did want a drink.

Maybe, he thought, he could still catch Gunther at the steakhouse if he took a cab there.

Finding Bauer & Bullock's webpage was easy. It was splashy, with a lot of photo carousels showing beef searing on different apparatuses. The one-hundred-and-forty-three-seat restaurant was apparently the choice for the Portland business diner looking to impress a client. Keith had always hated joints like these, even before he'd become a vegetarian. White guys in business suits eating slabs of meat and steak frites while talking about money always curtailed his appetite.

But Gunther had gone there, so now Keith wanted to be there too. He decided to check out the bar menu.

Pleasantly, though somewhat predictably, the website informed him that the bar stocked over five hundred different whiskeys. He picked up his phone and was just about to dial Gunther when the image on the carousel changed from a sizzling grill to a photograph of the owner.

The face was familiar but her name even more so: Cindy Bullock, wife of Trent Bullock, whom Keith had arrested for cannibalism in Dallas less than a year before.

He decided to pass on the whiskey after all.

Chapter Four

Gunther arrived at Keith's hotel room early the next day. The coffee maker had just started to gurgle and fill the hotel room with the scent of morning. Keith had neither dressed nor shaved and still wore the ragged old Misfits T-shirt and shorts he'd slept in.

"I just got an email from the lab." Gunther set his laptop down on the small hotel desk. "The blood sample taken from the mop head at Lulu's Flapjack Shack contained a mixture of human and bovine blood," he said.

"So the killer is stretching one with the other?"

"Or there might have been two separate sources of blood," Gunther said. "In addition to that, traces of methotrexate were present throughout the fibers, which would indicate that it had been combined with the blood mixture," Gunther went on.

"Is that some sort of exotic new food additive?"

"It's a prescription drug used to treat autoimmune diseases."

"Weird." Keith hunted through the cupboards for coffee cups. "I don't know what to make of that at all."

"Nor do I."

"Did you get your cookies?"

"Last box of the night," Gunther said.

"How did the restaurant seem?" Keith poured two cups of coffee and pulled the room's remaining chair up alongside his partner.

"Busy. Crowded bar." Gunther glanced up. "I sat down and had a superb whiskey sour. When you failed to appear to keep me company I decided to while away the time google-stalking you on my phone."

"Why?"

"Idle curiosity." Gunther's response came with such flirtatious ease that Keith initially mistook it for sarcasm.

"Did you stumble across anything good?"

"Your freshman yearbook photo. And a fine mullet you had then too. I particularly like the vaguely stoned look on your face and the ripped Whitesnake concert tee." Gunther looked pointedly at Keith's Misfits shirt. "Good to know you haven't changed too much."

Keith momentarily choked, embarrassed by the accuracy of the statement, but he recovered. "I was also wearing red parachute pants, but you can't see those."

"Nice." Gunther smiled. "Do you still listen to metal?"

"Sometimes." Keith took a sip of his coffee. Too harsh. He returned to the counter to swirl more sugar in.

"I always wanted to make some kind of rebellious adolescent statement on school photo day but never had the nerve," Gunther said. "I was always afraid that if I was anything but absolutely harmless and normal I'd be found out, charged with breaking the Secrecy Act and sent away."

Keith was ashamed to realize that he'd never thought of what it must be like to grow up with that kind of isolation. Sure, he'd had the experience of hiding the fact that he was gay from people, but that was different. At any point he'd had the freedom to tell anyone which gender he preferred to sleep with. The Secrecy Act mandated silence on pain of deportation.

Lamely, Keith said, "That must have been rough."

"It's a unique way to experience childhood." Gunther's tone told him nothing.

"Don't feel bad. My wearing a Whitesnake T-shirt was more an act of laziness than rebellion."

"For you, maybe, but my mother dressed me in slacks and a tie every day of my freshman year," Gunther said. "My classmates all thought I was a Mormon."

"I imagine you learned to fight pretty early, dressed like that."

"Some, but I also became adept at hiding other clothes in my backpack and changing in gas station bathrooms." Gunther punched a couple of keys and entered the NIAD database. "I never really had to learn to fight so much as how not to kill people. Humans are fragile."

Keith's discomfort rose to an intolerable level. He wondered what offhand remarks he had made about goblins. Had he called them butchers? Animals? Sick fucks? Any or all of those pejoratives was possible. He hadn't been in a good way when he'd met Gunther before—angry and full of rancor.

He sat down on the bed and said, "I did look up the address of the bar you were at."

"You did?" Gunther's expression brightened briefly before dimming again. "But you didn't come."

"It's not because of you," Keith said quickly. "It's because of the restaurant's owner. Bring up Trent Bullock's file in the NIAD base and you'll see what I mean."

Gunther complied and took a few minutes to read through the details of Keith's recent bust.

"So although the meat that these people had been eating was goblin sourced, the diners were all human?" Gunther finally asked.

"It surprised us too, but then after we reviewed their supper club, we realized that the same sort of people whose demand fueled the mermaid-flesh trade were branching out into this chic cannibalism. They were foodies gone very wrong."

"This is the case you were mentioning at the Flapjack Shack, isn't it?"

"Yeah, it is. Bauer & Bullock is owned lock, stock and barrel by Cindy Bullock, now Trent's ex-wife, since he went into Beaumont," Keith said.

"According to the file, Beaumont was just a stopover on his trip to the goblin high king's summer solstice table."

"As the main course, yeah," Keith said. "The wife was in Argentina researching sources for her new restaurant venture for the entire duration of my investigation. We had our South American counterparts monitor her movements while she was in their country, but her exploits were purely beef or beefcake related. We couldn't nail her on anything."

"Okay, so Bullock's widow is here slinging steaks. And?" Gunther asked.

"And it occurred to me that there are a few things we don't know about this case."

"Such as, everything?" Gunther gave a derisive snort.

"Such as: Where does the butchering take place?"

Gunther shook his head. "I don't know. I'm not sure anybody would risk the sentence for cannibalism if they actually knew the law, and I'm fairly certain that Cindy Bullock is familiar with it."

"I'd like to say that I agree with you, but when it comes to carnal pleasures like food, people will risk anything. Trust me on this. I want to question Cindy and take a look around the restaurant kitchen if I can. Even if she isn't involved in these murders, I guarantee that she is still in contact with at least a few of her old cronies." Keith drained his coffee and stood to get himself another cup.

"All right, but apart from the Dallas connection, do we have any reason to question the Bullock woman?"

"At least three ex-employees have called her a bloodsucker and a harpy," Keith offered.

"Do we have any hard evidence of either of those?"

"No, and it's pretty common for an ex-employee to call their boss a bloodsucker."

"That is a very tenuous connection. I don't think any judge, even one who was in the NIAD loop, would issue a search warrant based on accusations of harpydom," Gunther remarked.

"I realize that, but I don't see any reason not to see if we can shake something out of her," Keith said. "We'll hit her place on the way back from the vampires. Did the lab happen to know anything about what methotrexate is used for aside from arthritis?"

"It's a very strong antimetabolite with potentially fatal side effects taken by people to treat cancer, rheumatoid arthritis, psoriasis—things like that. It's a human drug with no known magical applications." Gunther paused, musing before he continued, "Maybe the victim was taking it. We could have a look at missing persons to see if any of them had a prescription for methotrexate. At least that way we might be able to identify one of the three unknown deceased, if nothing else."

"Can you do that in the car on the way to visit the vampires or would you like to stay back here?"

"My phone is mighty," Gunther said. "And I wouldn't want to send you off to visit vampires on your own."

"I'm twice as likely to be eaten by a shark as a vampire."

"While that is true, I'll just tag along anyway. After all, it only takes running across the right hungry individual and suddenly you find yourself contemplating lunch from the perspective of a hamburger."

"How do you know the vampire wouldn't just gobble you up as well?"

"I have it on the highest authority that vampires hate the taste of trans-goblin body fluids."

"Whose authority would that be?"

"Ex-boyfriend," Gunther said simply.

Keith gaped, unable to mask his sense of revulsion. Keith had once, like most teenagers, found vampires sexy. And why not? Films portrayed them, generally, as hot young people in leather. The true form of the vampire was more Nosferatu, less model-turned-actor. To Keith they resembled humanoid hagfish. Because of the necessity of hiding their extra-human nature from the population, all registered vampires wore glamours to disguise their pale, pointy faces and hide their bulbous eyes and round, jawless mouths.

The idea that Gunther had managed to have sex with one both fascinated and revolted him. Finally, he said, "I'm not sure I'm liberal enough to have a romance like that."

"You mean because of his true physical appearance?" Gunther asked.

"Right." That, Keith thought, and the fact that you qualify as a main course to him. Aloud he said, "Did you ever see it?"

"Yes, of course. But not often. He was self-conscious about his appearance, but it would have been shallow of me to insist he always disguise himself."

Shallow? Keith supposed so, but it might also be considered crucial by anyone who was made nervous by the prospect of sticking his dick into the mouth of a creature with more than a hundred and fifty razor-sharp teeth.

Gunther must have seen the skepticism on his face because he said, "I enjoy dating challenging men."

"Why did you break up?"

"He insisted on polyamory," Gunther answered. "That and he kept wanting me to call him 'master.' Ultimately, I was not that interested in pursuing a vampire-style relationship. Too hierarchical for me."

Chapter Five

The three registered vampires living in the Willamette Valley ran a business called Azalea Point Creamery. They produced goat-milk artisan cheeses sourced from their own humanely pastured herd. As Keith's rented sedan moved up the long, tree-lined drive, Keith's proximity alert buzzed. Blinking green nine.

Keith shut it off. Gunther glanced up from his phone.

"These individuals have no priors," he stated.

"I know. Procedure says I have to interview them, though, so here we are."

"What's your feeling?"

"My gut says they don't have anything to do with it, but rules is rules, and I've got to interview them anyway since evidence of exsanguination has been found." Keith pulled up alongside a long, corrugated tin goat shed. Three farmhands were at work there, forking hay and soiled wood chips out of the shed. The goats seemed to be out back in an enclosure. He wondered if the farmhands knew about their employers' true nature. Most likely not.

Keith put the car in park. "Do you ever wonder why these guys come here?"

"The vampires?" Gunther kept his voice low. "Probably the same reason as everybody else. They want the chance for a better life."

"I suppose so. It just seems like a lot to have to put up with—concealing your physical form, having agents routinely hassle you."

Gunther shrugged. "It depends on what they had to put up with in their own realm, I guess."

Keith casually unsnapped the holster of his mage pistol and said, "Well, I guess we should go wake them up."

The farmhands watched but did not intervene as the two of them walked to the front door and rang the bell. There came the slight whirring noise of the camera mounted above the door focusing and a groggy male voice on the intercom said, "Can I help you?"

"Joe Sounder?"

"Yes?"

"NIAD. We'd like to ask you a few questions." Keith held up his ID and the door popped open. They entered a small enclosed porch thickly hung with blackout curtains. Overhead lights switched on automatically. Gunther closed the door behind them. From a speaker somewhere above, Joe said, "Please make yourselves comfortable. I'll be right up."

Keith walked into the living room, which, apart from the blackout curtains, looked perfectly normal. He took a seat on the overstuffed beige couch. Gunther remained standing, apparently performing a survey of the numerous photographs of goats hung on the walls.

Joe appeared shortly thereafter. For his glamour he'd chosen the form of a fit, if slightly weathered, middle-aged man. His soft brown hair was rumpled, but attractively so. He wore a blue bathrobe over a set of striped flannel pajamas.

Keith introduced himself and Gunther.

Joe nodded, stretched and scratched his head. "I was wondering when you fellows would be coming around. You want to ask me if I know anything about the Cannibal Killings, right?"

"Just a routine inquiry," Keith assured him. He glanced down at his black book. Joe was listed as having two concubines. "Are Julie and Janice also still residing at this address?"

"Janice is visiting one of her friends in Boise. Julie is still asleep downstairs, but I can wake her if you'd like." Joe started back toward the hallway.

"I don't think that will be necessary at the moment," Keith said. "Have you heard anything about the killings?"

"Just what's been on the news. We don't get into town much." As Joe sat down, the cuff of his pajamas rose up to expose Joe's ankle and reveal the plastic tracking device all registered vampires wore. Keith noted it. "I guess I just assumed it was goblins. They've been coming around here looking for meat for the summer solstice. I told them I don't raise meat goats."

"Do you know anything about this?" Keith displayed the Theater of Blood Carnival Circus flyer.

Joe shook his head and shrugged. "Looks like some kids playing monster to me."

"Tell me a little more about the goblins who came looking for meat," Gunther said. He stood with his hands in his coat pockets, looking genial and harmless. Clearly his interrogation technique was based on gaining trust rather than inspiring fear—just the opposite of Keith's.

"Every year we get inquiries. Mostly over the phone, but sometimes guys will come out here to the dairy right before solstice hoping to make a last-minute deal," Sounder said, chuckling. "They're the same kind of guys who shop for all their gifts on Christmas Eve, you know?"

Gunther nodded. "Some things are universal constants."

Keith scowled slightly. He was himself one of those eleventh-hour shoppers.

Sounder cocked his head to one side, thinking. "There were three of them who came around just recently though. Young guys. I thought it was strange, them being so young."

Gunther nodded, then pulled out his phone and, after a few moments, turned the screen toward Sounder. "Is this one of the guys who came by?"

Keith didn't know why he was surprised to see Lancelot's face smiling out of Gunther's phone. He had been just about to show Sounder a photo of Lancelot himself. He shouldn't have supposed that Gunther would be a less thorough investigator than himself, but somehow he had.

He supposed he did still have some issues with goblins after all, if his unconscious assumption was that because of his race, Gunther wouldn't pursue all avenues of inquiry impartially.

The thought sobered Keith. He hadn't considered himself to contain the capacity for bigotry.

Sounder peered at Lancelot's picture carefully, squinting slightly against the backlit screen.

"Yeah, he was one of them," Sounder replied. "Seemed like a little bit of a kook."

"Can you remember exactly what he said when he came?" Keith leaned slightly forward, keen to catch the inferences of Sounder's delivery. Glamours made reading body language difficult, but the sound of a person's voice often communicated information the glamour erased.

"Well, let's see . . . They asked how much it would cost for two whole goats. I told them that we didn't sell meat goats, like I told you. And then the kooky one wanted to know if I ever heard of any vampires who drank blood on stage."

"On stage?" Gunther gave Keith a sidelong look.

Sounder nodded. "It was a really strange question. That's why I remember it."

"It does seem somewhat random," Keith remarked. "Why do you think he wanted to know?"

"I have no idea," Sounder said.

"What did you tell him?" Gunther asked.

"I told him that only an idiot would risk a run-in with NIAD over something like that, and I don't associate with idiots." Sounder shifted on the sofa and stifled a yawn. "Not if I can help it, anyway."

"And then?" Keith prompted.

"Then they left," Sounder said. He flashed a faint smile. "I think they might have been offended."

◆◆◆

During the drive back to Portland, neither he nor Gunther spoke too much. Keith was sunk in his own thoughts. Interviewing the vampires, which had seemed to him to be borderline harassment at first, had yielded a piece of information after all. Goblins had been there looking for meat. The arrows were all lining up and all confirming Keith's original suspicions.

He supposed Gunther's silence could also be attributed to this information.

They made good time and got into the city and to the Bauer & Bullock Steakhouse right in the thick of the dinner service.

Stepping into the dining room, Keith was struck by both the smell—searing flesh—and the decor—the predictable, yet still imposing combination of dark wooden paneling, leather and massive proportions. The whole place looked like a supersized fantasy of an old-time gentlemen's club. Even the silverware was slightly too large.

Keith made his way to the host station, where he very discreetly flashed his badge at a fragile-looking young host and asked to see the manager. It would do no good to antagonize the staff, especially if this turned out to be a dead end.

The busboy disappeared upstairs, only to return a few seconds later, Cindy Bullock in tow.

Bullock was a skinny, stylish woman with kinky blond hair and long, bony arms on which she wore a multitude of designer bangles. She took one look at Keith, crossed her arms, and said, "Agent Curry," by way of greeting.

"Hello, Ms. Bullock," Keith returned, undeterred. "This is my associate, Gunther Heartman. We'd like to ask you a few questions."

"About?"

"About your meat supplier," Keith said. "Who might that be?"

Cindy's expression darkened. "We serve grass-fed organic beef sourced from USDA-certified local ranchers. You can read all about them on our menu. Additional information can be found on the website."

Keith jotted down the address of the website in his black book, though he already had it. He wrote slowly and precisely. He wanted Cindy to squirm a little. She clenched her hands. The large rings on her fingers glittered.

"You have a really impressive selection of whiskeys," Gunther commented.

Cindy's initial bright response at being complimented dimmed with suspicion. "Yes, we have a discerning clientele."

"Do you do much catering?" Keith swept in with another question.

"A fair amount," Cindy replied.

"So you've got, what? Three jobs a week?" Keith asked.

"I'd have to look at my calendar. It's upstairs in the office if you'd like to follow me."

"Actually, what I'd really like to take a look at is your kitchen." Keith started for the kitchen door. Cindy rushed ahead of him.

"I'd really rather you didn't go back right now, Agent Curry. You know we're right in the middle of dinner service. If you could just wait—"

"Oh, I won't get underfoot," Keith said. "I've been a chef. I know how to keep out of the way."

Cindy placed herself between him and the kitchen door. She flung her arms out, bracelets jangling, ringed fingers flashing. "I must insist, Agent Curry. You have no right to go back there. This is my place. You have no right!"

A dishwasher who had been rounding the corner carrying a rack of clean plates stopped, reflexively backtracking at the sight of Cindy in what looked like full rage.

Keith's lip curled in disgust. Why was it that the completely insane gravitated so heavily into the hospitality industry? "Listen, ma'am, I can go get a warrant if you want, but I assume you that you don't want me coming in here during dinner service with a bunch of uniformed officers, right?"

"Are you threatening me?" Cindy lunged forward, skinny body flexing like a viper preparing to strike. "I know why you are harassing me."

"Neither Agent Heartman nor myself is attempting to harass you. All we'd like to do is have a look at where you do your butchering. That's all." Keith kept his tone calm, businesslike. "We can go get a warrant if you like, but all I need to do is look at your product."

"Well, you can't." Cindy crossed her arms, raising her chin triumphantly. "I won't let you because I don't have to and you know it."

Keith shrugged. "If that's the way you want to play it, ma'am, then we will. I'll be back with a warrant, a health inspector and a representative from the state liquor board. I might bring an auditor just to get it all over with at once." He turned and started toward the door. He needed to get out of this joint anyway. The smell of chargrilled meat was beginning to seriously nauseate him. He saw a slight motion out of the corner of his eye.

"Son of a bitch!" With a jangle of expensive bangles, Bullock smashed her fist directly into his jaw. He staggered back a step, pain exploding through the side of his face. In a moment, Gunther had caught her right arm, but she still lashed out with her left, raking her nails across his neck.

"That is really uncalled for, ma'am," Gunther said, tightly twisting her arm around her back and slapping one handcuff on. He caught hold of her left hand and managed to get it in the other cuff, but Bullock bolted. Keith stuck out a foot and hooked her ankle. She went down, screaming and cursing, on the damp tiled floor. Gunther wasted no time; he cuffed her ankles, then brought them up and hogtied her.

The kitchen had gone silent as the whole crew gaped at the scene. The dishwasher seemed to be working hard to suppress a smile.

Gunther leaned down and said very loudly and very close to her ear, "You are under arrest for assaulting a federal officer." Then, to Keith, he said, "You want to go have that look around now or wait till the police get here?"

"Yeah, sure." His jaw throbbed. He glanced at the dishwasher. "Show me to the meat locker, kid."

The dishwasher led the way back into the kitchen. They passed a busy line of grills. Flames and smoke leaped and billowed around the cooks as they tended the orders. Then they entered the back kitchen—a small, clean space whose walls were lined with steel prep tables and banks of shelves holding dry goods.

"The big one's right there." Tentatively the dishwasher pointed back toward a heavy door. "But there's another smaller one for the really expensive steaks that's padlocked."

"Who's got the key?"

"It's a combo lock." This came from a burly Black guy who had followed them from the line. Keith thought he might be the head grill man. "Ms. Bullock is the only one who knows it."

"Of course she is."

After a wait of approximately ten minutes, Portland Police Bureau arrived with a pair of bolt cutters for the padlock and a car to transport Ms. Bullock. Being a member of the strike force, Gunther could have probably performed a spell to open it, but there were far too many bystanders and it was just as easy to use a human tool. By the time PPB carried Bullock away, the deep bruise on Keith's jaw had begun to darken, but he refused to show any pain in front of the restaurant's staff. There was still no way to tell where any of their allegiances lay.

Keith entered the meat locker. He already felt ill. Very quickly he found himself fighting to avoid retching. Two naked bodies hung suspended upside down from chains, throats cut, blood collecting in buckets on the floor.

To the left, on a stainless steel rack, were more remains. This one had been skinned, cut apart at the joints, and separated into several metal hotel pans, but Keith recognized the anatomy immediately.

Gunther's cookie search had led them straight to the abattoir. Plainly, the butchering had taken place here. For all his commentary about humans not abandoning their carnal pleasures easily, Keith would have never seriously thought that Bullock's wife would have the sheer stupidity to continue her Thyestean feasting after her husband had been caught. Yet here she was.

Keith stepped back outside for some air. Gunther had been waiting just beyond the door.

"From your face I gather that you've found something?"

"Have a look for yourself," Keith suggested.

Gunther held up a demurring hand. "I trust you. What do you want to do now?"

Keith scanned the faces of the kitchen staff and of the servers who were looking anxiously on. It would be impossible for all members of the staff to be innocent. Cindy Bullock's manicure made it clear that she never picked up a kitchen knife.

"Put a uniform on this door, clear the dining room and call for a paddy wagon. We're detaining and questioning all staff. We'll also need to find the names of any not on shift tonight and have PPB bring them down to the station. Particularly the butchers. Someone with skills skinned those carcasses. I'm thinking we're looking for one front-of-the-house person and one or two members of kitchen staff who were in on it with Ms. Bullock."

Gunther gave a slight salute and departed the back kitchen. Keith walked up to the line but didn't walk through. Each and every one of those five guys had at least one knife. Plus, they'd be more cooperative if he respected both their territory and hierarchy. He held up his badge. "My name is Keith Curry. I'm a federal agent. Who is the person in charge here?"

Unsurprisingly, it was the Black guy who had spoken first. His name turned out to be Baratunde and he was the chef. He outweighed Keith by at least forty pounds but seemed overall even tempered. "I need to ask you to shut this down and bring your people out to the dining room to be interviewed."

"What about the tickets?" He indicated the unmade orders with a wave of his tongs.

Keith shook his head. "Shut it down. For tonight, anyway. We're already clearing the customers. This is a crime scene."

The other man nodded slowly. Behind him, Keith could see one of the cooks texting someone. "And I'm going to ask to hold your phones for the time being, starting with his."

Baratunde whipped his head around to fix the young cook with a glare. "Damn it, Jesse. Bring that here. Haven't you got any sense?"

Jesse cowered as he handed over the phone. "I was just texting my girlfriend to say I'd be late, chef."

"Your woman can wait."

Keith found it sentimentally amusing that as an agent he inspired less fear than the chef.

Baratunde collected the phones into a square plastic refrigerator insert. As he handed them to Keith, he said, "Jesse's just a dumb kid, sir. He wasn't trying to disrespect you."

"Sure, I understand." He waved the chef into the back kitchen where they could have relative privacy.

"I'm going to ask you straight-out. Have you ever been in this locker?"

"No, sir. It's Ms. Bullock's private refrigerator. No staff is allowed in there."

Keith leaned back against a stainless steel prep table. "You and I both know that somebody must be allowed in. Ms. Bullock is not cooking for herself."

This drew a slight smile from Baratunde.

"Not my staff." The chef's tone was final. "None of my boys have ever stepped foot in there."

"Who then?"

"There's a private catering company that uses this space on Monday nights when the restaurant is closed. Forbidden Pleasures, I think they're called."

Of course, Keith thought. "Do they share all this equipment?"

The chef nodded. "It's part of their rental contract. They clean up fine, but they're hell on the knives."

"Do you have contact information for this company?"

"No, sir. We're not allowed on the property on Mondays. Not even me."

"Did you ever think that maybe Ms. Bullock was hiding something?"

"Sure," the chef said. "Look at that big-ass lock."

"What do you think is in that refrigerator?"

"Heroin." The answer came without pause and with certainty. "Or maybe coke. Some kind of drugs anyway."

Keith nodded thoughtfully. That is exactly what he would have assumed in this guy's position. He said, "Do you read the newspaper?"

Baratunde's eyes narrowed slightly. "Sometimes. I'm more of a talk radio man, though."

"Have you heard anything about the Cannibal Killer?"

The chef's face paled to the color of ash. He swallowed and said, "Some."

"Inside that walk-in, lying in stainless hotel pans that you probably use every day, are the butchered remains of at least three people," Keith said. "You can see how I want to know more about this catering company that shares your kitchen, right?"

The chef did not immediately answer. Keith wondered briefly if he had misjudged Baratunde. Maybe he truly had been complicit. Then, with no warning, the man lunged sideways and puked loudly into the trash can. The uniform didn't look much better, but he, at least, hadn't been eating off the same dishes used to process human protein. Keith waited while the chef splashed his face with water and stood, leaning on the hand sink, breathing deeply. Finally, he said, "Sometimes the caterers have leftovers that they leave in our refrigerator for the staff to eat."

The cause of Baratunde's abrupt illness became sharply clear. "And?"

"This morning they left some posole in our walk-in. I— for lunch—" Tears rimmed the chef's eyes. Whether they were the result of impending further illness or horrifying remorse, Keith could not say.

"Is there any left?"

Baratunde nodded. "Ms. Bullock and I were the only ones who ate any. Nobody else wanted hominy. She kept talking about how back in the day the dish was made with human flesh."

"You better show me. We'll need to test it."

"I just need a second." He leaned far over the sink, jaw working, plainly fighting the urge to vomit again.

Keith said, "Take your time."

It only took Baratunde a few deep breaths to recover before he was able to lead Keith into the main walk-in, a long, narrow space. It was supremely clean and well organized. The chef plainly took pride in his profession.

"This is it." He handed Keith a long insert of quasi-congealed stew, taking obvious care not to touch the contents.

Gunther ducked into the walk-in. "We've got the dining room cleared."

"Thanks." Keith glanced at him and then at the chef, whose eyes were still glassy. The big man's hands shook slightly. Keith remained placid while he removed a small vial from his pocket. He pulled a piece of flesh from the stew and squeezed a couple of drops of tincture onto it. The tincture shone blue. He looked at the chef and said, "It's pork. We should keep it anyway. The container might have prints we can use."

The relief that swept across Baratunde's face was that of a condemned man released at the last minute.

"Thank the Lord."

"I'd appreciate it if you'd go and see how your crew is doing."

"Yes, sir." He went, smiling.

The second the door closed, Keith crumpled the meat in a napkin, whispering, "I'm sorry—whoever you were."

Gunther drew closer. "I thought blue meant human."

Keith nodded. "The chef doesn't need to know that though. He doesn't need to have that knowledge on him for the rest of his life—that he's a cannibal. It's bad enough that he's going to lose his job when this joint shuts down. Working here isn't going to be a resume builder, either. We'll still send it to the lab—just for documentation. And prints, like I said."

Gunther said, "Do you need a minute?"

"No, let's just go get this over with."

Chapter Six

Interviews at Bauer & Bullock went quickly. Few staff knew much about Forbidden Pleasures. Keith called it quits around nine, when his jaw started hurting him too much to pay attention to their uninformative answers. He decided to save Bullock's interview for the morning, when he was less tired and after she'd spent the night in jail.

Once they reached the hotel, Gunther went to the ice machine to make up a pack for Keith while Keith himself poured two vodka shots and drank them both in quick succession.

Returning with a softball-sized bag of ice, wrapped in a clean white towel, Gunther said, "By the way, it was bison."

"No, the carcass in the fridge was human. Trust me." Keith held the ice pack to his jaw, wincing at the cold against his tender flesh.

"I mean the preferred protein at my family's midsummer meal. It was bison. You asked and I never answered." Gunther sat down beside him on the bed. Keith's proximity alarm buzzed and buzzed again, warning him of Gunther's closeness. He pulled it off and threw it on the nightstand. He didn't need the watch to know how near the other man sat. Every part of Keith's body seemed to be responding to the nearness—to the smell of Gunther's faintly spicy cologne, to the knowledge of his sheer masculinity.

He needed to get laid and that was a fact.

Gunther said quietly, "Is your jaw hurting you a lot?"

"It hurts enough." The bruise did hurt, but if he was honest, the real wound had been mainly to his pride. He said, "Getting hit by a crazy, slap-happy bitch isn't what I wanted from this evening."

"I admit I had other hopes as well." After this remark, Gunther lay back and fell silent. Keith glanced sideways, wondering if the other man had somehow drifted to asleep. His eyes were closed, his fingers laced behind his head. His abdomen rose and fell slowly. His expression had softened. His mouth looked supremely kissable. Keith imagined himself leaning over and tasting Gunther's mouth, wondering if a hint of tobacco still lingered there.

And for so many reasons that was the stupidest impulse Keith had had in years.

Without opening his eyes Gunther said, "Are you hungry?"

"I'll make myself some grilled cheese in a minute."

"That's pretty much the only thing you eat now, isn't it?"

"Pretty much."

Gunther shook his head. "It doesn't seem like that could possibly be good for you."

"Says the man who ate two and a half packs of cigarettes today."

"I didn't say my diet was good. I'm just saying that you might want to take a multivitamin."

"I ate an orange last week," Keith said. "Grilled cheese is easy when you're cooking for one."

"Why don't you include me in your dinner plans then?"

"I don't cook meat anymore." Keith felt like a complete weakling admitting this but also knew that Gunther probably didn't truly understand how pathetic this made him seem in the professional cooking world.

"I didn't say it had to be meat." Gunther opened his eyes, regarding Keith with a steadiness that made him look away.

"You're a goblin. Meat is what you want."

"You know we prefer to be called Luminous Ones. And I think we don't know each other well enough for you to know what it is that I want."

"You're telling me that your favorite food isn't meat?"

Gunther shrugged. "When I was a little kid my favorite food was Christmas lights. I used to eat them right off the string like candy."

"You're shitting me."

"Not at all. My godfather used to bribe me with them so I'd stop sucking all the butane out of his lighter. So while it's true that I haven't eaten many vegetables in my life, I'm feeling very game today. So how about it?"

"I don't really want to cook," Keith said.

"What do you want to do then?"

"I don't know."

"You must want something."

Though he knew Gunther was still talking about their dinner plans, Keith felt so demoralized and tired and maybe slightly drunk from the vodka shot on an empty stomach that he found himself saying, "What I want, Heartman, is to fuck you and not have to talk about it afterward."

Gunther didn't immediately respond and Keith realized he'd gone too far, so he added, "That's just about the only thing that would make me feel okay about today."

Gunther sat up and then stood up. Keith stared down at the mottled brown carpet, expecting the other man to take his coat and go. He heard the rustle of fabric.

Soon I'll hear the click of a hotel door closing, Keith thought. Instead he just heard more rustling. He glanced up and to his astonishment realized that Gunther had shed his sport coat and tie. His cuffs hung, unfastened, while he worked the buttons of his dress shirt open.

Stupidly, Keith asked, "What are you doing?"

Gunther pulled a slow smile, looking him straight in the eye as he shrugged out of his shirt. He wore a white undershirt that molded to his flat abdomen. His biceps and forearms bulged, angular masses of muscle. "I'm preparing to make you feel better about today."

Keith gave a dry laugh. "Okay, nice one. You got me. How about we get Thai takeout from that joint around the corner?"

"Afterward." Gunther stepped out of his shoes and un-buckled his belt.

With a weird mix of pleasure and fear, Keith realized Gunther wasn't joking. He said, "I don't have anything . . . for that."

"I do. Inside pocket of my overcoat." He dropped his pants. Even in white boxer briefs and black dress socks, Gunther looked amazing. He didn't keep either of those on for very much longer, though. Nor did his undershirt remain in place. Naked, Gunther's pale body seemed like it could have been cut from paper. His legs were heavily roped with muscle. Though his chest was mostly bare, a fine line of dark hair ran from his navel to his groin. His cock, like the rest of him, seemed perfectly proportioned. Long, uncut and resting on a pair of the most even testicles Keith had ever seen.

Gunther stepped closer. Keith set his ice pack aside and rested his hands on Gunther's hips.

Gunther shuddered and murmured, "Chilly."

"Sorry." Keith ran his palms up over Gunther's abdomen, then around to his back, sliding down over his round ass, the tips of his fingers lightly brushing the tender inside flesh.

Keith watched Gunther's face as he gently explored Gunther's body. "You really were perfectly made."

"Through no effort of my own, unfortunately. But thank you." Gunther rested his hands on Keith's shoulders, spreading his legs slightly, allowing Keith greater access. Gunther's cock was fully erect now, the head bobbing very near Keith's face. He nuzzled the shaft, cheek pressed against Gunther's abdomen.

Gunther said, "I hope you will invite me into your bed soon."

"In a minute." Keith caught the head of Gunther's cock, sucking it, tasting it. Now that he knew Gunther was trans-goblin he half expected some vile Zippo-fuel flavor to assault his senses and kill his desire. But Gunther tasted just like he had before. He tasted just like he looked—perfectly human, while simultaneously being inhumanly perfect. Gunther arched into him, just slightly.

Keith stood and nibbled Gunther's lower lip, sampling that flavor too, though he'd never truly forgotten it. How could he? Spicy, fragrant, rich and slippery. Luscious as drawn butter. Gunther's lips parted, soft and passive to Keith's explorations. His hands rested lightly on Keith's sides, as if they were waiting to receive a permission slip before even attempting to touch Keith's chest.

Keith supposed that that was exactly what Gunther was waiting for, given Keith hadn't even loosened his tie. Cheek pressed against Gunther's throat, he said, "Lie down with me."

Gunther said nothing. He merely climbed onto the mattress and stretched out on his stomach as he had numerous times in the past.

At the small of his back, Gunther had a tattoo. A small triangular blackwork design with a point that dipped down toward the cleft of his ass. It was just about the last thing Keith expected to ever have the pleasure of seeing again, but once he did, he could not get his clothes off fast enough.

Face resting on his folded arms, Gunther watched. He said, "I have a condom in my inside jacket pocket."

Keith picked up the jacket, felt inside the pocket and laid the foil packet on the bedside table, along with a small tube of lube. He lay down next to Gunther and ran his hand along the other man's back till he reached the tattoo. He traced the inked lines, wondering what, if anything, they meant.

Keith had tattoos of his own. He'd never met a chef who didn't. His were slightly more embarrassing, though piecemeal, work that dotted his body like pictures scattered from a scrapbook. On his right shoulder, a Jolly Roger from his pirate phase—on his left, a Celtic maze, and on his inside left forearm, a line of black stars stretching from his wrist to inner elbow—a remnant from his club period.

"I always liked this." Keith gently traced the lines of Gunther's tattoo.

"It's goblin script." Gunther looked slightly embarrassed. "It's how you write the word 'love.' I got it on my eighteenth birthday."

Keith chuckled, ran his hand down over the curve of Gunther's buttock. "And you say you're not rebellious."

"It's my one and only display. I'd seen a picture online of a man who had a tattoo right there and I thought it was beautiful, so that's what I got. Imagine my surprise when it turned out to be called a tramp stamp." Gunther smiled up at him from under his lashes. "Will you still kiss me?"

"Why not?" Keith bent to press his mouth against Gunther's. The other man's lips were hot and soft and supple. Keith didn't think he'd ever kissed a man who seemed so relaxed and willing to let him take the lead. The very compliance seemed suspicious. Why in the world had Gunther taken his ludicrous bait? Had their positions been reversed, Keith would never have offered his own body—especially not to a guy like himself, with such questionable views and obvious anger issues. It seemed impossible that they should be here together this way. And yet, here they were.

By nature Keith was not a rough or aggressive lover. He never had been. He'd played at it, sure. Lied about it to the straight guys he worked with who didn't really understand that being gay wasn't about plundering ass after ass after ass—not to him anyway. He'd bragged with some bravado over slaying this or that twink at the bar. But inside he'd never thought about sex that way and he couldn't think about it that way now. He gave it his best, turning the ritual of condom and lube into teasing play, taking time to make sure Gunther was comfortable, relaxed and overall eager to accept him into his body. Keith murmured small compliments, telling Gunther how beautiful his body was—how hot inside—as he lay, chest pressed to Gunther's back, fingers entwined with his temporary partner's, hands flexing and contracting, mirroring the push and pulling of their bodies.

Gunther responded with more generosity, if it was possible to supersede the hospitality of allowing Keith within his body.

Keith wound his arm around Gunther. Feeling Gunther's questing hand, he laced their fingers together once more.

Friction became slick heat and he could no longer tell where his skin ended and Gunther's began. Dizzying scents and sensations flowed through him. The carnal pleasure of Gunther's skin far exceeded anything he'd ever known before or since he'd last had this man. Whether it was a trick of his goblin flesh or actual love, Keith did not know and he did not care. He thrust into Gunther's responsive flesh, kissing and consuming him as if he'd been starved and alone for years only to stumble upon some lush, wild bacchanalia.

No number of kisses or fevered thrusts seemed adequate to slake Keith's craving. He longed to consume Gunther utterly, selfishly. Gunther bucked back against him, then began a tense and shuddering climax. The beauty of seeing Gunther's pleasure, feeling the other man's delicious hunger, drove Keith to the blinding, inarticulate edge of sheer avarice. Then all at once ecstasy was upon him, rolling through his taut muscles, drawing tears from his eyes.

Afterward, Keith lay alongside Gunther and drifted, waking only briefly when Gunther rose, collected his clothes and silently departed.

CHAPTER SEVEN

Keith was up and out the door at six the next morning. He walked the block and a half to Whole Foods and bought a doughnut. But rather than returning immediately to the hotel, he found himself, for the first time, pacing the aisles. Soon he had an armful of ingredients—eggs, heavy cream, milk, butter, spinach, nutmeg, Gruyère—which he toted back to the hotel in a newly purchased green reusable bag. Without allowing himself to think about what he was doing, he began to cook. First came the crepes, completed one at a time and layered with sheets of waxed paper to keep them from sticking together. After that he prepped creamed spinach filling and grated Gruyère. He brewed coffee. He waited, surfing through television channels until his proximity alert informed him that Gunther had exited the elevator. Then he bounced to his feet and began to assemble breakfast, filling the first crepe before he heard a knock.

Gunther's manner was exactly the same as it had been the previous day. No casual observer would have suspected from looking at Gunther that they had made love less than twelve hours ago in this very bed.

Really, the only person displaying a change of behavior was himself.

Keith decided not to think about that at all.

"Want some breakfast?" he said. "I made crepes."

Gunther smiled. "Yes, please."

"Do you like spinach?"

"I've never really had a spinach crepe before, but I probably do. So far I like everything except banana pudding."

Keith folded the spinach filling into the four remaining crepes and handed the plate to Gunther, along with a fork.

"Aren't you going to have any?" Gunther asked.

"I already had a doughnut."

"So you made these specially for me?"

"I wanted to cook something this morning." Keith knew that this wasn't really an answer, but he wasn't ready to actually think about an answer either. He didn't want to plumb the murky depths of his own motivations. It was perfectly reasonable to want to make breakfast for a man you had sex with the previous night. The urge toward hospitality contained no special significance. And yet, he found himself carefully scrutinizing Gunther's reaction.

Again, nothing special. He was a chef. Chefs all wanted to know how their food had been received. He paid no special attention to Gunther, nor should he.

If he told himself this enough times, Keith thought, certainly he would eventually believe it.

Suddenly, Gunther glanced up, noting Keith's stare. "These are amazing, but I really feel awkward eating them all alone."

"I'll get myself some coffee." Keith rose, poured himself a cup and to change the conversation, asked, "So do you know many other gay goblins?"

"Trans-goblins," Gunther corrected, then added, "No, hardly any. During the transformation process virtually anything can be decided about a baby. Few parents want to give their child an orientation that will make their human lives less easy. My parents were the exception to this rule."

"Are you telling me that you were made gay on purpose?" Goblins, Keith thought, truly were a breed apart. Apart from common sense, mainly. But then he caught himself in his own disturbing condemnation. Why shouldn't parents want a gay child? Goblin or not?

"My parents thought my godfather was the ideal human, so they wanted me to be as much like him as possible.

I joined NIAD to follow in his footsteps. You've probably heard of him. Half-Dead Henry?"

"The Undead Bum?" The words leaped from Keith's mouth before he could jam his foot in to stop them from escaping. "I mean—"

"No, you got it right: the Undead Bum." Gunther took a forkful of crepe and chewed it thoughtfully. "You remind me of him, somewhat."

"How's that?" Keith tried to keep his tone neutral, but he couldn't help but be slightly offended by being compared to a famous hobo.

"Your tattoos. The way you don't seem to be able to express yourself emotionally. And your terrible diet. Henry eats cold chili right out of the can. Are you sure you won't have this last crepe? They're very good."

Keith hesitated, on the edge of turning back from a second refusal. Again that unthinking inspiration struck and he just said, "I would, but I'm too lazy right now to lift a fork."

"I could feed it to you," Gunther said. "That's what you want me to do, isn't it?"

"God, no. I'm not a little kid. Give me that." Keith took the plate and fork and ate the crepe in six bites. It tasted better than he expected. He wiped his mouth and, finding Gunther staring at him, leaned across the table and quickly kissed him.

"Are you—"

Keith held up a silencing hand. "I haven't changed my mind about talking about it."

"I didn't think you had. I was about to ask if you wanted to question Bullock now."

"I think it's about time. Is she still at PPB or was she moved to the NIAD detention facility?" Keith asked.

"I'll call." Gunther did so. Keith listened absently, while finishing the dishes. He heard Gunther say, "I see."

Gunther's tone alarmed him and Keith turned back to see that his partner's expression had grown dark. He said, "What is it?"

"Bullock was dead in her cell this morning. Suicide. I guess she knew the penalty for cannibalism after all."

CHAPTER EIGHT

While Gunther spent the day visiting homes and interviewing members of the local trans-goblin community, Keith
remained in his hotel room, staring at his own laptop, sifting
through tens of thousands of pieces of text.

Looking.

Searching for any connection.

Keith made grilled cheese, brewed coffee.

Around ten p.m., Gunther returned. "Find out anything
interesting?"

"Samantha Evans, the booker from Lulu's Flapjack Shack,
has gone missing. Her mother reported her disappearance
to the PPB and they sent out an officer to investigate, but
according to the PPB report, her boyfriend says it's not un-
common for her to take off for a couple of days without
telling anyone," Keith said. "What about you?"

"I had to drink seventeen cups of tea, but I did manage
to catch up on every piece of trans-goblin gossip for the last
fifteen years. Lancelot, our goat-seeking goblin musician,
has recently lost both his parents in a boating accident."

"A suspicious accident?"

"Not at all." Gunther leaned back, closed his eyes.
"Nothing even remotely suspicious about him. Everybody
loves him as far as I can tell."

Gunther yawned mightily. Keith waited for him to continue. He did not. A minute later Keith said, "You can take
the bed if you want, Heartman."

Gunther complied, lurched up out of the chair and
flopped onto the bed limp as a side of salmon slapping
down onto a chopping board.

Thinking that he should persevere, but tempted beyond
all reasonable measure, Keith made it ten more minutes before

joining Gunther on the ugly bedspread, then between the freshly changed hotel sheets.

Approximately five hours later, at 3:06 a.m., PPB called them out to take a look at a foot.

The foot in question had been found lodged under some fallen wood near an observation point in the Smith and Bybee Wetlands Natural Area. The foot was pale as wax. It had four toes—all of them very long. Each greasy white digit ended in a hornlike yellow talon. The most striking feature of the foot, though, was its NIAD vampire-identification bracelet looping the burned and slimy ankle stump.

"We called this cuff into the office and they gave us your number," the police officer said. "I would have called the department of wildlife myself. Since it doesn't look like a human foot."

"It's not a human foot." Keith knew he stated the obvious but felt the need to say something. "Don't worry, I've got the gear to take care of it."

"Who found this?" Gunther asked.

"And ornithology professor from PSU. He was trying to set up in a blind before sunrise to observe the waterfowl when he ran across it. We sent him home. We wouldn't have called you except for the cuff."

"It's no problem," Gunther said.

"Do you mind if I ask what that thing is?"

"It's an animal limb. We'll know more about it after it goes to the lab in San Francisco." Keith opened up a lightproof bag and prepared to remove the evidence from the scene. They'd need to buy some dry ice on the way back to the hotel to keep it fresh during shipping.

"It doesn't really look like any kind of animal around here," the officer remarked. "I've hunted here all my life, you know."

Gunther stepped smoothly between them. "I strongly suspect that this is part of a highly endangered animal."

"Endangered animal?"

"Yes, the Argentinean four-toed sloth. Have you ever heard if it?"

"No. I've seen a sloth in Costa Rica before, but never heard of the Argentinean one."

"Well, until recently, they were considered extinct. I'm actually collecting money for habitat preservation right now. Do you think you'd be interested in helping with a donation? Anything at all would be appreciated."

The officer demurred, claiming to have left his wallet in the car, and sidled away.

"What would you have done if he'd given you money?"

"That guy? It was never a possibility," Gunther said, smiling.

Keith crouched down. The stench of decay filled his nostrils. He gloved up and gingerly picked up the limb. After wiping the goo away he read out the serial number on the tracking cuff while Gunther typed it into the database, via his phone.

"Janice Sounder," Gunther pronounced. "No surprise there. The question is—is the rest of Janice alive somewhere?"

"I don't think so." Keith finished bagging the foot, then poked at the ground with his pen. Though footprints and rain marred the scene, traces of ash remained. "I think she burned here."

"Wouldn't there be clothes left behind? Or remnants anyway?"

"Only if she was wearing them." Keith beckoned the PPB liaison forward. "You say the foot was found in the woodpile?"

"Yes, sir."

"Was any of the wood around it burned?"

"Yes, sir. We have those in evidence. We're testing them for traces of accelerant. We did find some metal as well.

Some fragments of silver and also a piece of metal we think might have been a wedding ring, sir."

"Why do you think that?"

"It was gold and about the right shape."

Driving up the road, Keith could see a small procession of nondescript black SUVs approaching. The forensic team had arrived, probably via some sort of portal. Through his NIAD glasses, he could see the faint blue tracers still clinging to them.

"Well," he said. "I suppose we need to go turn this over to the team."

By the time they'd relinquished Janice's foot to the Irregulars forensic team and signed all the requisite papers, it was seven a.m. Keith was hungry and on the delirious level of fatigue. He pulled into an old-school doughnut shop called the Tulip Bakery, glanced over to Gunther, and said, "You want to go in or should I just get a dozen and head back to the hotel?"

Gunther leaned back in his seat, eyes closed. "I trust you."

Tulip Bakery turned out to have the sort of doughnuts he remembered from his childhood back east. No coffee milk, though—in fact, no coffee at all. He got an assortment of cakes and raised and a couple of maple bars. He set the box in Gunther's lap—the other man didn't open his eyes but held the box instinctively as Keith pulled out of the parking lot, heading back to downtown.

"Okay, so we've got the butchery venue and we've got one dead vampire who was supposed to have gone to Boise but never made it." Keith rubbed his face, not relishing the drive back. "There is no reason to believe that these two occurrences are connected except for proximity."

Gunther reclined his seat. "Let's say, for the sake of argument, that they are."

"All right."

"What if Janice was somehow connected to the killings—maybe not as a killer, but as a purchaser of blood?"

"Why kill her then?" Keith asked.

"Maybe she wanted out. Maybe she was blackmailing the real killer."

"I don't know. The Sounders have been here for a hundred and forty-five years without a single incident," Gunther pointed out.

"Okay, let's go at it from another angle. Who was Janice meeting in Boise?"

"A vampire named Silas DuPree. According to our office there he hasn't even left his house for the last fifteen years." Gunther cracked an eye long enough to paw a coconut twist out of the doughnut box.

"How does Silas survive?"

"Blood delivered weekly by courier." Gunther took a bite of his doughnut. "He's basically a shut-in."

"Where does he get the money for the home-delivery bloodmobile?"

"He wrote a series of romance novels featuring sexy reclusive loners. Before that he performed on stage, but that would have been in the pre-electricity era." Gunther inhaled at least half his doughnut in one massive bite. "Damn, these are good. Any coffee?"

"There's some cold stuff from yesterday in the cupholder if you don't mind my backwash."

Gunther looked like he might make some sort of droll remark, then seemed to think better of it. He slugged back Keith's leftover black with two sugars, then fished around in his pocket for his cigarettes.

They turned and were heading straight into the rising sun. Keith scowled. More than likely this was the last sight that Janice Sounder had seen. "Did our office actually send an agent to speak with DuPree or did they just check the computer tracking system?"

"I don't know." Apparently reinvigorated by fried dough, Gunther adjusted his seat back to alert passenger position. "Are you thinking that he's not really there?"

"I'm thinking that a vampire can survive losing a foot, no matter how it gets removed."

"That's true," Gunther said. "And speaking of surviving losing a foot, we've also just seen that a foot can survive losing a vampire."

"What's your point?"

"It's really convenient that we should find Janice's ankle cuff still attached to her foot. I think she might have deliberately shoved her foot out of the sunlight when she knew that she was going to die."

"It's not like the sunlight would have destroyed the cuff. We would have found that eventually via the GPS tracking."

"But what would that have looked like? Just a ring of plastic. It's nothing that anyone would call the police over," Gunther said. "Someone needs to contact Janice's friend in Boise directly."

"I'd like to do it myself."

"That's just what I was thinking. I'll call for air transport." Gunther applied himself to locating his phone.

While Keith focused on staying awake so as not to kill them both in a tragic car wreck, Gunther spent the next few minutes arranging for a plane to take them from Portland to Boise. "A NIAD plane can take us at four and bring us back tonight."

Keith nodded.

Gunther finished off his doughnut, then paused thoughtfully. "That was pretty good. Could have used some hot sauce though."

"I could use a nap and shower."

To Keith it seemed inevitable that they would end up having sex again. They were both too exhausted to feel inhibited and also pumped up on half a dozen doughnuts each. It felt natural in the surreal, sugary morning to invite Gunther into his room, then into his shower, then finally into his bed.

Afterward, Gunther lay next to him, his chest heaving. Keith stared up at the hotel ceiling for a few minutes, catching his breath.

Gunther said, "Want something to drink?"

"Anything that contains alcohol."

Gunther rose, opened the refrigerator. The chill and artificial light flowed out across Keith's damp skin and silhouetted Gunther's perfect body as he grabbed a beer and twisted the cap off. He handed it to Keith, then delved back into the refrigerator. From inside the door, he chose a bottle of Dave's Insanity Sauce, unscrewed the top, then tipped his head back and chugged the entire thing, ending with a satisfied sigh.

He climbed back into the bed and pressed his lips against Keith's cheek.

Keith lay awake as Gunther fell into a doze, feeling the slight warmth of pure capsaicin left behind in the shape of a kiss and wondering what the hell he was going to do now.

Chapter Nine

For the first time in two years, Keith dreamed about his old restaurant. He had thought that he would dream about it more than he did. It was as though even his subconscious mind remained too wounded to venture back into his own kitchen.

He knew he was in a dream. The department had trained him in lucid dreaming, trances and astral projections as part of his basic course. But knowing one is in a dream and being able to control that dream world remained two different activities.

He stood behind the long, old-fashioned counter, regarding his sole customer, who sat drinking coffee and reading the paper. A snow goblin. A creature made of angular bone with smoldering red slits for eyes. The goblin turned a page of paper, took a sip of coffee, and then shook a few dashes of hot pepper sauce into the liquid. He said, "I think we should check out that film festival."

"Can't. I'm working."

The goblin folded the paper shut and said, "Not everything is about food, you know."

"To me it is. This is my whole life. It's everything I know." He became aware of the fact that he hadn't finished his prep work for the dinner rush. Customers would be coming in hungry and wanting to be fed. Shadows moved outside his restaurant's front window, some stopping to read the menu posted there. Somewhere in the background he could hear the sound of the dishwasher playing reggae and clanking dishes together. He had to get to work. Keith went to pick up his chef's knife from the cutting board, but he couldn't find it. Instead his mage pistol sat atop a neatly folded bar towel. How could he have left it sitting out? He lifted it and slid it into the holster under his left shoulder. The goblin, Gunther, glanced up.

"You look good wearing that," he remarked, tapping a cigarette out of a pack. "It suits you."

He felt a slight bump, then a hand on his knee. The restaurant dissolved. He opened his eyes to see the inside of a plane cabin. The private plane used by agents on assignment. Gunther sat across from him, leaning forward, shaking his knee slightly.

"We're touching down," he said.

Outside Keith could see the flat expanse of the Boise airport. The evening sky had gone the color of cantaloupe and cured ham, tinged at the edges with lavender. A Provençal-flavored sky, Keith thought.

"I was dreaming," he said blearily.

"Was it prophetic?"

"No, just a normal dream." Keith shifted in his seat to pull on his coat. "You were in it though."

"Was I?" Gunther sat back, apparently pleased by this information.

"You were made of bone."

"How did I look?"

Keith thought of telling him. Frightening. Strange. The shape of his nightmares. Instead he said, "Good . . . You looked good."

♦♦♦

As was standard, a government car was waiting for them—a big one. Keith had never been to Idaho before. As far as he could tell everything had been made to accommodate at least a family of six. Especially the cars. Or rather, the SUVs. They crowded the roads and lined up in neat rows in the ample parking lots.

DuPree's house was located in a section of the old town called the Bench, which was what the natives called the one bluff that bisected the city. Houses there were, like everything else, large. Even DuPree's old arts-and-crafts-style home, which must have been a mansion when it had been built in the early forties.

The house looked exactly like a place where a vampire would live. Surrounded by a wrought-iron fence posted with pressed-tin Keep Out and Beware of Dog signs.

"Do you think he really has a dog?" Gunther asked.

"If the dog is as old as the sign, it must be a revenant by now." Keith pressed the button mounted on the front gate. He expected a voice to come at him from some hidden intercom speaker. Instead the front door opened fractionally. A man's pale face peeked out. He appeared to be in his midfifties with thick, gray-streaked hair and a thin, beaky face.

"Who's there?" The voice was thin and reedy.

"NIAD." Keith held up his identification. He didn't know if DuPree could read it in the dark. Probably. "We have some questions to ask you."

DuPree crept from the door, looking furtively to the now-dark sky, then toward the neighbors on either side, before he slunk down the sidewalk toward them. He was dressed in a black turtleneck and slacks, which made his spindly limbs seem even more spidery.

He gave Keith a long, suspicious look, then turned to Gunther. DuPree sniffed the air obtrusively, his mouth half open. When he did, his expression brightened considerably. He whispered, "You're trans-goblin, aren't you?"

"Yes, sir. Gunther Heartman." He, too, showed his ID.

"Oh, good." DuPree seemed inordinately relieved by this. He unlocked the gate and Keith started through. DuPree leaped back.

"Please don't come too close, Agent Curry. I don't mean to be disrespectful, but I have a phobia of humans." His voice shook slightly.

This was new. Keith didn't think he'd ever heard of anything so ridiculous in his life. A hunter being afraid of his prey.

"May we come inside?" Keith said.

"I certainly can't stop you, can I?" DuPree remarked. He said this without particular malice, just making a statement of fact.

After waiting for DuPree to lock the gate behind them, they followed him into his disheveled old living room. Books and papers were everywhere: stacked on tables and chairs, forming leaning, waist-high towers against the wall. Most of the furniture seemed to have been acquired in the forties as well. There were a couple of deco beige couches and silver modernist lamps.

"Please sit down." DuPree indicated the only clear couch in the room. He kept well away from Keith. "Can I get you a soda? I have several flavors."

"No, thank you. Would you mind showing your cuff, please?" The vampire's nervousness was making Keith edgy. Gunther didn't seem fazed by it. "We need to verify that it's working."

"Could Agent Heartman do the cuff verification please? I mean no offense, Agent Curry, but if you come too close I might hyperventilate." DuPree said this apologetically.

Gunther smiled easily. "Sure."

He approached DuPree with no obvious caution or concern and this seemed to settle the vampire somewhat. Once Gunther had established that DuPree's cuff was both present and sending out the correct signal, he took his seat beside Keith on the couch.

DuPree remained standing, hand on the mantelpiece of his empty fireplace. "What can I do for you?"

"We're here about Janice Sounder. Her husband said she was supposed to be here visiting you." Gunther took the lead.

"Yes, but she never arrived. I phoned several times, but she isn't answering her cell," DuPree said. "I even called her awful master, but he says he hasn't seen her. I'm terribly worried about her."

"Why is that?" Keith asked. He didn't miss DuPree's use of the word "master"—nor did he miss the fact that DuPree didn't seem fond of Sounder. DuPree also appeared to be under the impression that Janice was still alive, but he could just be casting a good glamour. A person couldn't trust body language when an extra-human's real body wasn't visible.

"Because she hasn't arrived." DuPree seemed to feel he was stating the obvious. "She was flying on a night flight, but you can never be sure about airplanes these days. Flights get delayed. I've been checking the news to see if there were any cases of spontaneous combustion."

"What is your relationship to Janice?" Gunther asked.

"She wrote me a fan letter about ten years ago," DuPree said. "We started a correspondence. At first neither of us knew the other was a vampire, but after a couple of years we discovered we were kindred spirits, so to speak."

"And Mr. Sounder knew you two were writing letters?" Keith pulled out his notebook.

"Yes, of course. Janice had a very traditional concubine relationship. She keeps nothing from her master." DuPree seemed displeased as he said this.

"Do you think her master had a problem with her writing to another vampire?" Gunther asked.

"No, I don't think so. I don't think she would have written to me if he had." DuPree paused, alarm rising up through his expression. "What do you mean by 'had a problem'? Why are you speaking in the past tense? Has something happened to her?" DuPree started forward toward Gunther, then recoiled slightly as he remembered that Keith was also present.

"I'm sorry to inform you that Janice Sounder has been killed," Gunther said.

"Was it Sounder?" DuPree asked.

"We're looking at a variety of suspects. Why would you think it was Sounder?" Keith kept his voice very neutral. He had perceived that, though he was more comfortable playing the heavy with Gunther taking the more sympathetic angle, DuPree truly was experiencing a tremendous degree of distress. He didn't want to shut the vampire down with ham-fisted tough-guy talk, no matter how easily it came to him.

"Because Janice and I had planned to leave this realm together. Surely you must know. I've filed all the paperwork. Oh, Janice . . ." DuPree crumpled down to the sofa facing them. A thin red tear trickled down his gaunt cheek. "She didn't even have a chance to file her papers, did she?"

"No record of a petition exists as far as we know." Gunther rose and handed DuPree a handkerchief. "When you said you and she were kindred spirits, what did you mean, exactly?"

"We were born into the same cult. Polygamists, you know. That's why we were all exiled here. I had thought that that was common knowledge."

"Not as common as you might think," Gunther said.

"So you have concubines as well?" Keith was a little at sea. How could this information not have been covered in basic training? Then again, there was so much information—so many realms. Realms upon realms upon realms, all stacked atop one another, existing at once in layers.

DuPree sniffed and wiped his eyes, leaving Gunther's handkerchief streaked with blood. "No, I came as a concubine to my mistress."

"And where is she?"

"Gone. Burned along with my two brother concubines. It's why I'm so afraid of humans, you see?" DuPree spoke to Gunther. "I've seen such horrible things. And the mass media just reinforces all stereotypes about us. Encourages our murder."

"Mass media doesn't cover actual vampire deaths," Keith remarked before he realized how callous his statement sounded.

"Have you seen a vampire movie?" DuPree demanded. "They're horribly violent. Full of wooden stakes and decapitations." DuPree choked on his last words. A sob escaped him.

Keith felt his sympathy for DuPree unexpectedly rising. Was it actually possible that Janice Sounder's death had been merely a case of spousal abuse? Much more gently he asked, "Do you think that Sounder would kill Janice for leaving him?"

"Why not? She was his property, wasn't she? In his mind anyway. In her mind too, at first. But after living among humans for so long, Janice had started to have her own ambitions. She had decided to write her own mystery novel. I thought she had tremendous potential. When we returned to our own world we were going to write together."

Keith was momentarily too stunned by the idea that the vampire realm had a publishing industry to think of a follow-up question. Gunther saved him.

"Do you think we could read part of Janice's novel?"

DuPree shook his head. "She had only just started writing it. She'd written only short stories before—mostly about farm life and rearing goats. But those killings in Portland had given her inspiration. She was asking me a lot of questions about how the police investigate crimes. I didn't know the answers, of course, because I write only romance. I believe in love, you know."

Keith exchanged a glance with Gunther.

"Were you in love with Janice?" Gunther asked.

"Yes, oh yes." He broke off again, sobbing.

"What do you think happened to her?" Keith asked.

"I think that Sounder found out that she planned to leave and . . . ," DuPree said, lifting his face from Gunther's now-scarlet handkerchief, "and he burned her. That's what happened to her, isn't it? That's how masters punish disloyal concubines. And it's never investigated."

"We're investigating it now," Gunther said.

"But you'll never prove it," DuPree said. "How could you? There won't be any evidence. Like those poor girls who get drowned in Saudi Arabia or honor killings of rape victims in Pakistan. No one cares what happens to concubines. One less vampire—that's all anyone ever thinks."

Gunther stood. "I assure you, Mr. DuPree, that we will see this investigation to its conclusion. In the meantime, I'm afraid we will need you to remain here in Idaho."

"Do you really think I am a suspect? I haven't left this house in two decades."

"No," Keith said quickly, causing DuPree to start. "But if Sounder is behind it, we will need your testimony."

"Please . . . I just want to leave this place. Meeting Janice, I finally had the courage to try and start again. Even if . . ." DuPree took a deep shuddering breath, but then recovered. "Even if Janice won't be with me physically, she'll be with me as the beautiful, shining spirit that she was."

Keith said, "We'll be in touch."

Once they were back en route to the airport, Keith said, "That was not what I expected to happen."

Gunther shrugged. "As it turns out, not everything is about food."

Pushing through a profound sense of déjà vu, Keith returned, "It is to me. Plainly, Janice's interest in the Cannibal Killings could not have been coincidental. Coincidences don't leave combusted vampires behind."

"Agreed. We need to pay Sounder another visit. Even if he's not connected to the Cannibal Killings, he's certainly the number one suspect in Janice's death."

"Then we're officially calling Janice's death a murder?" Keith didn't even know how to begin to file the paperwork on that one. Who would investigate? NIAD, he supposed.

"Vampiric concubines are citizens like anyone else, right?" Gunther's phone rang. He answered and after a perfunctory conversation turned to Keith and said, "They found bones from the club booker's body. Lots of butchery marks. Same MO as before."

"And?" Even without the déjà vu Keith knew there had to be an and.

"They found them in our friendly rocker kook Lancelot's garbage. He's being held at the NIAD detention center."

Chapter Ten

On the way to the NIAD detention center the next morning, Keith picked up a copy of the *Willamette Week*. He did this as a matter of reflex. Weekly papers often gave a better snapshot of the restaurant and bar scene in an area than anything else did. Not that he was sure this case really did still have to do with food anymore. Janice Sounder's death, at least, appeared to be a jealous master vampire disciplining his concubine.

As a matter of course, they'd ordered a search of Azalea Point Creamery and the Sounder residence. The homicide team was there now, going over the joint with spectrometers and witches. At last report, Sounder and his remaining concubine were both cooperative, but then he didn't have much choice but to be cooperative while the sun shone.

Gunther drove while Keith leafed through the paper. Among the usual local political rants, cult cartoons and ads for escort services, he found the food column.

"This is interesting," he said.

"What?"

"This food critic is talking about the Bauer & Bullock closure. He's missing the cookies."

"I can see why. They're great cookies," Gunther remarked. "Rake's going to be brokenhearted when he learns he's had his last box."

Keith continued to leaf through the paper, looking for live music listings. Carnivore Circus had a Friday show booked at a club called the Greenhouse. He found no listings for Theater of Blood. Was it because they'd gone underground or because they were just a bad band who nobody wanted playing their club? Hard to say.

As Keith could have predicted, when at last they sat in an interrogation room with Lancelot, they found him not terrified that he would be arrested and tried for cannibalism. Instead, he wanted to know whether or not he would be out of jail in time to make it to his gig on Friday night. Gunther glanced to the legal advocate. She was some sort of faerie with long pink hair and longer legs. She shrugged and shook her head slightly. Gunther turned his attention back to Lancelot.

To Keith's surprise, Gunther's amicable cool evaporated. He let loose a long string of growling goblin syllables that, from Lancelot's reaction, were seriously profane.

"If you could stick to English, I'd appreciate it, Heart-man," Keith remarked.

"Lancelot," Gunther snapped. "Disappointing your bandmates is the least of your problems right now."

"I know, I just can't think about it. I don't know what to do." Lancelot hung his head in misery. "My legal advocate says I don't have to talk to you, but I didn't do anything. I don't know anything. I don't know what to do."

"Why isn't your family here with you?" Gunther shot back.

Keith thought it an odd question for Gunther to ask, but then, he supposed he'd underestimated the filial connectedness of goblins.

"My parents are dead," Lancelot replied. "They were in a boat accident last year. I don't have anyone else." Lancelot's hands shook.

Much as he valued aggressive questioning, Keith didn't think badgering Lancelot would yield much profitable information. The kid—and he was clearly a kid, Keith could see that now—was visibly retreating into himself. He said, "Would you like a cigarette?"

"I sure would." Lancelot raised his eyes fractionally.

Keith signaled to Gunther, who grudgingly placed his own pack of Luckys on the table. Lancelot took one and chewed the end nervously. He looked up to Gunther and said, "I know you're disappointed in me, but I didn't do anything."

The rest of the interrogation revealed nothing of value. No one could provide Lancelot with an alibi for the time of the murder. He had been at home, alone.

They left Lancelot in the interrogation cell and headed back downtown.

Gunther wanted to walk along the river, so Keith parked and soon they walked shoulder to shoulder along the greenbelt, the Willamette River on one side, the sky-scrapers of downtown on the other. Gunther chewed three cigarettes, one after another in silence, before finally saying, "The latest victim of the Cannibal Killer was dumped directly in Lancelot's backyard. There has to be a goblin connection. Only another trans-goblin would know about Lancelot's status."

"But the question is, is the connection to Lancelot or to Carnivore Circus?"

"When I interviewed the other two band members, they alibied out. No, I think the connection must be to Lancelot, but . . ."

"But?" Keith prompted.

"But I don't think he's a killer." Gunther shook his last smoke out of the pack and crumpled the empty box.

"Are you suggesting he was framed?" Keith sat down on a bench overlooking the water.

"To me it feels like someone is going out of their way to make it look like he is the killer. Not just any old goblin, but him."

"All right, what's special about him? Apart from the fact that he's in a band?"

"He can't make change?" Keith suggested.

"Well, you can't expect that. He hasn't been working at the market all that long."

For the first time, Gunther's reflexive defense of Lancelot's abilities didn't annoy Keith. It was true. He hadn't worked there long. "We know he's an orphan, if you can call a twenty-one-year-old guy an orphan. He owns nothing of value. No car, no savings. His house is rented. He hadn't even finished paying off his guitar. He lives off the nominal cash he gets from his band and his recycled-sweater stall."

"Didn't his parents leave him anything?" Gunther asked.

"Just the hereditary table. Lancelot's mother sold hand-crafted knitwear."

"There has to be a connection between these things," Keith said. "I'd be willing to bet it's money. Somehow."

"Not food?"

"Food is money," Keith said simply. "In other contexts, food can be love, art and culture. But in this case I feel comfortable saying that if food is involved, it's in the form of money."

"Agreed." Gunther gazed out at the river. "Maybe if Lancelot needed money enough he would start hunting and selling human flesh, but I don't think it would have been his idea. Maybe Bullock or one of her cronies lured him into it?"

"I don't buy the money angle there. Lancelot's market reporting shows that he made enough cash to support himself," Keith said. "And he has absolutely no connection to Bullock."

"That we've found yet," Gunther countered grimly.

"It's not like we haven't looked. There's none. Zip." Keith flipped his paper open, once again reading the article on the Bauer & Bullock closure, looking for anything he'd missed. What was surprising about the article, from a law enforcement standpoint, was the complete lack of apparent concern the writer had about the restaurant being shut down by the police under suspicious circumstances.

Rather, the author was simply obsessed to the point of torment by the idea that he wouldn't have any more *alfajores* described lovingly as "a three-tiered sandwich cookie filled with alternating layers of feijoa jam, goat *cajeta*, and hazelnut pastry biscuit dipped in white and black chocolate for the signature Bauer & Bullock half-moon effect. An Argentinean delight made native to the Pacific Northwest. Local hazelnuts were supplied by Peabody Orchards. The luscious cajeta goat caramel was sourced locally from Azalea Point Creamery."

Keith did a double take. Gunther, who had been reading over his shoulder, seemed to notice the name at the same moment. He said, "Don't I recognize that brand?"

"Holy shit," Keith breathed. "It's the fucking vampire after all."

"I don't disagree, but why? And where's the evidence? We already searched his property and came up empty."

"I don't know yet." Keith popped his knuckles in irritation. But the pieces refused to assemble themselves into any sort of picture. "The connection we have is the cookie."

"If only we could interrogate pastry," Gunther remarked dryly. "I suppose we could have it analyzed, but what for?"

"Don't you still have that box you got for your old partner?"

They drove back to the hotel under flashing lights and Keith parked illegally while Gunther legged it up to his room to retrieve the souvenir. He flopped back into the passenger seat just as the hotel manager was approaching the loading zone. Keith zipped around the corner into the alley, put on the hazard lights, and said, "Let's see them."

Gunther opened the beautifully wrapped box and handed over a cookie. Keith broke it in half. A delicious, fruity scent floated up. Instantly, his mouth began to water.

He wanted nothing more than to put it in his mouth but knew better.

"This jam is not made with feijoa." Keith had experienced this amazing aroma before. He'd confiscated twenty-seven jars once in a quaint teashop in Madison, Wisconsin. "This is heartfruit."

"I don't know what that is."

"It's a fruit that grows exclusively in necrotic human organ meat, specifically the heart and liver. It's incredibly rare. I busted a manufacturing operation last January. A guy who worked at a funeral home was harvesting organs and selling them to a nice little grandma who used them for growing material."

"But Bauer & Bullock sells hundreds of these cookies every week. How could they farm that many organs?"

"Heartfruit is so potent that one fruit can flavor an industrial vat, and there isn't much jam in each cookie. I can't believe I've been so stupid. Bauer & Bullock pulled in fifty percent of its take from the sale of these cookies." Excitement rose in his chest. They might just be able to prove Lancelot's innocence. "This isn't about cannibalism. That was just a fringe benefit. It's about money. It's about jam."

"That doesn't connect Sounder," Gunther warned. "Or Lancelot."

"No, it doesn't. But we know Bullock was in a business relationship with Sounder already. Maybe . . ."

"Maybe it was a trade," Gunther said. "Maybe Sounder traded something with Bullock."

"Like what?"

"If we assume that Sounder provided the bodies for Bullock, which is a pretty good bet, she must have agreed to do something for him. Standard pact," Gunther said.

"You think she or her accomplices, since she clearly had some, agreed to set Lancelot up in exchange for bodies?"

"Right. But there's no connection between Sounder and Lancelot either."

Keith thought about this. Finally he said, "If Lancelot has no direct heirs, who will his goblin market table go to?"

"I don't know. Getting into those markets is really competitive but . . ." Gunther suddenly smiled. "But I bet they have a waiting list. But that is insane. Killing over a table at a market?"

"It's not a table. The food industry is incredibly competitive. Fifty percent of all food-related business ventures fail in the first year. That table represents market penetration. It's exposure for the product. It's direct sales. It's—"

"It's money," Gunther finished for him. "Regardless, we still have no evidence of anything but a legitimate business arrangement between the steakhouse and the dairy."

"You're right. We need to find the grow operation. Somebody there will know who drops off the ingredient for processing," Keith said. "Is the jam made locally?"

Gunther flashed a smile. "It's Portland. What do you think?"

Chapter Eleven

The manufacturing facility for Cascadia Jams and Preserves was located in a light industrial area in Hillsboro. As it turned out, the flavoring agent for Bauer & Bullock's exclusive house jam was shrouded in such tremendous secrecy that the company's owner, Mike Grady, had to be called back from his afternoon orchard tour in order to speak to them.

Mike was a rotund man with dark circles under his eyes and quick, aggressive body language. Keith had met literally dozens of guys just like him. Cooks with ADD and one-track minds. This guy's brain had been consumed by the idea of jam early on so that every culinary idea that occurred to him, savory or sweet, had to be expressed in the form of jam. Or jelly. Or syrup.

Other cooks he'd met had been obsessed with pizza or hot sauce or ice cream as an expressive format. Keith had often wondered if this kind of focus constituted a form of autism. One-dish thinking combined with inevitably poor social skills created one of the most unpleasant, yet widely dispersed, character types in the culinary world. Often they were very successful business-wise specifically because they stuck to one product.

Chances were good that Mike, though ambitious, was too self-absorbed to be directly involved.

Keith knew exactly what would happen next. Mike would try to make them sample every product in his entire line while evading their questions about Bauer & Bullock.

"Our newest product is a line of savory honey syrups," Mike said, unscrewing the lid from a tiny jar of golden liquid. "White pepper truffle honey is going to go through the roof. I can feel it. It's just amazing on chicken. Here, try some."

"Sounds great." Gunther politely accepted a toothpick dipped in the fragrant syrup.

Keith demurred. "We need to see the ingredient list for the Bauer & Bullock private-label jam."

Mike smiled the typical, sneering smile that all guys like him never knew they were making. "No can do. That's top secret. I had to sign a legal agreement and everything. Sorry, boys."

"I can get a court order, but that's going to bring a lot of unwanted attention to your facility. Especially when it's about to be revealed that Cindy Bullock was butchering humans at her restaurant," Keith said.

Mike paled. "You're bullshitting me."

"Not at all," Gunther said. "In a couple of days anybody with even the slightest connection to Bauer & Bullock is going under the magnifying glass. If I were you I'd start distancing myself now. And I'd start by giving us a full ingredient list for that jam."

"I don't know . . . ," Mike began. His cheeks went gray and waxy.

"Look, would it help you if I told you that I already know what's in it?" Keith said.

"Then you're one ahead of me," Mike said. "It's flavored with a secret liquid compound. She said it was feijoa, but it isn't."

"Who brings you the flavor compound?" Keith asked. "Was it Bullock herself?"

"It's delivered by courier. I just got a bottle yesterday." Mike pulled out a key ring and unlocked his lower right desk drawer. He removed a two-pint plastic screw-top jar that had the words "Bauer & Bullock" written on it in Sharpie. "I have the receipt here. You can have it all."

Mike held up his hands, shaking his head slowly as if denying that the jar had ever been in his possession. This was why Keith didn't like guys like Mike. The cowardly pendulum of their emotions only swung between bullying people and rolling over and pissing on themselves.

With the courier's receipt it was easy to find the pickup address—another industrial park only half a mile away—and a business called B&B Extract Company.

Like most industrial parks, this one consisted of a series of low, large buildings whose sides were intermittently punctuated by bay doors. Occasionally a regular door appeared in the corrugated siding, and it was on one of these that Keith found a small, dull sign that indicated the existence of B&B Extract Company.

"You want to ring the bell or just go ahead in?" Keith asked.

"I think it would be wise to let ourselves in." Gunther pulled a skeleton key from his coat and inserted it into the lock. The spells etched into the key's surface blazed to life—first showing red, then slowly turning to green.

Gunther removed the key and Keith carefully tried the knob, moving his hand only slightly, to make sure the knob was unlocked.

Keith opened the door. Inside was a regular-looking front office with an old desk and a couple of chairs. Beyond that was a closed door. The faint sound of music could be heard thumping from beyond it. They moved forward, mage pistols drawn, standing on either side of the doorframe. Keith could smell the dense, lush perfume of heartfruit flowers in bloom. The fragrance made him salivate instantly and nearly managed to cover the sweet stink of rotting meat. How many plants did they have in there?

"Please don't let it be trans-goblins running this operation," Gunther muttered.

For the first time since he'd joined the Irregulars, Keith found himself hoping the same thing.

They burst through the door into a dank, humid, sweet-smelling greenhouse.

At the back of the room Keith could see a bank of grow lights. Seven slim heartfruit stalks rose beneath them. Five of these ended in white flowers. The other two had already developed fat, white seedpods.

Three pallid individuals, who had been apparently been engaged in tending the drip-irrigation system, looked up at them in what Keith could only describe as muted alarm. All wore black. Two had fangs. The third wore red cat's-eye contact lenses that Keith imagined greatly impaired his vision. Downbeat electronica pulsed through the air. A stack of Theater of Blood flyers and a staple gun sat on a metal table.

"Yes!" Gunther said into the silence. "Fake vampires!"

Then came a slight buzz at Keith's wrist. Without lowering his mage pistol, Keith glanced at his watch. Numeral nine blinking green.

"I don't think so."

"Are you kidding? Look at them." Gunther waved dismissively at the trio, then said, "You three idiots are under arrest, by the way."

"Master?" The guy wearing the cat's-eye contacts finally spoke but not, Keith thought, to them.

"Blinking green nine, Heartman." Keith kept the mage pistol trained on the three wannabes while scanning the room. In the upper corner of the room, a shadow moved against the ceiling. "Nosferatu. Ten o'clock."

The black shape moved like a spider across the ceiling toward them. Its strange, shapeless jaw undulated. He didn't know if this was Sounder or the remaining concubine.

It didn't really matter.

"Freeze, asshole." He retargeted his mage pistol. The vampire slid along the ceiling, still coming toward them, saying nothing. Saying nothing was a bad sign.

Gunther seemed unperturbed, even slightly annoyed by this. He said, "I order you to stop and identify yourself."

The vampire launched himself at Keith. Gunther threw himself between them. The vampire sank its teeth into Gunther's shoulder, narrowly missing his neck. The three humans bolted, running toward the back entrance. Keith slammed the butt of his mage pistol into the vampire's head. He couldn't risk firing while the vampire was still attached to Gunther. Though he was trans-goblin, the mage pistol would still have an effect on him.

"Get off him, you fucking lamprey." Keith pried but couldn't loosen even one of the vampire's inhumanly strong fingers.

He wished he'd had the sense to bring a wooden stake or flamethrower.

Flamethrower . . .

He shoved his hand into Gunther's inside pocket, groping for the flask of lighter fluid there. He got the top off and sprayed the vampire with it, straight into the eyes and down its undulating throat. The vampire released its grip and sprang away out of range of any lighters. Keith brought his mage pistol up immediately and fired. Three spell-inscribed bullets spiraled out, leaving blue tracers. The first shot went wide, but the next two found their target.

The vampire shrieked as the bullets penetrated its flesh, writhing against the ceiling like a vortex of angry smoke. Then, abruptly, the sound ended and a ring of plastic dropped to the floor. Carefully, keeping his mage pistol trained on the traces of lingering smoke overhead, Keith bent to read the name.

He stood and turned back to Gunther, who stood with one hand pressed against his shoulder to stanch the blood trickling out.

Keith holstered his pistol and phoned the ambulance.

CHAPTER TWELVE

PPB apprehended the fake vampires within a mile of the warehouse. Although the transformation from human to vampire was technically impossible, all three fake vampires claimed to have been made Nosferatu by Sounder. None of them was anything but a misguided human.

"Sounder really did a number on them," Gunther said. "He used the administration of methotrexate to induce photoallergic reactions when any of these kids went into sunlight. He let movie mythology do the rest of his convincing. After that he had himself a nice little set of minions."

"And we got this from the remaining concubine?" Keith glanced at the clock. Ten minutes till checkout. Not enough time to have one last hurrah with Gunther. Not that Gunther was in any shape for sex. His shoulder was a mess of stitches and bandages. Keith gathered up the last of his clothes and shoved them into his suitcase.

"She made a deal. Her lawyer claims that she was acting with Sounder under duress. I believe her." Gunther shifted in the stiff-backed hotel chair.

Keith nodded. "Well, we saw what happened to the concubine who didn't cooperate."

"Exactly. Administration at the Portland Saturday Market confirms that Azalea Point Creamery was next on the waiting list for a market booth. It's hard to believe that Sounder would do all this just for money."

"People have done worse for less," Keith commented. "Ultimately, Sounder only ever saw humans as prey."

"That doesn't explain why Bullock went ahead with it."

"She was just sick, like every other gourmet looking for the ultimate thrill. PPB managed to round up a couple of people associated with Forbidden Pleasures. They've been handed over to NIAD. I'm pretty sure at least one of them will be willing to talk, once they've found out what kind of death sentence they're looking at." Keith zipped his suitcase. Time to check out. Time for him to head back to DC.

"Want to ride to the airport with me?" Keith squared himself, assembling his expression into professional cool. Gunther didn't appear to be fooled. He reached out, smoothing Keith's lapel.

Gunther said, "So it's over, just like that?"

"I already saw housekeeping lurking in the hallway." Keith knew that wasn't what Gunther was asking, but he'd never been good at saying goodbye.

"There are literally dozens of portals between DC and San Francisco," Gunther said. "It would be easy to pop over there. Maybe you could make me dinner sometime. Or even breakfast, if you're in the mood."

Keith caught Gunther's hand and pulled it to his lips.

"I think I could be in the mood." He heard the creaking of a disinfectant-laden trolley outside in the hallway. "Time to hit the road."

They made their way down to the parking lot, passing by a line of food carts just opening for lunch. Keith felt a familiar pang of loss as he watched them open. He missed that world. He missed it a lot. But then again, being an Irregular wasn't so bad. It had its perks. And watching Gunther slide into the passenger seat beside him, he thought maybe he'd found a regular customer to cook for again.

Gunther folded a smoke into his mouth, then unwrapped the Carnivore Circus CD he'd left on the dashboard.

"Want to find out what they sound like?"

"Why not?"

Massive, heavy beats exploded out of the speakers. Growls and screams like the howling of the damned pounded through the rental. Bombastic blasts of sheer sound vibrated from the speakers.

Above the noise, Gunther shouted, "I kinda like it."

Keith nodded. "Me too. What's the track called?"

Gunther searched the homemade packaging a moment, then said, "'Chunderfuck.' Next one is: 'Thy Doom Approacheth, Shithead.'"

They listened to the song. It didn't take long, being comprised of only seventy-two seconds of bowel-jangling guitar. Keith turned the volume down. Gunther gave him an inquisitive look.

"I'm not a nice goblin boy," Keith said, then added, "I'm not even nice."

Gunther gazed out the windshield, smiled in that slow way he had, and replied, "I know, but you sure can cook."

Cookie Jamboree

A Christmas Coda from the world of NIAD

Despite having once been a professional chef, Special Agent Keith Curry didn't know a lot about cookie cutters. He understood that they were used to cut sturdy dough into decoratable shapes—generally circles, unless it was a holiday—and that was all.

But Gunther knew all about them.

"These are the collectibles." Gunther waved his hand over a box of tin shapes as if he were a presenter on some home shopping network. Granted, with his dark hair and long, toned body he was handsome enough to be on TV. But the gleam in Gunther's blue eyes as he displayed his precious beauties held a hint of mania. "Sometimes I think they're my only addiction—apart from kerosene and cigarettes."

Really, Keith wasn't sure which was worse. Neither the kerosene nor the cigarettes could do Gunther, a transmogrified goblin, much damage.

Collecting cookie cutters, on the other hand, represented a foray into dorkville that somewhat detracted from Gunther's mighty sex appeal. Insofar as Keith now considered Gunther long-term-relationship material, he had to weigh things like cookie cutter collections against his own ideas of what should be in a home kitchen. Not that Gunther and he were swirling around the vortex of inevitable cohabitation. Far from it. Like most trans-goblin children, Gunther still lived with his parents.

Keith's reluctance to have sex in the garden-level bedroom of a ranch house in Marin County while his boyfriend's parents slept overhead had been the source of many tense conversations and one genuine argument. Gunther didn't understand why Keith didn't want to transfer from DC headquarters to the West Coast. Keith couldn't explain how uncomfortable Gunther's extra-human family made him without sounding like a racist.

So they'd argued and made up and gotten a little stronger every time—understood each other better as the days went on. Keith was pretty sure he was in love with Gunther. He'd have to be to willingly attend this awkward Christmas party after having gone so far as volunteering to work for the winter holidays just to avoid having to celebrate so many other holiday gatherings.

Gunther delved into the box and pulled out a tiny tin rocket and held it up. "I really love this one. You can make it look dirty really easily."

"Are you sure we want to bust all these out?" Keith rustled through the box. "It's supposed to be a Christmas cookie party. Don't we just need a star and a gingerbread man?"

"A lot of the returnees don't have a very fixed idea of Christmas and I like to give them a lot of options." Gunther continued setting the cutters out in lines. "Who says Christmas can't be celebrated with rockets?"

"Or muscle cars, apparently." Keith nudged a vehicle-shaped cutter back into line. "I always thought modern Santa would drive a red Cadillac."

"I don't really know what car Santa drives these days," Gunther replied. "Probably something Swedish."

That's the trouble with working for NIAD, Keith thought. You mention some guy you think is fake and he turns out to be real. Never fails . . .

"Does your family make a big deal of Christmas?" Gunther asked.

"Sure, I guess." Keith finally found the gingerbread man. It was a good-sized cookie cutter. Eight inches high.

"Are we going to go visit them?" Gunther kept his eye on the cookie cutters. "Or do you think it's too early for me to meet them?"

In the six months that he and Gunther had been seriously dating, Gunther had never once inquired about Keith's family, which had been odd, given the close connections in the trans-goblin community, but also relieving, since Keith hadn't wanted to talk about it.

"We don't really communicate," Keith said. "They weren't stoked about me turning queer on them."

"I see. . ." Gunther flashed him a smile. "I guess it's good I spent their present money on you then."

"You bought me a Vitamix 5200?"

"How much do you think I was planning to spend on them?" Gunther asked, with a laugh. "I'm just a civil servant, after all."

With four hours till the party started, they still had a lot of work to do, so Keith put on some tunes and fell into the rhythm of rolling dough and cutting out shapes. They used every single cutter, no matter how odd or seasonally inappropriate. The only criteria that needed to be satisfied were that he had four hundred cookies at the end of it and that twenty-six of them were gingerbread men. Keith had no idea why they needed such a specific number of those, but he complied.

As the cookies were cooling and Keith was mixing food coloring into icing, other agents from the San Francisco office began to arrive. It was still early—an hour before the weirdos would show up to try and become more human-socialized via application of frosting, silver dragées and red and green sprinkles.

Not to mention the assortment of edible glitters.

He didn't remember so many agents being there the previous year, but then he figured maybe he hadn't been as able to distinguish the guards from the inmates—so to speak—back then.

Even Gunther's retired ex-partner, Rake, showed up. A hulking, dark-haired man, he looked like he should be clumsy, but moved with the grace of water. He wore a sticker that read "VISITOR" in large letters and had a devious expression on his face.

But he was an actual demon, so Keith supposed he would. Still, Keith was about to go over and see what he might be up to when he caught Rake sneaking a handful of chocolate jimmies.

Mystery solved.

Keith went back to baking while Gunther greeted the arrivals with volleys of enthusiastic hugs, handshakes and high fives.

As Keith transferred the final sheet of gingerbread men into the oven, he noticed Gunther's godfather, Henry, lingering near the tall cooling rack. How any man who looked and acted so much like a dirty old hobo could have snagged such a hot boyfriend as Jason Shamir, Keith would never know. To Keith, Henry looked like a grizzled blond scarecrow who had hopped a train in 1933 and somehow ridden it all the way to the twenty-first century. The last time he'd had Henry over for dinner, the guy had pronounced the appetizer, Gunther's favorite salmon tartare dressed with lemon confit, to be "the best cat food I ever ate."

Unaware of Keith's watchful eye, Henry reached into the pocket of his stained and battered trench coat and removed a handful of white iridescent powder, which he started to sprinkle over the freshly baked cookies.

Keith felt certain that nothing pulled out of that guy's pocket should be applied to food. He started forward, but was stopped by a hand on his arm.

"Don't worry. It's part of the plan," a male voice whispered in his ear. From the lingering scent of chocolate jimmies, he guessed it was Rake before he turned around. "He has to get this done while they're still hot and pliable."

"What crazy shit did you put on those?" Keith glared at Henry, who just grinned.

"It's edible . . . I think." Henry licked his finger, then after a moment of contemplation said, "Yeah, I'm pretty sure."

The powder he'd sprinkled on the gingerbread men shimmered and twinkled like starlight glinting off newly fallen snow. Then one of the cookies began to twitch. At first Keith thought it was a trick of the light and shifting parchment paper; then the little guy sat up. It twisted from side to side as if cracking its back.

Keith's reaction was immediate. He brought the spatula down hard. The gingerbread man caught it, struggling against him with strength and will that should have been impossible in a cookie.

"Ease up, kiddo, you'll squish him," Henry chided.

Keith relaxed his grip on the utensil and the gingerbread man shoved the spatula away. It stood up, teetering on its rounded legs. It hopped from the cooling rack to the table, gave Keith the *bras d'honneur*, then gave Rake a more military salute.

Rake handed the gingerbread man a small roll of paper. The cookie accepted the banner before marching, drill-sergeant style, toward the end of the table.

As it strutted, others began to rise as well, moving clumsily, like baby cartoon pandas awakening from nap time. The scent of hot ginger and molasses saturated the air.

One by one the guests started to notice. They pointed and smiled, but were much less surprised than he would have expected even NIAD agents to be.

Gunther broke out into a wide smile as he watched the gingerbread men line up on the counter. Then they unfurled the paper Rake had given them. In large block letters it read "Good Luck, Gunther!"

"You guys!" Gunther looked around, grinning.

Keith looked around too, but he was more baffled.

"We just thought you should have a good send-off," a dark-haired agent said.

Keith leaned toward Rake, who had left the jimmies behind and was applying himself to a saucer of heart-shaped candy confetti.

"What is going on?" Keith whispered.

"Gunther's transfer came through. He's headed for DC." The big man's voice rumbled beneath the congratulatory noises made by the agents who surged around Gunther.

Rake daubed a finger into a nearby bowl of pink icing. "Maybe it's supposed to be your Christmas present." He licked the icing from his finger with a tongue that was too long, too agile and too red. Forget tying a knot in a cherry stem—this guy could make a whole macramé-owl wall hanging with his lingual appendage.

Keith snatched up the icing before Rake could double dip. Rather than being deterred, Rake simply grabbed a gingerbread man and bit its head off. The cookie's arms and legs flapped and flailed, but nothing could stop the progress of Rake's teeth through its torso.

As Rake noshed, a strange, blissful expression lit his face. Catching Keith watching him, he shoved the gingerbread man's kicking feet into his mouth, swallowed and then murmured, "Just like the good old days."

Rake sauntered toward the group of agents who surrounded Gunther, shouldering through them easily.

The rest of the gingerbread men were slowing down now, gradually hardening as they cooled.

"Are they alive?"

"Nah, they're just animated. Like puppets. See, the pixie dust is already wearing off. Wouldn't want to scare the new returnees." Henry took a swig of something from a flask and then stuck his hands deep in the pockets of his coat. "So I guess you're getting a new roommate."

"If you mean Gunther, he hasn't said anything."

"Seems like the classy thing to do would be to invite him then. Meantime I've gotta run. Gunther asked me to break the news to his parents for him."

"You aren't going to stay to decorate cookies?"

"Not this year. I think I made enough of a mess of it last year." Henry looked chagrined. "In hindsight I can now say spiking the punch was a bad idea. Look at that—Carrera is already giving me the evil eye." He saluted the San Francisco bureau chief. She neither smiled nor waved back. Behind her stood a few of the guests—all humans, all with the fashion sense of recently released mental patients. One young girl wore what looked like a live lobster on her head as if it were a tiara. Another, a middle-aged man, wore candy-cane pajama bottoms, a sweater with Santa's face knit into it, and a tangle of battery-operated LED lights around his neck. The festive, flashing necklace failed to hide a Frankenstein-like scar.

Time to get this party started.

Keith went to greet them, meeting up with Gunther along the way. All in all thirteen returnees attended. Though their number swelled to fifty once all the agent-volunteers, handlers and integration liaisons had been accounted for— fifty-one if he counted the girl's symbiont crustacean, which Gunther said they should not, since it would be surgically removed the following week.

After two hours of unparalleled weirdness with frosting, the guests retreated to the NIAD residence facility, the room emptied and only Keith and Gunther remained to do the last of the sweeping up.

"I think it went pretty well," Keith said, just to break the silence. Gunther seemed unnaturally preoccupied with getting every last rainbow jimmie into the dustpan, so Keith continued, "What are you going to be doing in DC?"

"Same as here. Assault team. Volunteer goblin community liaison." Gunther still hadn't looked up at him. "I thought it would be nice to be in the same city as you."

Diplomatic as always, Gunther left it open for him to decide whether or not they'd live together. Keith could almost feel Henry's breath on the back of his neck whispering, "Now's the time, kid. Don't blow it."

He knew it wasn't true. Or at least it probably wasn't really the old bum's voice—just the sound of his own conscience. He felt his face reddening. How was it possible that he could be nervous? Gunther had made it just about as easy as it could be. Still, he'd never lived with any boyfriend before and he knew that to Gunther's family, this step was the first on an inevitable road toward marriage. Goblins were just conservative that way.

"I guess I always figured that you'd live with me. If you ever did come back east," Keith said.

"Yeah?" Gunther finally lifted his face so that Keith could see the blue of his eyes.

"I mean, I thought I'd have more time to plan than this, but—"

"It's not till after New Year's," Gunther put in.

"Then I guess I better start looking for a bigger place."

"There's a two-bedroom condo for sale in Dupont Circle that has a beautiful kitchen with an induction range." Gunther fished his phone out of his pocket and started swiping through screens of DC-area realty ads. "Hardwood floors too."

"Why would we need two bedrooms?" He didn't immediately address the rest of what was wrong with Gunther's plans, including actually buying a pricey condo.

"For when Mom and Dad come to visit." Gunther glanced over shyly.

Keith felt objection after objection rising up within him, then realized that none of those issues needed to be addressed right this second. He took the broom and dustpan out of Gunther's hands, leaned in and pressed his mouth to Gunther's. He tasted like caramelized sugar and butane—like the top of a crème brûlée.

"Baby, I know it's your first place away from Mom and Dad and you're excited. But you've never even paid an electrical bill."

Gunther smiled, leaned in close and whispered, "Maybe I've been living with my parents for thirty-seven years, but that just means I've got a million bucks in the bank and nobody to spend it on but you."

"Well then." Keith slid his hand down Gunther's back. "I got a hotel with room service. Why don't I give a brief overview of my long-standing grudge against the Potomac Electric Power Company over breakfast in bed?"

"Then can we look for a place?"

"As long as the Pepco bill is in your name," Keith said, "we can live anywhere you want."

The Little Golden Book of Goblin Stories

A coda from the world of NIAD

Special Agent Keith Curry did not excel at shopping. Unless it was for kitchen equipment. Or rare punk rock on colored vinyl.

But books? No, he'd never been too much of a reader—not even as a young child. His boyfriend, Gunther, however, had established a bibliophile identity before he had adult teeth and vigorously maintained a well-used library account ever since.

He even had a special book from his childhood that he loved, a Little Golden Book edition of *The Hidden Goblin*.

"That story could have been written about me," Gunther had said the previous night. "It was about a goblin boy who has been transmogrified to be like a human. He lives with his mother and father, who are goblins living in the human realm."

"Was he sizzling hot like you?" Keith asked absently. He was making himself a grilled cheese sandwich for dinner. Gunther had picked up a bucket of fried chicken for himself, which he was steadily working his way through.

Gunther rolled his eyes, poured himself a shot of kerosene and took a sip. "He was just a little boy. But he did have dark hair and blue eyes like mine."

Keith nodded. He was constantly amazed at Gunther's ability to remember the tiniest details of his childhood and also at the ingenuity of the trans-goblin community. Most had emigrated to the human realm as refugees from tyrannical rule by the sidhe. They'd gone from life as mercenaries living on snowy mountaintops to working as bank tellers or recycled-sweater salesmen. Yet, like other émigrés, they held fast to their goblin traditions.

Or to most of them. Eating humans had necessarily been crossed off the list of traditional goblin solstice activities. But Gunther's mother insisted she'd never liked hunting and eating humans, so it was no great loss.

"Anyway," Gunther said, "this boy gets rejected by the other goblins because he looks different. He has fingernails instead of talons and his eyes are blue instead of red. And his teeth are tiny and square and all on the inside of his mouth."

Gunther paused to eat a chicken leg, bone and all, then continued, "Then a faerie comes with a magical mirror and sees that the boy is sad. She shows him that he's still a goblin inside, even if he looks different on the outside." Gunther sighed then. "I loved that book so much! It's why I want to give it to Audrey for her baby shower on Sunday. It's not easy to understand being one thing on the inside and another on the outside when you're a little kid."

"Why don't you buy a copy then?"

"I've tried! I can't find it anywhere online. And no bookstores in DC have even heard of it," Gunther said, exasperated. "I think it might be out of print."

"It could be that you have to visit the Grand Goblin Bazaar to find a copy," Keith remarked.

"I don't have time! I have to be out on maneuvers all Saturday with the rest of the strike force."

Now Keith understood where all this nostalgia had been headed. "I'm off Saturday. Do you want me to pick a copy up for you?"

"Could you?" Gunther asked.

Which was why it pained Keith to be standing in his living room late Saturday night having visited all seven layers of the Grand Goblin Bazaar's book market and still come home empty-handed. Even the famous vampire booksellers, whose stores of texts were so vast that they extended miles into the realm of darkness, shook their heads at him.

The one goblin bookseller he'd found had simply said, "We don't have any golden books. Just ones made of paper."

Gunther came home freshly showered, as he always did after maneuvers. He dropped his gym bag on the sofa and pulled his best men's-magazine-cologne-ad smile.

"Did you find it?" he asked. Keith shook his head no. Gunther frowned and tapped a cigarette out of his packet. He chewed the end despondently.

"Are you sure you have the right title?" Keith asked.

"I think so," Gunther replied. "But I can always check."

He stood and went to the bedroom closet. From the top shelf he removed an old cardboard box. Inside, beneath a couple of stuffed toys and an undersize baseball mitt, lay a book.

What became immediately obvious about this book, to Keith, was that it was absolutely not a real Little Golden Book. A new cover had been pasted on top of the previous one and the pages had been replaced as well with well-drawn but obviously handwritten text. Gunther examined the book curiously, as though he'd never noticed these details about the slim volume before.

"Well, that explains why you can't find another copy," Keith ventured into the silence.

"I think my mom must have made this," Gunther said. "It's her handwriting."

"That's a fair bet."

"How did I never notice this before?" Gunther wondered aloud. "I mean, the character's name is even Gunther."

"You were a little kid," Keith said with a shrug. "My question is: Why take apart a Little Golden Book? Seems like it would have been easier to buy a blank one and write in it."

"All goblins love gold," Gunther replied.

"You never wear gold."

"I have that tie tack and cuff links. It's a small hoard, but it's mine. And it's not like I'm a dragon or anything." Gunther dismissed Keith's contrary observation with an impatient wave. "Anyway, all the other human kids had Golden Books. I remember specifically asking her for a Golden Book, like everybody else had."

Gazing down at the homemade book in Gunther's hands, Keith found himself getting unexpectedly choked up at the thought of Gunther's human-hunting mother meticulously studying dozens of children's books, then replicating the details to make a special story to help her son feel better—a story just for little goblins like him.

Once all danger of sounding teary had passed Keith said, "I guess we'd better get to work."

Gunther glanced up, eyes a bit shiny as he, too, fought to retain his manly composure.

"Doing what?" he asked.

"Finding an all-night copy store and a Little Golden Book," Keith said, grabbing his coat and hat. "We've got an arts and crafts project to do."

Magically Delicious

Special Agent Keith Curry didn't like going nowhere. But where else could a guy go on a stationary bike? Not that he didn't like to work out. He liked free weights just fine. Cardio day? He wished he could pass on it. But even when he was in top shape, being 100 percent human in NIAD, NATO's Irregular Affairs Division, had some disadvantages. When arresting an extra-human suspect, he could not turn invisible, shoot geysers of flame or fly. The only magic he had access to resided in his shoulder holster in the form of his mage pistol.

And besides, he had to try and compete with Gunther. Well, he couldn't compete with his boyfriend, but he could try not to look too bad by comparison.

Tall, dark, handsome and naturally fit, Gunther did not need to tag along with Keith to the company gym. His perfect physique had been bestowed on him by the mages who had transmogrified his goblin body in utero so that he could look consistent with the human world. But most mornings he came along to the gym anyway. Insofar as Keith knew, Gunther only ever worked out to be social.

Whereas Keith could have epitomized the word "average." Not good-looking or bad looking. Brown hair and eyes. Nothing beyond that to report. He was the kind of man nobody noticed for very long. And that worked out well for him when he was on an investigation, but was a constant source of mild unease for him the rest of the time.

Gunther was hot enough to get any so-inclined man and maybe a few who were just curious. His blue eyes twinkled like chips of lapis lazuli as he sat his duffel bag down on the gray carpet and started scrolling through the messages on his phone.

"Looks like strike force is on call for the Saint Patrick's Day parade again," Gunther commented.

"Damn leprechauns," Keith muttered.

"Their labor dispute sounds like it's getting intense." Gunther held up his phone to display for Keith a photo of six nasty-looking specimens forming a three-layer pyramid that stood about hip high to a normal man. The one on top held a sign reading "Pixies Go Home"; another held a card that said "NIAD Busts Unions!"

"I do not envy you. They look like ball biters," Keith observed. "What's their beef, anyway?"

"They worked for one of the NIAD contractors, who replaced them with pixies because they came cheaper."

"So, angry ball biters." Keith let out a low whistle. "Be careful."

"I'm always careful. And I'm a good planner. I brought you some breakfast." He reached into his gym bag and pulled out a can of Primal Thunder Power Shake and waggled it at him.

"That's not breakfast. It's a meal-replacement product." Keith pushed the pedals harder as his velocity-free vehicle simulated a steep incline. Sweat prickled beneath his Slayer T-shirt and trickled down his stomach. "It tastes like baby aspirin sprinkled on sawdust."

"But it has twenty grams of protein and its new, improved flavor makes it taste like a ray of Creamsicle-flavored sunshine." Gunther sat on the bike next to Keith's and idly pushed one of the pedals around.

"I've got my own breakfast."

"I hope you don't mean that baggie with a tofu dog in it I saw you put in your pocket this morning." Disapproval darkened Gunther's expression.

"No, that's my lunch." Keith kept a straight face, unable to stop himself from winding Gunther up. They'd been living together for a year now and although many of their domestic conflicts had been smoothed out, Gunther still found Keith's eating habits appalling. Which Keith thought was pretty rich coming from a guy whose goblin origins allowed him to eat cigarettes and swig lighter fluid.

"Are you sure you used to be a chef?" Gunther asked.

"Either that or I just loved wearing checkered pants and a ridiculous hat." Keith grinned up at his boyfriend. "Seriously though, I've got a hard-boiled egg as well. And a couple of Dijon mustard packets I swiped from the fancy grocery store. I'm fine."

Keith reached a plateau in his imaginary bike ride and took the opportunity to get his wind back. He glanced out the fifth-story window. If he looked between two buildings he could just see the Washington Monument poking up at the midpoint of the National Mall. Beyond that lay the Lincoln Memorial, where, in the vaulted basement beneath, NIAD mages worked strange spells that controlled the flow of magic in this, the earthly realm.

But if Keith and the other agents did their jobs right, neither the chilly tourists nor the tired commuters filing into office buildings all around would ever know about the mages, the leprechaun labor dispute or any other magic.

To them it was business as usual in the nation's capital. Dismal winter fog still clung to the tops of the buildings. Dirty slush coated the sidewalk below.

As a native Californian, Gunther had been game about his first East Coast winter, getting very excited about owning his first pair of snow boots. But then, Gunther's outgoing nature and high spirits were hard to deflate by any means—the exact opposite of Keith's own inborn pessimism and suspicion.

"Is there any more news on the security breeches?" Keith asked.

Gunther returned his attention to his phone. "No one has claimed responsibility and the spells leave no residue to analyze. Pixie-pure magic. That's what they say."

Keith rolled his shoulders to try and remove the tension building there. For the past three weeks, seven NIAD agents had been attacked by a bizarre and completely incapacitating spell that caused severe hallucinations that lasted from hours to several days. During that time, the agents became convinced that they'd been abducted, recognized no one around them and often had to be physically restrained. Afterward, the agents remembered little about the experience, but seemed mostly to be unharmed.

While it was true that many extra-humans, especially in the fae community, might regard this sort of attack as more of a prank than a terrorist assault, NIAD took a dim view of any kind of breech of security.

"I suppose they haven't bothered to interview the local pixies yet, then," Keith asked.

"Anybody with a handful of jelly beans can score a thimbleful of pixie dust these days," Gunther replied, giving a shrug. "It's half of what the leprechauns are so pissed about. Apart from being made redundant at work, all that magic dust flying around is completely ruining the market for three wishes, or so they say."

"I would say the three wishes racket also suffers from some credibility issues that are unrelated to pixies." Keith didn't like to think of himself as prejudiced, but the antics of leprechauns often rubbed him the wrong way.

"Such as?" Gunther glanced up from his phone.

"Oh, like a bald guy wishes for hair and ends up getting a rabbit. You know, a hare? Douchebag leprechaun humor."

"Yeah, that's probably true. Still, if the pixies don't get on the self-regulation ball, our brass is going to step in and do it for them. Then nobody will be happy. Especially not that sugar junkie Buttercup," Gunther said absently, his eyes still glued to the small screen.

Doubtless he was scanning some social media feed for news of his huge West Coast family. Gunther had more cousins than anyone Keith had ever met, as well as apparently endless interest in looking at photos of their babies, pets and favorite outfits. Suddenly his expression brightened and Gunther glanced up at him.

Keith steeled himself against the shock of whatever photograph he was about to be shown.

Snow goblins—that is, goblins who had not undergone transmogrification—looked like creatures of nightmare. They seemed to be made entirely of spiky, white bone. Blood-red pits smoldered where their eyes should have been and they had more teeth than a barracuda, even when just born. Keith had now gazed upon many small, toothy creatures being held by proud parents or grandparents.

He mentally crossed his fingers, hoping for a pink or blue hat that would help him figure out the gender, at least. Instead Gunther turned the phone around to reveal a photograph of Keith's old restaurant.

"It's a five-star review!" Gunther offered his phone for Keith's perusal.

Keith broke into a smile. Before coming to NIAD, he'd owned his own place, called KC's. When he'd decided to use his knowledge of food to help NIAD root out extra-planar contraband, he'd sold the tiny diner to his sous chef, Candy. At first she'd kept the place going strong using his menu and recipe book. But lately, she'd been switching it up—making the joint hers, which made Keith proud. He'd picked a winner when he hired her. That was for sure.

Though as the reviewer glowingly described the cozy surroundings and carefully crafted plates, it still gratified him to see that one of the five standout dishes mentioned was his own.

"This is great. We should definitely go see her next time we're in Providence," Keith said.

"Maybe we can make a weekend out of it in June. I hear their pride parade is the only nighttime parade in New England."

"That is correct," Keith said.

"And KC's is right on the parade route."

"Have you had this plan for a long time or did you come up with it now?" Keith felt he should ask.

"Just now." Gunther took his phone back, pocketed it and picked up the Primal Thunder again. "If you're not going to drink this I will."

"Knock yourself out." Keith bore down on the pedals again, pushing against the last incline in the computerized interval training. Sweat slicked his palms. Beside him Gunther cracked the top of the can and chugged the entire twelve ounces. Even then he looked good, like a guy in a commercial. He finished, crumpled the can in his hand and gazed out the window.

"I'm also really looking forward to seeing the cherry blossoms this spring," he said. "I just missed them last year."

"They're pretty good . . . if you like pink trees." Keith dismounted from the bike and scrubbed his face with a dry towel. When he glanced back up he found Gunther's expression had filled with sadness.

The sudden change of mood puzzled Keith, as it went against Gunther's usual equanimity. He stepped forward and put a hand on Gunther's shoulder.

"You okay?"

Gunther didn't reply. He moved closer to the window until his forehead pressed right against the glass and his breath fogged the pane. Though his lips moved, Keith couldn't hear what he said.

Keith glanced around the workout room. They were

hardly the only agents present. Eight or nine other agents occupied the space. A couple of Gunther's strike force buddies gathered at the back, pumping iron. One of them noticed Gunther's dejected posture and gave Keith the stink eye.

His name was Haakon and he was half dark elf, though Keith would never have used the word "fae" to describe him. He always stood too close to Gunther in the cafeteria lunch line and Keith suspected him of unnecessarily flexing his big black 3-D delts while using the free weights. To Keith, Haakon always seemed to be thinking something like, "How does a scrub like you keep a stone-cold fox like Gunther? He could definitely do better." Or at least that's what Keith assumed Haakon thought, since they were the only two sentences Haakon had ever spoken to him.

Keith ignored Haakon's glower and turned back to Gunther. Quietly, he said, "Hey, what's up?"

Slowly Gunther turned to face him. His blue eyes shone with tears.

"I have to get out of here," Gunther whispered.

"Out of DC?" Sure, the city could be dreary at this time of year, but he thought Gunther might be overreacting a little. Could it be homesickness?

"Out of here!" Gunther's voice rose with each word. "I have to get out!" He spun to face the window and smashed his fist directly into a window designed to withstand a mage blast. Blood exploded across the glass as his knuckles split and popped against the unyielding surface.

Gunther howled with rage and threw himself at the glass, thrashing against it like an eel caught in a net. Keith lunged forward and caught him around the waist, pulling him back from the impenetrable barrier.

"I need some help here!" Keith bellowed.

Gunther fought him, throwing an elbow that caught him like a club in the gut. Keith curled over in pain, but managed to keep hold of his boyfriend long enough for

Gunther's strike force buddies and a couple other agents to get across the room. While Keith tried to stand, Haakon tackled Gunther like the high school linebacker he'd probably been. Someone hit the alarm. A red light coalesced in the center of the room, spinning and flashing like the light atop an old-time cop car.

Gunther struggled against his opponents, wailing and writhing on the gray carpet. His already injured hand smashed against the pedal of an elliptical trainer. Blood spattered across the device. Being goblin inside, Gunther easily overwhelmed the men restraining him. He kicked Haakon back against a weight rack, sending dumbbells crashing down.

On-duty security came through the door, stun guns drawn.

"Clear off!" one shouted.

"What the fuck are you doing?" Keith rushed forward, but not in time. The point man leveled the gun and fired. A silver bolt of magic flared from the muzzle, slamming into Gunther's chest. Gunther went still.

Completely still. Keith couldn't even see the rise and fall of his breath.

For Keith all time stopped. Though he knew that the security guy had fired a stun gun, he also knew that stun guns could kill, especially when fired at close range.

Keith dropped to his knees, leaning forward to listen for breath, and heard nothing. Suddenly he felt hands on his shoulders urging him away from Gunther's unmoving body. Blind with rage, Keith shook them off and launched himself at the shooter, screaming, "I'll kill you, you stupid fuck!"

Two on-duty agents caught Keith by both arms and held him back. One of them was shouting something in Keith's ear.

". . . he's been compromised. That's what happens when you stun a goblin. Calm down. He'll be fine."

Keith stopped struggling as he saw a medical team also coming through the door. They crowded around Gunther's fallen form so densely that all Keith could see were Gunther's feet. One of his running shoes was missing—lost in the struggle.

"Let me go," Keith growled. "I want to see him."

"No, you'll just get in their way." Haakon came forward, rubbing his shoulder as he did so. "You need to let them do their job."

"Where are they taking him?"

"To the medical unit." Haakon did not actually look at Keith as he spoke, which did nothing to soothe Keith's nerves. But he stopped fighting and the two security guards holding him loosed their grip.

"What the hell just happened?" Keith tried to mute the panic in his voice, but he couldn't.

Haakon finally met his eyes and said, "I think he just became the eighth agent to get pixie-dusted."

Chapter Two

Keith went to the medical unit but wasn't able to enter, as Gunther had been quarantined until he regained cognizance. The witchdoctor in charge shook a couple of rattles around Keith's head to make sure he was clear of magical influence, then said, "We'll call you when you're allowed to visit. Would you like me to inform Agent Heartman's family?"

"I can call them," Keith said quickly. He knew Mr. and Mrs. Heartman would react badly to any official NIAD phone calls.

Phoning Gunther's family with bad news was harder than Keith had imagined possible. It had been a long time since he'd been a contributing member of a family and he'd forgotten how it felt to participate as an insider. Now he would have to tell them that their son had been attacked, while he stood by, powerless. But at least he knew that Gunther's parents were the only two people in the world who loved Gunther as much as he did.

Despite Keith's delicate wording, Gunther's mother, Agnes, broke down right away, crying and handing the phone to Gunther's bewildered father, Gerald, who seemed certain that Gunther had been killed.

Once Keith managed to explain that Gunther was at the hospital under sedation and was expected to make a full recovery, he had to wait while Gerald explained this to Agnes. Finally, Gerald finished by saying, "We'll be there in five minutes. We'll just have to tell our supervisor what's happened."

Since Gerald and Agnes worked in the translation office of the San Francisco NIAD branch, they had access to the travel portals that connected all the offices. This proved convenient during the holiday season, but could be overwhelming as well.

"You don't have to rush," Keith said. Even he hadn't made it into the medical unit yet. "They won't let you in to see him anyway. Not until he starts to come around. And I still have to go be debriefed about the incident."

"Agnes and I would rather be there just in case," Gerald said.

"At least go home to pack a bag," Keith said.

"No need. Gunther keeps a suitcase of ours in the closet of the spare room. We'll have everything we need for a few of days." Gerald had the tone of a man announcing an obvious fact that Keith should have already known.

"Right." Keith sagged against the wall. Of course Gunther would have an emergency suitcase for his parents. He'd only moved out of their place to move in with Keith. "Look, I'm not at home right now. But I guess you probably have your own key."

"That's right. You just get on with what you're doing." This last came from Agnes, who had apparently just found the extension handset.

On the one hand Keith was relieved to know that someone understood how he might feel about Gunther, but he also felt a twinge of annoyance at how easily the not-even-in-laws-yet decided to invade his space. He pushed it aside. He had work to do, so he said, "Thanks, you too."

◆◆◆

Clad all in black and seated around a circular table of the dim, circular room beneath the Lincoln Memorial, the twelve men and women in charge of maintaining the magical barriers surrounding NIAD DC headquarters looked like they'd come directly from some big funeral for a corporate incense manufacturer. Thin, perfumed trails of smoke coiled against the ceiling and swirled into the recessed lighting fixtures like gravity-defying serpents.

For a group of people who had all decided to wear the same color to work, the mages varied wildly in their personal style in that they appeared to have chosen to survey the entirety of fashion history. One man looked like he'd stopped moving forward with fashion in the midseventeenth century. The female closest to Keith wore latex pants that were arguably inspired by the dystopian necro-future. She held a lit cigarette that smelled like cloves.

Keith thought, Things to bring up to my union rep: mages being unfairly exempt from dress code and flouting citywide indoor smoking ban.

The joke helped calm his nerves.

Taking turns, the mages quizzed him on his and Gunther's actions leading up to the event. As he spoke, spells moved the smoke in the air to re-create his actions in a three-dimensional representation.

"And you did nothing unusual?" another mage asked. She was a dead ringer for Morticia Addams, and Keith wondered whether she imitated the costume ironically to creep people out, or if the character herself had been the inspiration. "No one contacted Gunther or handed him any packages, for example? Tapped him on the shoulder, maybe? Was there anyone smoking a cigarette on the street nearby that Agent Heartman could have inhaled the smoke from?"

"Not that I know of," Keith replied. The mention of this caused a twinge of anxiety about the amount and contents of the smoke he currently inhaled.

The Morticia clone steepled her fingers and leaned back in her chair. Another mage, an elderly man whose neat Savile Row suit contrasted sharply with the jewel-encrusted crown he wore, leaned forward to take his turn as interrogator.

"You said Agent Heartman was looking through his phone messages just before the attack? Did he receive any calls?" As the King spoke, Keith thought he caught a whiff of formaldehyde.

"I don't think so. But I have his phone here. You can check." Keith slid the device across the table toward the

King. The man removed a silver pen from his pocket and used that to manipulate the phone while murmuring a string of incantations. Finally he said, "There's nothing here," and pushed the device back to Keith, who caught it just before it spun off the edge of the table.

Morticia straightened in her seat. "That will be all. You may return to your duties, Agent Curry."

As one, the mages turned from him. Without speaking, they stretched out their arms and linked hands. Then, following some unknown cue, they began a loud, slow chant in what sounded like Latin, but could have been anything.

Keith didn't know if he'd ever experienced such a summary dismissal in his life. He'd wanted to ask questions—find out if they had any real leads. But they just kept chanting as if he didn't exist.

Dejected, he mounted the stairs and climbed back up into the chill winter air and headed returned to his office. By the time he got there, his coworkers had both already gone on their assignments, so he was left alone in his undecorated cubicle.

As an agent, Keith specialized in investigations involving contraband food items. Everything from illegal unearthly fruit importation to busting human protein rings fell within his purview. Among the new cases in Keith's inbox were fresh allegations of glycerin adulteration of vampiric meal supplements. He also needed to finish up the paperwork on what had turned out to be spurious allegations of mermaid flesh dealers working the Florida Keys. After a cursory investigation, Keith had determined that the mermaid flesh was really manatee—also illegal, but not his department—and passed the case along to the Department of Fish and Wildlife.

He needed to file paperwork for both but he couldn't just file reports knowing that the person who had caused Gunther to break his own hand was just waltzing around somewhere free and happy.

He considered asking his supervisor, Nancy Noble, to reassign him to Gunther's case, then realized it would be quicker and easier to just reassign himself, as his supervisor had stepped out to lunch.

Gunther had said that the magic was pixie-pure, and the biggest known dealer of pixie dust just happened to be an associate of the Heartman Clan. Her name was Buttercup and she, like a lot of fairies, spent a lot of time dressed up like an insect—a moth, to be precise. She lived in the Elysian Fields, a former paradise that now served as a kind of way station en route to the Grand Goblin Bazaar. Keith could have easily traveled there via the official system of NIAD portals, but he would have had to file a travel plan, so he elected to use the goblin market transportation system instead.

The Grand Goblin Bazaar existed over many different realms simultaneously, linked together by portals that allowed a shopper to move from one market to another via a system of entry points.

Prior to being associated with the Heartmans, Keith had disliked this method of travel, fearing both uncertainty and ambush. But since becoming close with Gunther's family, Keith had lost nearly all fear of goblins. More than that, he wore a tooth-shaped pendant affiliating him with the Heartman Clan, which had helped a lot on the one occasion he'd gotten lost.

The only market currently open in DC in March was the fish market at the wharf, so that's where Keith headed. He donned his spectral lenses, which allowed him to see objects concealed by magic. These might include living creatures who altered their appearance to blend better with human society, or signs and symbols written in spectral ink. In DC, as with the entire Eastern Seaboard, leprechaun graffiti covered the bottom foot of most walls.

He walked through the lunchtime crowd, heading toward the bathrooms. There he found an out-of-order stall marked with a sign whose plain block letters glowed vibrant green when viewed through the spell-revealing lenses and changed from reading "out of order" to "Elysian Fields."

Unfortunately the glasses also revealed the presence of a line of six leprechauns forming a blockade in front of the stall. Standing shoulder to shoulder with their arms linked, they formed a barrier the approximate height of a rabbit fence. Easy to step over? Not if a guy wanted to come out of it with his nutsack intact. After glancing at the urinals to make certain no other guys were present, Keith pulled out his ID and said, "Official business. Step aside."

The leprechauns looked at each other with expressions of such exaggerated incredulity that Keith thought it might have been faster to file the paperwork to use the NIAD portals after all.

"He's from NIAD, don't you know?" The leprechaun whose crinkly orange beard poked down toward his pointed shoes like a fuzzy carrot spoke not to Keith but to a compatriot, whose green felt hat sported not one but three decorative buckles.

"NIAD, you say?" Three Buckles said. "Doesn't that stand for something?"

"Nasty, idjit, arsehole, dingleberries, I think it is," Carrot Beard replied.

"Oh no, them letters means nosy, insulting, arrogant, dickholes," a third leprechaun, who was clean-shaven but sported a nose the relative size and shape of a toucan's beak, chimed in.

Keith remained unmoved. Years of experience had proved to him that he couldn't out-insult a leprechaun. Instead he pocketed the ID and crouched down to as close to their eye level as possible.

"What are you doing here, guys? What's the point of hanging out in this shitter all day?" He tried to sound reasonable rather than frustrated, as the wee men tended to thrive on conflict and general strife.

"We're committing an action!" Carrot Beard cried, his ruddy face reddening even further.

"It's our right to demonstrate," Three Buckles said.

"So this is a protest?"

"That it is." Carrot Beard nodded. "Against them damn union-busting scabby pixies, may they rot in eternal hell forever."

"May their wee heads be squashed like grapes and may goblins suck the marrow from their tiny broken femurs," Toucan Beak added solemnly.

"I don't think it's wise for professional wish-granters such as yourselves to be cursing anyone aloud. It could constitute a criminal threat," Keith remarked. He kept his tone calm, and resisted the urge to crack his knuckles, an action that he tended to perform unconsciously when irritated.

"I was merely speaking figuratively." Toucan Beak pulled an obsequious pout.

"Look, I'm not here to bust you. I just need to use this portal. Do you have any literature I could take? A pamphlet maybe?"

"Yes, sir, we do!" Three Buckles reached into his small waistcoat and pulled out an even tinier piece of paper. From what Keith could make out, the leprechauns had been on strike against their employer, Taranis Inc., for several weeks. The leprechauns claimed that the pixie scab labor had been brought in by NIAD itself, to ensure production would continue uninterrupted.

"It's an interesting theory," Keith said.

Carrot Beard grinned. "How about a monetary donation to help our cause then?"

"How many wishes do I get for it?" As Keith said it, he realized that this was how people fell for the wish racket. He knew if the little bastard said yes that he would pay up and wish for Gunther to be better.

"None. Ha! We wouldn't grant a dirty badge's wishes even if we weren't on strike, which we are, so fuck off, ball bag!" Carrot Beard said.

Keith didn't know if he was happy or sad about the wish being denied, because whatever emotion he felt was immediately subsumed by a wave of overwhelming anger. His hand was around the butt of his mage pistol before he even registered that he'd made a decision to draw it.

Five leprechauns scattered, but Carrot Beard stood his ground, spitting, "You don't have the guts!"

Keith's finger tensed around the trigger, but some part of his mind that had remained free from homicidal rage stilled his hand.

"Don't count on that," Keith said. "I'm an East Coast chef. I've killed more living creatures on a busy Friday night than most agents grease in a lifetime. But I don't want to kill you. I just want you to know that I'm serious about going through this portal."

"And I'm telling you no! I know what you really want."

"And what's that?"

"To buy the dust from Big Wings. Her and her mob are the reason we're here protesting instead of working. Why can't you badges shut her down?"

"By Big Wings I assume you mean Buttercup?" Keith said. "What do you know about her customers?"

"Don't tell him anything," Three Buckles shouted from behind the toilet.

"I'm no squealer," Carrot Beard yelled, as much at Three Buckles as at Keith. "You'll get nothing out of me."

"But I think we can both agree that I caught you, so you do owe me three wishes," Keith said. "So for the first, I wish you would tell me everything you know about pixie dust being used for terrorist attacks on NIAD agents."

Keith watched Carrot Beard's face writhe and contort, but he had the little man dead to rights. "I only know that nobody's claimed responsibility. Nobody knows who's doing it. What's your second wish? For me to know the answer? The magic doesn't work like that. Even if you wished it into me, chances are I'd be whisked away and changed into one of the villains doing this and then I wouldn't be interested in telling you, and owe you nothing. The magic does what it wants and takes its own payment. It obeys your words the way it wants to."

Keith considered this. He'd often wondered why leprechauns were so consistently obstructive in their wish-granting. He hadn't considered that magic might be capable of creating perverse manifestations of its own accord.

"All right then, I wish you'd step aside and allow me to go though the portal."

"Fine, you may." Carrot Beard did as Keith asked and beckoned him forward.

Keith holstered his pistol and took a step inside.

"Wait, what about the third wish?" Carrot Beard rushed up and caught the leg of Keith's pants.

"I'll keep it for when I need it," Keith replied, shaking the little creep off.

"Careful, badge-boy, one slip of the tongue and your mother's on the surface of the moon."

"I'll take that under advisement."

Then he stepped inside the portal.

◆◆◆

The experience of travel through portals was unnerving because of its lack of drama. There was no sense of vertigo or travel at all, just a slight tension in the air and a strange bending of the light, and then Keith's surroundings changed from the dingy bathroom stall to the interior of a blue plastic port-o-let. Opening the door, Keith squinted at the intense light flowing in from the vast green meadow outside.

The wind smelled sweetly of flowers and hay. A brilliant sun shone in a blue sky. Keith had been to this realm three times now and it always seemed to be the same time of day—around three o'clock, when the shadows lengthen slightly.

Maybe it was the only time the portal opened there. Then again, maybe time held still in this realm. Who knew?

He scanned the verdant grass for his target.

Finally, about fifty feet away he saw a large yellow moth fluttering toward him. As it drew near it fluttered in a circle around him, then hovered in the air around his belt. A swirling ribbon of yellow light shimmered through the air as Buttercup expanded her body. When she was finished she stood about belt height. She wore nothing, and her small breasts jiggled as she put her hands on her hips. He was crotch to face with Buttercup, the undisputed master of this realm.

"Well met, badge," she said. As she spoke Keith could see that her tongue, like her lips and hair, was a vibrant yellow.

"Well met, Miss Buttercup." Keith produced the badge of which she spoke, just as a formality. Obviously she'd already pegged him as a NIAD agent.

"Spooky to see a human badge wearing a goblin pendant," Buttercup said. She flapped her wings to bring herself closer to his throat, twisting her head this way and that as if looking at hidden dimensions in the jewelry, which, for all he knew, she could see. Finally she squeezed her eyes closed and crinkled up her nose to take a long sniff. "You smell like kerosene kisses and forbidden love! How romantic . . ." She rolled back in a little flip, as though bowled over by the wonderfulness of it. Tiny yellow hearts manifested in the air between them.

"There's nothing forbidden about my love," Keith said. It wasn't true. Not by a long shot. But he wasn't going to let some half-pint fairy yank his chain again. He'd already committed a major infraction drawing a mage pistol on civilians engaged in a legal protest. Even if they were leprechauns, they still had rights.

"Love between a goblin and a human? Only as much as the adoration of a cat for a mouse." Buttercup's face went serious. "You want to watch out if she brings home a pot big enough to hold you, badge-boy."

Keith considered correcting any of Buttercup's errone-ous assumptions, but decided that, on the whole, it wouldn't be worth it. Instead he pulled out his notebook.

"I came to ask you a few questions," he said.

"It took you long enough."

"Oh? Why would you say that?"

"I've sent hundreds of letters," Buttercup said.

"Letters?" Keith couldn't help glancing around for any sign of even a building, let alone a post office box, on the broad, green expanse of the fields. The lone structure was the blue port-o-let that he'd stepped out of minutes before. As he gazed at it, wondering where the letter slot could be, the port-o-let vanished as the layover ended. The sight of the gate fading caused a cold stab of anxiety to move through his gut.

It will reappear in three minutes, he told himself. And then disappear again three minutes after that. It's the way the gates work.

Still, he checked his watch.

"You said you've sent letters?" he prompted.

"Every day. Hundreds and hundreds of messages. I've written about it on every single leaf and flower petal I could find, but no one answered." Buttercup raised a sorrowful hand to her forehead, then added, "Until you! Forget what I said about your forbidden love. I'm sure she's very nice. And you! You must be a great knight! Pray, illustrated stranger, find my little pixies, I beg you. They are so tiny. And cats are everywhere in the earthly realm."

The "illustrated" took him aback until he realized Buttercup was staring at the tattoos on his forearms. Keith resigned himself to missing several cycles of the gate. He sighed and said, "Okay, describe what happened."

"I was just fluttering over there by the riverbank when I saw three men come through the port-o-let. They wore white paper clothes and smelled like bleach." Buttercup wrinkled her nose. "One of the men began to sprinkle wondrous delights on the ground."

"Do you know what they were?"

Buttercup nodded vigorously. She leaned forward, venal desire showing in her yellow eyes. "Pop Rocks."

Of course, Keith thought. He wondered how Buttercup would respond to the string of Zotz he had in his pocket, but decided not to play that card yet.

"And these attracted the pixies?"

"I knew it was a trap right away," Buttercup said. "No one just throws magical marvels such as those on the ground! I yelled for my little girls to stop, but they were already there, swarming. Then out came the butterfly nets. I tried to stop them, but they had a hateful orange cat, and then in an instant they snatched my girls away through the stinky toilet door."

Keith finished writing this down, as well as the names of each of the pixies: Butterbur, Artemesia, Lorraine—the list went on and on.

"I don't suppose you have any pictures of them?"

Buttercup cocked her head, then swept her hand over her heart and pulled away a bit of gray dust. This she cast into the air, where it became a glittering image of a small woman with wings like a dragonfly and shimmering azure hair and lips.

"That's Lorraine," Buttercup said.

Keith pulled out his phone and took a photo. From the corner of his eye he saw the port-o-let begin to coalesce into existence. Knowing he was about to leave, he said, "So the leprechauns say that you deliberately sent your girls into the earthly realm to eliminate competition for sales of your pixie dust."

Buttercup looked aghast. She jumped back and flitted up into the air. "That's a dirty lie! What do they know? Little finks."

Keith pressed the issue. "But you do sell pixie dust, right?"

"To my friends," Buttercup conceded. "Or to people with candy."

"When was the last time you sold dust?"

"You're not a knight after all, are you, fish-foot? You're another nasty badge trying to put your laws on my body." Buttercup zipped into the air. "What I do with my dust in my kingdom is my own business."

"Wait!" Keith whipped the Zotz out of his pocket and waved the string of candies in the air. "I didn't say I believed them. I was just telling you what they said."

Buttercup circled just out of reach, eyes never leaving the Zotz. She dived in and snatched at them, but Keith pulled them away.

"Give it!"

"Tell me who you last sold dust to."

"Another badge called Half-Dead. He used it to disguise a boy who smelled like Half-Dead's semen." Buttercup's humor seemed to have returned.

"I remember the case. The guy was in protective custody," Keith said, nodding. Half-Dead was a veteran NIAD agent and also Gunther's godfather, so chances of him being the kidnapping culprit were slim. "But no one else since then?"

"No one."

"But there's been a lot of illegal dust around DC recently," he said. "Where do you think it could be coming from?"

"How would I know?" Buttercup came back to the ground, crossing her arms in a sulk. Then her expression changed to one of total distress. "Those bleach men. What if they're taking it from my little girls?" She threw back her head and let out a wail that filled the air like a siren and grated like the screech of an owl. It reverberated through the air, shaking the petals from the yellow flowers nearby.

"We don't know anything for certain," Keith said, shouting through the terrible noise. Buttercup did not relent. In desperation he pressed the strip of Zotz into her hand. It took her a moment to notice them, but when she did she tore open one of them and thrust it into her mouth, sucking it violently as saffron-colored tears streaked her cheeks. Keith glanced at his watch. He had one minute. He said, "I'm going to file a report. And I'll make sure that another agent contacts you with an update. Don't worry. We'll do everything we can to find your girls and bring them back safely."

Chapter Three

As he walked back through the fish market to the Metro, Keith took stock of what he'd learned. A group of humans— or at least humanoids with human candy—had kidnapped more than twenty pixies. That meant that there was more than enough contraband power of illusion floating around the earthly realm to perpetrate the intrusions on NIAD. But who had those so-called bleach men been? Few humans knew how to use the port-o-lets to travel, and fewer still would be so familiar as to know that one of them had a layover in Buttercup's realm.

As he stood, swaying with the motion of the subway car, Keith pondered the circumstances of Gunther's attack as rationally as he could.

What if it had been an inside job? A mole in NIAD was hard for him to imagine. The pledges of loyalty, secrecy and disclosure an agent took when being instated were magically binding. But pixie dust was powerful stuff—strong enough to allow an infiltrator to cast a glamour on himself and appear to be any agent.

The key would be to review the security camera footage, he decided. He should look at every single agent entering the building that morning and establish that they were really there, as well as scanning for duplicates. He entered NIAD headquarters with the plan firmly in mind.

The moment he stepped past the security door, two agents escorted him straight back to the Lincoln Memorial, where he once again descended into the vaulted chamber beneath the scrotum of Honest Abe to meet Morticia and the funereal fashion of the mage gang.

They did not seem happy. And neither did Keith's direct superior, Nancy Noble. She stood just inside the doorway, arms crossed and eyes narrowed.

Usually Keith liked Nancy. Though she was in her early forties, she shared his taste for metal music. He found her boxy pantsuits and perennial frosted eighties mullet soothing. But Nancy's adherence to rules could sometimes cause a rift in their relationship.

"Agent Curry has arrived, Mage Melchior," Nancy intoned.

The mage who Keith had dubbed "the King" slowly turned to face him, looking for all the world like an animatronic figure in the world's creepiest theme park.

"What can I do for you?" Keith asked, trying for a pretense of nonchalance.

"We have received a complaint from a member of the extra-human community regarding your conduct." As Melchior spoke, a coil of smoke slithered down from the ceiling and wormed its way into Keith's nose.

Keith sneezed and tried to rub away the tingling sensation it left behind.

"Now please tell us how you've been spending your morning." Melchior smiled as he spoke. Keith took a breath to collect himself and to figure out how to put the most positive spin on his actions. While he was thinking, he heard a voice begin to relate his actions. With mounting horror, he realized that the voice was coming out of his own mouth. The mages had put a spell on him. Rather than being able to choose his own words, the spell drew an account that sounded like court testimony, as if his subconscious had been duped into giving evidence.

He could do nothing to stop speaking long enough to collect his thoughts and nothing to stop himself from cracking his knuckles, one by one, as he grew more and more furious.

"And then I returned to the office with the intention of reviewing the security footage to scan for the presence of doppelgangers," Keith heard himself finish.

Melchior gave him a long, appraising look and then, with the expression of a man who has been offered chicken gizzards when he expected foie gras, he said, "Agent Curry, your job is to act as a food inspector. You are neither cleared nor qualified to investigate security breeches. If you persist in making incursions beyond your station I will ask for your dismissal. Is that clear?"

Still under the influence of the smoke, he said, "Yes, I understand. And just for the record, you don't need to put the whammy on me to get me to tell the truth, you ridiculous old mummy. I'm an agent, not an offender."

The mage's eyes flashed wide. Keith thought he could see tiny lightning bolts flashing across them. Necro-future girl snickered, then took a hasty drag of her cigarette to cover it.

"We're within our rights to use enhanced interrogation," Morticia said. "So long as your superior officer is present."

"And I'm within my rights to file a complaint about it anyway," Keith said. "Which is what I'm going to do."

The King narrowed his eyes and said, "Agent Noble, please escort Agent Curry back to his desk."

Nancy nodded, caught Keith by the elbow and guided him out of the room. Once they'd reached the chilly winter air of the mall, he expected her to turn to him and crack a joke—possibly about which archeological dig the King might have been unearthed during. Instead she stalked silently alongside him. Keith spent the walk sneezing over and over, causing his abs to ache like hell by the time they reached the NIAD building and climbed up to their floor.

Nancy remained wordless as they returned to their department, not even giving him a single gesundheit. She motioned him to follow her to her private office.

"Shut the door behind you," she said.

"So . . . ," he said. "Am I in big trouble?"

Nancy turned to face him. At that point he noticed her right eye twitching slightly.

"If you embarrass me like that again I will rip off your dick and shove it right into your disrespectful, permission-avoiding rectum," she said. "Do you hear me?"

"Yes, ma'am."

"I don't like apologizing to those creepy old fossils," she said.

"Right. I get that. I'm sorry."

"And I hate being summoned to their underground lair. Now I'm going to smell like I threw a séance at an undertaker's all goddamn day." Nancy flung herself into her rolling chair and unbuttoned her suit coat.

Nancy had never been this angry with him before. He felt hurt and slightly scared, which was weird for him. Normally being admonished by his employers evoked sensations of rage and personal affront.

Maybe worrying over Gunther's condition was affecting him more than he knew.

"Do you want me to pay for your dry cleaning?" Keith didn't know if it was appropriate to offer but needed something to say.

"No," she said, sighing. "But you are going to have to hand over your mage pistol."

"What?" Here comes the affronted rage, he thought, with grim satisfaction.

"Your weapons privileges have been revoked pending the investigation into allegations that you brandished it at innocent civilians." Nancy held out her hand to receive the weapon.

Keith left it snuggled into his holster, protesting, "Those were not innocent. They were leprechauns."

"What the hell were they doing? Jacking your Lucky Charms?"

"You and I both know those little runts are dangerous."

"One of those little runts also claims that you extorted three wishes from him." Nancy leaned back in her chair. "Did you?"

"Not extortion, exactly. I caught him, fair and square."

"Agents soliciting or accepting magical items from extra-humans is expressly forbidden!" Nancy said, eyes wide. "You know that, Keith."

"It happened in the heat of the moment," Keith said. "I just wanted to find the people who attacked Gunther."

"Listen, I know you do, but unfortunately Mage Melchior is right. You don't have any authorization to investigate anything outside of this department. Now give me your pistol."

"You can't take my weapon. It's not fair. It's the only thing I have against all that magic. When I'm killed out there by some shitty vampire, my blood will be on your hands." Keith felt his face flushing. His hands shook with rage.

"Don't be so dramatic. It's only temporary."

With the reluctance of a drowning man letting go of a life preserver, Keith handed over his weapon. He knew he'd broken the rules, but why did that mean he had to part with the sole piece of equipment that gave him any chance of surviving a magical encounter?

"When do I get it back?" Keith asked, abandoning all pretense at civility.

"It could be as long as a week, presuming you get it back at all." Nancy stood and locked the pistol into the office armory cabinet. "Until then you can help catch up on permitting paperwork."

Keith had thought that NIAD could not insult him any further. "You aren't seriously confining me to the office, are you?"

"Not confining, but without your weapon all you can safely do is permits and recertifications." Nancy spoke as though everything she said was perfectly reasonable, rather that salt in his open wound.

"So that's it? For trying to find the bastards who attacked my boyfriend, I really have been busted down to being some kind of food safety inspector?"

"Now you know why the rest of us don't wave our pistols around in public bathrooms," Nancy said with a shrug. "Now get back to your desk. Or better yet, go visit your boyfriend at the hospital."

"He isn't allowed visitors yet."

"Apparently the situation has changed. He called while you were gallivanting with the fae folk. When you see him, give him a big hug from me."

◆◆◆

After a brief detour at Gunther's locker, Keith made his way back to the elevator and up to the on-site medical unit, which took up an entire floor of NIAD's primary office. While standing in the hallway waiting to be admitted his phone rang.

"Curry speaking," he said.

"I prefer my curry silent and in a bowl, but we can't have everything we want." The voice on the other end had a lilting accent—distinctly reminiscent of an Irish Spring deodorant soap commercial.

"Okay, who is this?"

"Never you mind my name, let's just say we have some unfinished business—a matter of an unfulfilled wish."

Carrot Beard, then.

"So why are you calling me?" Keith leaned against the wall, scanning the hallway from behind his mage-enhanced spectacles, wondering if he would spot the leprechaun hiding out behind a chair leg, whispering down his sleeve. The only knee-high creatures he saw were a couple of brownie orderlies dressed in white smocks.

"I was hoping you wouldn't mind going ahead and making your wish now to settle the business between us," Carrot Beard said.

"I was hoping you wouldn't run tattling to my boss like a little snitch, but we can't have everything we want." Keith wouldn't normally have antagonized one of the fae folk like this, but the loss of his mage pistol left a raw mark on his pride and temper. "But you did, so why would I do you any favors?"

"That wasn't me! I was against it! The others forced me against my will," Carrot Beard protested. "Listen, Agent Officer Curry, sir, you've got to help me out. My nerves are shot. The magic wakes up and listens every time you say a word. It's driving me fucking bonkers! Just close out your wishes, for the love of God."

"You can hear everything I say?"

"Not me, the magic," Carrot Beard said. "It's giving me the mother of all headaches."

"Good. I think I'll let it go a little longer then." Keith hung up, despite the continuing protests coming from the phone's tiny speaker.

He got directions to Gunther's room. As he went, Keith passed other, stranger rooms. One held what looked like an incubator full of sparkling red smoke, while another room, completely blacked out, had a sign that read "CAUTION! VAMPIRIC PATIENT! ADMIT NO NATURAL LIGHT!"

Gunther lay on a regular-sized hospital bed, near a window in a regular room designed for the more human-looking of NIAD's extra-human agents.

He looked surprisingly well. He reclined casually, wearing a faded blue-and-white checked hospital gown. His hair was tousled but still silky and black as a raven's wing. His right hand had been extensively splinted and bandaged, so that only the tips of his fingers were visible. And those looked swollen.

Keith went to him immediately. Gunther's expression lit when he saw Keith approaching.

"Hey there, how was your day?" Gunther spoke with such casual ease that Keith simply told him, ending with Nancy's revoking his gun privileges.

"So, I guess Haakon's right," Keith finished. "I'm a fuckup

and you could definitely do better."

"That's just mean." Gunther reached out to pat his hand. "And it's not even true."

"I'm pretty sure it is." Keith stroked Gunther's long fingers. Then, remembering he'd brought a gift, he dug into his pocket and produced Gunther's half-finished pack of Lucky Strike filterless. "But I did remember to bring your smokes."

Gunther's eyes lit up. He snatched the pack with his good hand, shook a bent white tube out, folded it in half and popped it in his mouth. Gunther chewed and then swallowed the entire thing, paper and all. His eyes closed in bliss as he leaned back against the pillows.

"Thank you so much," he said. "All those little brownie orderlies only eat Drum shag."

"There's no accounting for taste," Keith remarked. As surreptitiously as he could, he took stock of Gunther's body. He didn't appear to be hooked up to anything but a pulse monitor, which Keith found infinitely relieving. "So you ready to talk about what happened to you yet?"

"Well, one minute I was in the gym and the next I was tripping and then I woke up in here," Gunther said, shrugging. "The witchdoctor said I recovered from the hallucinations more quickly than the fully human agents on account of my goblin blood. But that didn't help my hand at all. I broke almost every bone in it. It's going to have to be magically reconfigured once the swelling goes down."

Keith winced. "I am so sorry. That's awful. You must feel like shit."

"I don't know about shit. More like really weird." Gunther shifted on the propped-up pillows.

"When they took you away, I didn't know what to think," Keith admitted. "I thought the security guys had killed you."

"I heard you unleashed your fury on them," Gunther teased.

"Don't laugh about it," Keith said, still feeling raw over the incident.

"I'm not. I'm touched. I'm pretty sure you could have taken at least one of them out before the rest of them started tasing you."

"So everybody's talking about how I lost it?"

"No, just Haakon. He told me when I came to." Gunther smoothed the pale yellow blanket that lay over his lap.

"He was waiting here?" Keith tried to keep the outrage from his voice, but seriously: Did the guy have no shame? Trying to bird-dog Gunther in a hospital bed?

"No, they paged him because he's my team leader. They paged you first but you were still out pounding the pavement." Gunther gave him a warm smile, as if proud that Keith would be so dogged in his pursuit of justice.

"It was mostly standing around in a lush, green, sweet-smelling field," Keith said.

"Yeah," Gunther said, closing his eyes. "It smelled pretty green where I was, too."

"Where? In your hallucination?"

"That's right. I can't really remember too much about it but it smelled really green—like grass or something. And there was this big pile of gold coins. It was so weird." Gunther opened his eyes. "I was really scared, but there wasn't anything to be afraid of. Like how in a nightmare sometimes blue is terrifying."

Keith gripped his good hand harder. "I haven't ever been scared of blue, but I get what you mean. Do you remember what you were saying when you were first attacked?"

"Not at all."

"You were saying that you had to get out."

Gunther shrugged. "I don't remember anything about that."

Keith thought a moment. "But you did see a pile of gold coins?"

"Right." Gunther peered into the middle distance as if trying to access the hallucination again.

"Like a pot of gold, maybe?"

"If it was a pot of gold, I definitely don't want to go to find the end of the rainbow again," Gunther said. He flashed a smile, then his expression dimmed. "You don't think leprechauns had anything to do with this, do you?"

"When I met them this morning they said they were committing an action. Maybe attacking you was part of that action."

Gunther lay quiet for a moment, staring silently out the window, which caused a thrill of alarm to go through Keith. His face had the same sad expression that had crossed it moments before he'd flung himself at the exercise room window.

Then he said, "I don't like that word."

"What word?" Keith spoke as gently as he knew how.

Gunther looked right at him, "Attack. What happened to me didn't feel like an attack. It didn't feel like I was being targeted to be hurt. It felt like . . . like I stopped being me."

Keith did his best to hide the intense relief he felt at Gunther's lucidity.

"Did you tell that to Haakon?"

"Sure. Him, the medic, the witchdoctor, that mage who looks like Elvira—"

"I thought she looked more like Morticia Addams."

"Oh, yeah, right, I see that. Anyway, I told everybody who came to question me."

Keith sighed, and lifted Gunther's good hand to his lips. He pressed a kiss against Gunther's skin.

"Do you know how long they're going to keep you here?" he asked.

Gunther cocked his head as if he didn't understand Keith's question, then said, "They're not keeping me. It's voluntary. I can check myself out whenever I like."

"Then why are you still here?"

Gunther hunched slightly and whispered, "My parents came."

"I know they came. I called them."

"They're going to be at the house when we get home." Gunther's expression went furtive.

"Is there something wrong with that?"

"I just hoped I could avoid talking to them about what happened." Gunther looked miserable, then sat up straight and rang the bell to summon the nurse. "I guess I just have to face them like a man."

"We could always run away to a motel. Dye our hair. Buy fake beards."

Gunther gave him a tired smile and slid his hand across Keith's now-stubbly jaw. "It wouldn't work. My mom would just hunt us down by scent. Her nickname used to be Bloodhound back when she was a mercenary in the old country. Best to just go home."

Chapter Four

Even before Keith reached his front door, he could tell Agnes was making dinner. And not just any dinner. She was making a good old-fashioned goblin dinner to help her little Gunther regain his strength. Keith's eyes began to water preemptively as he imagined the capsaicin-laden steam that would be filling his house.

It wasn't that Gunther's mother was a bad cook—indeed, in goblin circles she was considered a model homemaker—it's just that she wasn't human and therefore did not cook to human tastes. She didn't stew meat so much as weaponize it by use of fistfuls of hot peppers.

On the day that Gunther had moved in with Keith, she had taken Keith aside and pressed a small spiral notebook into his hand. Written on the pages were her precious, famous and well-guarded recipes for goblin favorites such as Cracked Hot-Pepper Marrow Bones, Sheep Skull Surprise (the surprise turned out to be extra eyeballs sewn into the sheep's mouth), and Goblin-Style Pig Trotters, which were traditionally served raw in a bowl of vinegar and garnished with whole bulbs of garlic cut crosswise and seared on the edge of a heated scimitar. On the first page of the notebook she'd made a special note that Gunther, like all goblins, was sensitive to salt and could only abide the smallest amount on special occasions. Then she'd drawn a little, anatomically correct heart.

When she'd handed over the book, Agnes had made him pinky swear to never reveal the secret blends of peppers, and Keith had done so without even crossing the fingers on his other hand. He had been touched by the gift and, after reading it through, dutifully hid it in a locked filing cabinet, where it remained unconsulted to this day.

As he turned the key in the lock of the front door he glanced over to Gunther, whose worn-out expression lifted as he obtrusively sniffed the air.

"Mom's making knucklebones," he said with a grin. Then, anticipating Keith's reaction he added, in a whisper, "Maybe we should order you a pizza?"

Keith shook his head. "I'm sure she's made me something too."

As they crossed the threshold into the living room, Keith sneezed. Gunther's father looked up from his seat on the new sectional couch that Gunther had purchased specifically with his parents in mind.

Like Gunther, Gerald's body had been reconfigured to appear more human. Gunther had once told Keith that the magician who had chosen his parents' human appearances had been a big fan of romantic comedies and that was the reason that they closely resembled Gary Cooper and Barbara Stanwyk. Gerald was an older version of the great screen actor now, but not less formal, wearing shirtsleeves and a tie while watching television.

Gerald appeared to be using the television's screen-within-a-screen function to watch two separate curling tournaments simultaneously. He stood when they entered and embraced his son with an affection that Keith found embarrassingly dorky, yet couldn't help but be jealous of Gunther for inspiring. Keith's own father had given up dispensing hugs the second Keith had acquired secondary sex traits, as was the way in his family. So when Gerald next turned to embrace him, Keith found himself paralyzed in confusion. Gerald didn't seem to notice. He turned his attention back to Gunther.

"Your mother went straight to the butcher shop from the hospital," he said. "There's no stopping her when she's in a cooking frenzy."

"I guess I'm the lucky one today," Gunther replied.

Gunther's father's expression faltered as Gunther passed by him on the way to the kitchen. There, Gunther's mother had every one of Keith's six burners cranked up to high. The blue flames heated stockpots full of bubbling liquid. Keith did a quick volume calculation and decided that it would be a tight squeeze, but yes, he could have fit into the biggest pot. Bones protruded from the top of one, while another held a tangled knot of simmering chicken feet so big it could have been mistaken for a tumbleweed.

Agnes smiled at them as she shoved a bobbing organ that Keith thought might be a lamb's heart back under the simmering broth with a long wooden spoon. The end of the utensil she used was stained vivid orange from peppers and grease. The kitchen table had been set with the plain white plates that Keith preferred. In the center of the table sat a heaping dish of peeled raw onions.

"Dinner's almost done, so you boys should go wash up," she said.

"Thank you, Mom." Gunther kissed her on the cheek.

"You're welcome, sweetheart," she said. "And don't think I've forgotten you, Keith. I bought those veggie burgers. They have . . . carrots. I hope you don't mind."

"I have no beef with carrots," Keith said.

"Oh thank goodness," she replied.

For reasons that Keith had never discovered, snow goblins like Gunther's family despised the carrot above all other vegetables. Rabbit food, they called it, with a look of extreme disgust.

Keith took the upstairs bathroom, while Gunther used the one on the ground floor. He considered losing his shoulder holster and mage pistol, then, with a dismal, sinking feeling, remembered that he was no longer in possession of his mage pistol. He divested himself of the impotent holster immediately.

Back in the kitchen Agnes used tongs to heap hunks of meat and bone down onto three plates. The fourth contained eight veggie burgers and a party-sized bowl of potato chips. Keith noted that she'd drawn the curtains, and failed to put out any utensils.

This dinner would be fully goblin style. There was no getting around it. But Gunther needed it. Keith would just have to man up and endure the spectacle.

Though Gunther and his parents had been transmogrified to appear to be human, they were still magical creatures who retained certain qualities and abilities. They could and did consider substances like kerosene to be beverages, for example. And they could crush and eat bones with their deceptively human-looking teeth.

True goblin dinners were hands-on affairs full of chomping, gnashing and splintering of bone. Gunther tucked into his bowl of ribs with gusto, chomping the slender bones as one might eat a french fry, alternating with bites of raw onion, which he ate as though it were an apple. Agnes elected to start with a whole heart, which she bit and shook as though it were still alive. Her gold earrings glinted with the motion.

Gerald seemed unusually reserved as he slowly munched a chicken foot.

"You okay, Gerald?" Keith asked.

"Well, no, Keith, I guess I'm not," he replied. "Not after what happened today."

"I'm completely fine." Gunther rolled his eyes like an exasperated teenager.

"Your father's not talking about the pixie dust attack," Agnes said.

"He isn't?" Gunther glanced askance at Keith, who could only reply with a shrug. "What's up, Dad?"

"I guess I'm just hurt, Gunther," the older Heartman said.

Keith took a bite of his veggie burger in order to completely preclude his entry into the conversation. Gunther's parents, despite their frightening eating habits, were nice people.

"Why are you hurt?" Gunther's immediate guilt showed on his face.

"You fibbed." Agnes did not look up from her bowl.

Gunther froze, then hung his head in shame, which caused Keith to nearly choke. What could Gunther have possibly been lying about? He couldn't imagine. The veggie burger went thick as concrete in his mouth. Finally, he managed to swallow and ask, "What did Gunther fib about?"

"Why don't you tell him, son?" Gerald said.

"I said that I worked in the mage office as a researcher," Gunther said.

Keith felt his brow furrow in puzzlement. But before he could ask for clarification, Agnes said, "When really he's in the strike force!"

Again Keith paused, not sure what, if anything, to say. Then, inspired, he said, "How do you know Gunther's on the strike force?"

"Well," Gerald said, "his team leader was wearing a jacket that had those very words stenciled on the back in big white letters. That was my first indication. Then he introduced himself as the leader of Strike Force Team A and said that Gunther was a valuable member of the team. So after that I had a notion that it might be the case." The scorn in Gerald's voice could have been used to peel paint from the wall if the hot pepper steam hadn't already been hard at work there.

"I suppose you knew, Keith," Agnes said.

"Well, yeah," Keith replied.

"Do you know how dangerous that is? Gunther could be deployed to battle anything! Monsters, even!" She spoke with conviction that subsumed the fundamental irony of goblins being worried about attacking monsters. "We absolutely forbade him to interview for strike force. Gunther has gone directly against our wishes."

"He is a big boy now," Keith ventured into the conversation, though he worried where it might lead. Family arguments in his own childhood home often led to fistfights and rivers of tears. He didn't think he could take Agnes, or shoulder the guilt of making her cry, for that matter.

"Son, we want you to resign," Gerald said. "Strike force is too dangerous."

"Dad!"

"Absolutely not." The words were out of Keith's mouth before he could weigh the consequences—not that consequences would have mattered. Once he decided to say his piece nothing could stop him. "Gunther is exactly the agent strike force needs. He's strong, he's smart and he's ethical. And he's not afraid to bring a gun to a swordfight."

All three Heartmans stared at him in shock. Then Agnes said, "You've been in a swordfight? Oh, Gunther! How could you be so reckless?"

"Hell, yeah, Gunther's been in a swordfight," Keith cut in before Gunther could reply. "More than one! And he's also rescued baby centaurs from an illegal breeding farm and gone on a shitload of other operations that are too classified for any of us to know about. I'm proud of him. You should be too."

"We are proud of him, but we don't want to see him in the hospital ever again," Gerald said.

"That had nothing to do with strike force," Keith said. "That was a random attack that could have hit any agent. The one thing we do know, though, is that Gunther recovered three times as fast as a born human would have. Besides, the other guys on strike force would never let anything happen to Gunther. They all love him. It actually creeps me out how protective they are."

"Of course they love him. How could they not?" Indignation colored Agnes's cheeks at the implication that anyone could fail to love her son. "And yes, they were very nice to us when they came to visit Gunther in the hospital."

Silence, punctuated by the muffled snapping of bones beneath goblin teeth, descended over the table. For reasons mystifying to Keith, Gerald, Agnes and Gunther seemed to have come to an accord. Did that mean Gunther could stay on Haakon's team? For the sake of Gunther's pride and dignity, he hoped so, though privately he would have been relieved if Gunther transferred to a less violent unit.

"So, I don't mean to tell you your business, Keith, but I couldn't help but notice that we didn't see you there," Gerald said.

"Keith had to work," Gunther said. "His job is important."

"I'm sure his supervisor would have given him the day off if he'd asked," Gerald said.

It was the truth, and it stung. Sure, he could have been there holding Gunther's hand. He probably should have been. But he'd never been that guy.

"I thought my time could be better spent investigating the attack than hanging around the hospital hallway," Keith said. His reply sounded terse and defensive, even to him.

"And it was!" Gunther said. "Keith found out the probable source of the pixie dust used in the attack."

After a short silence, Gerald sighed and picked up a chicken foot.

"It's nice to see you boys are so quick to defend each other, I suppose." He bit off a long toe and chewed it.

"Oh, I know! Isn't it?" Agnes said, flashing a sudden smile. "Now you two finish your dinner."

Following the meal, Agnes started washing up, despite Keith's protests that he should do that since she'd cooked. Finally she relented when Gerald called her into the conversation to help him relate all the gossip Gunther had been missing since he moved away from the West Coast trans-goblin community. Keith scrubbed the greasy pots while listening to tales of abject normalcy. So-and-so went to college, someone else had a nice vacation in Hawaii. Only once did the tone of the conversation falter—when Gerald revealed that one of Gunther's distant cousins had been cited for violating the Secrecy Act and revealing that he was a goblin to a human reporter.

The leak had been sealed and sufficient disinformation broadcast to discredit the cousin as well as the journalist, but he was now unable to return to the earthly realm, even though he'd been born here.

Creatures with fae blood lived a precarious existence here, whether they were sprites, dark elves or goblins—facing deportation or exile for ever revealing their true nature. Keith didn't know if it was right or not. But it was the way it was.

Still, hearing of the sadness of Gunther's aunt and uncle, he wondered if it always had to be.

The conversation lightened after that and Gunther brought out the brand-new Scrabble game that he'd bought in anticipation of his parent's first overnight visit. Being professional translators, Gerald and Agnes wiped the floor with Gunther and Keith, even when they gave them a handicap and allowed them extra tiles. But it was a pleasant way to pass the evening—certainly different from Keith's own childhood home, where the television was a necessary guest at every meal.

Just after nine, yawning and stinging with defeat, he and Gunther adjourned to their bedroom. As the door shut, he pulled Gunther close.

"Do you think your parents are really mad at me for not being at the hospital?" he whispered.

Gunther shrugged, then shook his head. "When they're angry they don't say anything at all. I think . . . they think they know how we should be acting, but we're not them, you know? You're not my mother. You don't have to be standing around next to me ready to feed me your own leg to show me you love me. You can just text."

"What the hell are you talking about?"

"You know, the story where the mother secretly cuts off parts of her body to feed to her starving husband and children?"

"I've never heard of that—ever. I'm completely sure I would remember if I had ever heard that story," Keith said. "It must be a goblin thing. Is it set on a craggy, snowy mountaintop under a blood-red sky?"

"It is, but . . . are you sure you don't know that story? There's a children's picture book and everything," Gunther said.

Keith just shook his head, partially to answer Gunther's question and partially at the idea that he would have ever come across such a book. Though now that he thought of it, it did sort of resemble the plot of *The Giving Tree*.

"Anyway, that's not the point," Gunther continued. "What I'm saying is that they don't understand you, but they're trying. And at the same time they're trying to accept the fact that I'm grown up now and can make my own decisions. That's probably harder for them."

He stripped down to his boxer briefs and climbed onto the bed, careful to shield his injured hand from harm. Keith followed suit, though he removed all his clothes, as was his habit.

Nowhere did Gunther's physical superiority become more apparent than when they were alone and naked. Accessories like clothes and jewelry and epic attitude gave Keith moderate visual impact. Once they were removed, he had only his tattoos and his imperfect body to represent him. Whereas Gunther—Gunther achieved male perfection to Keith's eye. He could have been carved from marble and put on a pedestal in some Italian museum.

For the first year that Keith and Gunther dated, Gunther still lived with his parents. For that reason, Keith had a lot of experience not only having quiet sex, but also having sex while knowing that his boyfriend's parents lay sleeping only a floor away.

It had been a year since then and Keith had to remind himself to be quiet—very quiet—when he slid into bed beside Gunther. The first thing he noticed was the red mark where the bolt from the stun gun had slammed into Gunther's chest.

"Does it hurt?"

"A little. It's not too bad though. We all get mage-stunned during strike force training. It doesn't hurt as much as being tasered, but it makes you super groggy."

"Too groggy for this?" Keith ran his hand down Gunther's perfect abs to find the warm flesh beneath Gunther's boxer briefs. Keith couldn't actually believe that Gunther still wore anything to sleep with him, but he supposed that's the kind of habit a guy developed after living with his parents into his thirties.

And besides, if he was honest, Keith had to admit that he enjoyed the sense of transgression every time he slid his hand beneath the flat elastic band. It recalled the thrill of his first high school gropes.

"I can fight through the fatigue." Gunther began to roll toward him, then winced, rubbing the red mark on his chest where the mage bolt had hit him. "Maybe not on my side though."

"Don't worry. I got this one." Keith leaned in for a kiss and found Gunther shying away. "You really want me to stop?"

"No, I'm just . . ." Gunther turned away. "I can't believe my mom served raw onions."

"You're worried about your breath?" Keith almost laughed but stopped himself. Gunther could be sensitive about his extra-human qualities. "You brushed your teeth for practically an hour. You're fine."

"If you say so." Gunther allowed himself to be coaxed into a kiss, which, when deepened, tasted mostly of cinnamon toothpaste.

Keith luxuriated in the moment, careful not to put his weight on Gunther's chest or jostle his bandaged right hand. He decided the best course of action would be to head south. Not only would that avoid the injury zones—it would keep Gunther from trying too hard to get Keith off. Because the fact was that Keith owed him one.

He hadn't come to the medical unit when Gunther needed him. Why? 'Cause he would have broken down. No matter what kind of man-of-action rationalization he gave himself or others, the fact was seeing Gunther hurt tore at him worse than he'd imagined it could. And he hadn't wanted to break down in front of those people. So he'd been absent instead.

He definitely owned Gunther a righteous pole-smoking.

Gunther's reaction when Keith closed his lips around the head of his cock was both charming and predictable. He nestled closer into the pillows, smiling down at Keith as though he'd never seen anything better in his life. He tucked his bandaged hand over his stomach and reached down to stroke Keith's shoulder.

Keith decided then to make a performance of it. Not just to give the best head he could but look good doing it. He tried to incorporate a sense of drama and flair to his long licks and tongue swirls. He tried to keep all the eye contact he could while working Gunther to a feverish tremble, quivering right on the edge of orgasm, then withholding it at the last moment, causing Gunther to writhe against the pillows and clench his fingers in the screwed-up sheets.

Keith reckoned this must be the best job, blow or otherwise, that he'd ever done getting Gunther off. And the pride he took in that went straight to his dick, making it stand up to accept the honor, as if saying, "I'd like to thank Gunther's smoking-hot cock and its two ball companions for giving me the inspiration to be fucking amazing."

He dropped one hand down to his own tool to give it a little pat on the head, to acknowledge its participation in this award-winning event. Then he dived back down for his closing move, bobbing, nuzzling, snuggling and sucking with the confidence of a man who knows his efforts are appreciated.

He managed to time it so they came almost at the same time, with Gunther lagging a couple of seconds to watch Keith work himself before surrendering to Keith's final deep kiss.

He lay on Gunther's thigh, panting to catch his breath while Gunther stroked the sticky hair back from his face. Finally, he urged Keith back up into place beside him. They kissed again, which made Keith's already reddened lips tingle.

Just as he started to slip from the edge of consciousness, Keith heard Gunther say, "Even if I could do better. I wouldn't want to. Cause you're the best to me."

Chapter Five

The next morning brought news of another agent attacked—another member of the strike force. Keith found out about it from Nancy, who shook her head sadly as she related the information. "They now seem to be targeting Strike Force A directly. A lot of people are worried that it's a specific retaliation."

The idea of a person or persons going after the strike force specifically twisted Keith's gut and sent him rummaging around his desk for antacids before he even sat down.

He told himself Gunther would be fine. His parents were staying on a few days to help until his bandages came off so he wasn't alone and would be taken care of if he had a relapse or there was a new attack.

He forced himself to focus on his work.

Keith shared his office with two other employees, Inspector Daisy and Inspector Sandborne. Together with Nancy they constituted NIAD's Division of Magical and Extra-Human Drugs and Food, or "MED/Food" for short. Normally, Daisy and Sandborne carried out site inspections and recertifications while Keith investigated—investigated, despite what that tiara-wearing mage-puke King Douchebag Melchior thought—cases of criminal wrongdoing.

Stripped of his weapon, Keith had very little to do. He finished his own paperwork just before lunch. Then both his coworkers donned their MED/Food jackets and headed out.

Keith was left alone with the backlog.

A better punishment could not possibly have been devised for his insubordination. He spent three hours shifting paper, checking stamps and dispensing stamps on up-to-date companies before getting to the "request delay in filing paperwork" pile. Here he found a wide variety of semiliterate and partially illegible forms wherein the owners of various magical businesses alternately pleaded for more time in filing or attempted to explain their circumstances.

The forms ranged from weird, "primary stakeholders disappeared while dealing with trolls—request more time to acquire ransom," to the lackluster, "flood in records room makes it impossible to submit appropriate documentation." He gave the poor woman dealing with the troll kidnapping a ninety-day extension and flagged the flood for investigation.

It just sounded too much like a "dog ate my homework" to him—especially in this digital age. Moreover, it was Taranis, the company that manufactured Primal Thunder Power Shake. That wouldn't have, in itself, been a cause for punishment. But Keith happened to note that Mage Melchior served on the board of directors for that particular company. He figured as long as the mage was set on thinking of Keith as a mere functionary in the bureaucracy of the NIAD lunchroom, he should act the part. And in his experience, hell hath no fury like a health inspector scorned.

He grabbed a MED/Food windbreaker prepared to be the most pedantic, unfeeling obstructionist dick imaginable.

He paused only to stick his head into Nancy's office to tell her where he would be.

"You're doing a site inspection?" She lifted a quizzical brow.

"Primal Thunder has an exclusive on the exercise room vending machine. I'd hate for all those strike force guys to go thirsty because Taranis allowed their permit to lapse," Keith replied.

"I thought you didn't want to investigate without your gun."

"I'm not investigating. I'm just helping out Daisy and Sandborne." He brandished his new weapon for her to see. "Have clipboard—will travel."

"I find this suspicious, but I'm going to let you do it anyway, since this is the second time the company has missed their deadline for filing and it's all the way out in North Dakota." Nancy took a moment to write him the portal permit to the NIAD office in Bismarck, then said, "No expenses. I want you back here by five."

"Yes, ma'am."

◆◆◆

The portal to Bismarck deposited Keith in the closet-like toilet of a run-down filling station. There, a single, grizzled attendant sat behind a counter, reading the paper. He glanced up in mild surprise as Keith emerged from the out-of-order toilet. Keith thought he was human, but couldn't be sure.

"Didn't know I would be expecting a traveler today," the attendant remarked. "Especially not from MED/Food."

"That's why it's called a surprise inspection." Keith flashed his badge. "But not for you," he added when the old man began, very slowly, to become alarmed. "I'm on my way to the Taranis corporate office. My boss told me I'd have a car to use here?"

"Let's see." The attendant grunted slightly as he bent to perform some unseen preparation that Keith sincerely hoped did not include retrieving a shotgun or hiding some half-eaten human body. He didn't want to be suspicious of the guy, but since he'd entered law enforcement, he'd become cautious as a hypochondriac.

To keep from staring at the man like a creep, he took stock of the refreshments on hand. The tidy rows of cigarette packs, candy bars and breath mints looked strange and antiquated next to the Primal Thunder Power Shake machine's splashy blue facade.

The attendant straightened up and handed Keith what turned out to be a battered old key on a North Dakota State Capitol souvenir key ring.

"It's the silver Escort around back," he said. He rang some numbers into the register, then printed out a thin paper receipt. "No need to fill it up before you bring it back. Just sign here to take it out."

Outside, the weather in North Dakota was not as cold as Keith had expected. Crisp, but the air was pleasantly sweet and distinctly free of the smog and sorcerous residue that clogged the air filters of his home base. He found the car and slumped down into the seat, taking time to adjust the mirrors before donning his spectral lenses. Through these he could see two small, hidden readouts. These were located near the speedometer and alerted him to the presence of portals nearby.

The spectacles also allowed him to see the leprechaun sitting on the seat next to him.

Carrot Beard stared straight ahead with his arms folded in front of him, though because of his height the only thing to glare at was the bottom of the glove compartment.

Only NIAD's extensive agent training kept Keith from jumping. Instead, after a steadying breath, he said, "Trespassing on NIAD property can result in exile from the human realm for no less than one hundred days up to one hundred years."

"You think I care, badge? I have to protect myself from your loose lips," Carrot Beard said. "No jury would convict me."

"I think you'll find that even if you were entitled to a jury, which you are not, that would not the case. Now scram."

"Wait now, Agent Curry, let's not be hasty," Carrot Beard backpedaled in the way that Keith had come to expect, alternating between bluster and obsequiousness. "You don't want to go into that beverage facility alone, I guarantee."

"Why is that?"

"I used to work there, you know, before the pixies did me out of my job, curse their—"

"Watch it now."

Carrot Beard scowled. "Bless their little scabby hearts, I meant to say."

"So why would I need you with me to do a routine inspection?"

"Come on now, Agent Curry, you and I know you're not an inspector. You're the filth, if you'll pardon my vernacular."

"I don't think I will." Keith leaned back. "But okay, go on. What do you think I would be investigating there?"

"Any of their so-called natural flavorings, for one thing," Carrot Beard replied.

"Are you saying that they're made with contraband food items?"

"I'm saying that many of them are what you'd call magically delicious." The leprechaun pulled a smug smile, which almost caused the tip of his chin and nose to touch.

Keith took a moment to consider Carrot Beard's offer. He did have a floor plan of the factory—all food producers were required by law to submit one—but his specialty did not lie in factory-scale productions.

But it would never work. If leprechauns had been employed at Primal Thunder, then Carrot Beard would be spotted immediately.

Besides, he really wasn't investigating anything.

And yet, if Carrot Beard's accusations were true, there could be unauthorized adulterants in the company's line of energy drinks. The fact that Gunther liked them so much was reason alone to make sure that the ingredients were authorized.

As he thought this, Keith felt a wave of intuition sweep over him. Now that he was thinking along these lines, Gunther had been drinking a Primal Thunder beverage seconds before he'd been attacked or possessed or whatever had happened to him. The mages had asked if Gunther had inhaled any secondhand smoke before his attack. What if the magical agent that had allowed interlopers to take control of Gunther's body had been contained in the drink instead?

Of course Keith knew his immediate urge to condemn Taranis Inc. was based partially on his dislike of Mage Melchior, but still, once the idea entered his head he couldn't let it go.

He could think of one man who might know.

He got his phone and dialed a number he never thought he'd call on purpose.

The dark elf used a single word to answer and that single word was his name. "Haakon."

"It's Keith Curry."

"Yeah?" Haakon clearly didn't find Keith hard-core enough to handle entire sentences.

"When Santiago went down this morning, what was he doing?" Keith asked.

"Nothing," Haakon said.

"Was he drinking a Primal Thunder drink, by any chance?"

"What?"

"The protein shake," Keith said. "Did he drink one before his attack?"

"Well . . ." Haakon paused and Keith worried that that was the end of the sentence, but Haakon continued, "Now that you mention it, he was drinking one just before he was compromised."

"Do you remember what flavor?" He glanced askance at Carrot Beard, who nodded at him in an I-told-you-so fashion.

Another long silence, then, "Orange. I remember it spilled on the sidewalk."

"That's what I needed to know. Thank you."

"What does this have to do with Santiago?" Haakon's tone grew demanding, but also tinged with worry. He truly did care about his team, Keith supposed.

"I'm not sure yet. Just don't let anybody drink any of that shit until I get back." Keith rang off and turned to Carrot Beard. "How good are you at casting a glamour on yourself? Not turning invisible. A real glamour."

"It's interesting that you should ask, because I do have one fine disguise I use quite often." Carrot Beard's chest swelled with pride.

"Show me."

The leprechaun took a deep breath, then pinched his fingers over his nose as though he was about to jump into a dunk tank. Then he made a motion as if to blow out, but instead of opening his mouth, he kept it clamped shut.

He began to grow. His neck stretched upward and his legs stretched down. Another deep breath brought his head up to the level of Keith's shoulder and a third lengthened his legs to the floor. Then as Keith watched, the leprechaun's beard retracted into his face, only to emerge from the top of his head in a shock of bushy red hair.

Carrot Beard's face had changed as well, growing younger, his cheeks covered with a smattering of freckles. When he spoke it was with the voice of what he appeared to be—a ten- or eleven-year-old boy. Keith glanced over his spectacles to make sure Carrot Beard appeared the same to the human eye. He did.

"It's good, isn't it?" the boy, whom Keith now mentally referred to as Carrot Top, asked.

"That's not going to work," Keith said.

"Don't you worry. All I need is a clipboard and I'll make a fine assistant. I won't swear at all. I promise."

Keith rubbed his eyes in annoyance and said, "Little kids don't have jobs as food inspection assistants."

"Just tell them it's Take Your Son to Work Day." Carrot Top blinked. His green eyes twinkled. The freckles spattered across his milky cheeks seemed even more adorable than before. He leaned close to Keith. "I'd be ever so happy if you'd show me how you make money to buy me toys, Daddy."

Keith didn't know what was worse—the sudden horror and revulsion at some apparent kid calling him Daddy or his guilt at feeling revolted by it. Still, Carrot Top had come up with a pretty workable strategy. It would be foolish not to take advantage of it.

"Okay, we'll go with you being my son, but don't call me Daddy," Keith said.

"Whatever you say, Pops." Carrot Top immediately started playing with the electric window, rolling it up and down. Keith briefly wondered at the location of the child-safety control panel, then decided it didn't matter. If the leprechaun-now-posing-as-a-child fell out the window, it would be one less thing he had to worry about.

CHAPTER SIX

Driving through Bismarck's wide streets under the big clear sky would normally have been a pleasure. Keith spared only a glance for the historical town center and well-kempt lawns before heading to the outskirts of town.

There, nestled between two rolling hillocks covered in winter-yellowed buffalo grass, stood the head office of Taranis, and the adjacent Primal Thunder Bottling Company. It looked much the same as any other facility of its kind—a gray and cream corporate facade that somewhat resembled an airline hanger on one side with loading docks along the other. Shining blue trucks backed up to the docks to receive pallet loads of fruity drink.

No fence encircled the facility, but two security guards flanked the front entrance, which Keith supposed was not that unusual in corporate buildings these days—even in North Dakota. Keith's spectral lenses revealed that though one was human, the other appeared to have some ogre blood. Again, Keith found nothing suspicious about discovering extra-humans working in a facility with a NIAD contract.

The entry foyer held a big, round desk staffed by a bland receptionist. When Keith flashed his NIAD badge, the young man directed him to Mr. Taylor's office on the third floor.

While Keith negotiated the large, echoing room and oversize elevator buttons, Carrot Top tagged along behind him, staring up at the ceiling and occasionally picking his nose.

"Stop that," Keith said.

"It's part of my character," Carrot Top replied. "It's what boys do."

Keith watched Carrot Top twist his hand around to get

what appeared to be a deeply satisfying dig on. Then, as if possessed by some innate reflex, he dope-slapped the leprechaun in the back of the head.

Carrot Top whipped around, furious, but before he could speak, Keith said, "It's what fathers do."

Carrot Top just scowled. The mirrored interior of the elevator reflected back the image of them together, plausibly father and son, he supposed. The sight unsettled him more than he would have thought. Probably because it reminded him so much of his childhood interactions with his own father.

Gunther had most likely not been the recipient of even well-deserved dope slaps. Gerald and Agnes had probably been the type of parents who used their words and expected Gunther to, as well. The many photographs of Gunther and his assorted family members that hung in the home he shared with Gunther spoke of a close-knit, understanding, non-dope-slapping crew.

A thought occurred to him that had never before crossed his mind: did Gunther want to be a father? The notion of Keith himself acquiring a taste for parenting seemed ludicrous, but Gunther had a nice family and traditional tastes. Would he truly be telling some kid to get his finger out of his nose someday? Time would tell, he supposed.

The elevator reached the third floor, happily releasing Keith from any further contemplation of his future as a parent or how apt Carrot Top's imitation might be of any future progeny.

The letters stenciled on the door said "Rick Taylor, CEO." The rest of the office said, "I love hunting." From the framed page from *Bowhunting* magazine featuring Taylor in camo gear standing over a fallen moose to the head of what Keith suspected to be the very same moose mounted on the wall, Taylor's office transmitted a pervasive interest in trophy-centered aggression. Several gold plaques identified

Taylor as a winner, just in case Keith had failed to notice. Taylor had trounced the competition at numerous shooting and archery competitions, and had even achieved excellence in bowfishing, which Keith hadn't even known existed before this moment.

Taylor stood just slightly taller than Keith—somewhere around five ten, but outweighed him by at least twenty pounds. He had a thick shock of hay-colored hair and a mustache that looked strong enough to jump off his face and go on safari by itself.

He'd been named CEO of the year by *Food and Beverage Weekly* for his management of the Primal Thunder Power Shake brand for six consecutive years, if the series of plaques on the wall were to be believed.

Taylor shook Keith's hand and smiled at Carrot Top when introduced. Then he turned and gestured to the two chairs. "Please have a seat."

Keith did so, noting that Taylor failed to sit himself. Rather, he perched on the corner of his desk in a relaxed, informal, congressman-meets-his-constituents way that Keith, as a resident of Washington, DC, immediately mistrusted. But Taylor wasn't looking at Keith, instead keeping his eye on Carrot Top.

Keith glanced back at Carrot Top, whose illusory boy-like form turned out to be the perfect disguise for standing and gawking at the assorted deer and antelope heads keeping the prize moose company.

"What do you think?" Taylor asked.

"You must be descended from Herne the Huntsman!" Carrot Top said.

"No," Taylor laughed, then continued. "We're not related, but we do take down an elk together now and again."

Keith hoped that this was not literally true, but feared it might be. Taylor winked at him, which didn't clarify.

"Now what can I do for you?"

"I'm just here to finish your inspection." Keith held up his clipboard as though its presence proved his veracity. "You haven't had a walk-through in at least three years."

"Has it been that long?" Taylor asked, smiling.

Keith resisted the urge to put a check mark in an imaginary box on the form marked: This asshole is jerking me around. Instead he said, "That's right. And this year I gather your paperwork hasn't been submitted either."

"That would be because of the flood," Taylor said. "Five hundred gallons of orange beverage all over the floor. Mage Melchior himself came to help us with the cleanup. He's on the board of directors, you know."

"That's right, isn't it?" Keith said. He wondered if he should play it hard and question Taylor's obtrusive name-drop or just play dumb. Dumb seemed like a better option— easier to sustain. "Will Mage Melchior be joining us for the inspection then?"

"Oh, no, he's much too busy to hang around here." Taylor gave a laugh. "So what can I do for you?"

"I just need to establish that this floor plan is still accurate. It will only take twenty minutes or so. I've even brought my own hardhat." Keith rapped his knuckle on the thing to emphasize its sturdiness.

"I brought one too!" Carrot Top chimed in. He plopped the oversize headgear onto his ginger noggin. "Do we get free samples, Daddy?"

Keith fought not to roll his eyes. "You'll have to ask Mr. Taylor that."

"Can we, mister?" Carrot Top exuded the breathless excitement of a high school thespian chewing the scenery.

Taylor didn't seem to notice the overacting. He just said, "Sure, big guy, let's get started. I just have to make one phone call to let them know we're coming down. It might seem like fun, but this is a real factory and parts of it are dangerous. Do you promise to behave?"

Carrot Top nodded solemnly, though from his vantage point, Keith could see that he had his fingers crossed.

Taylor picked up the phone, dialed and, in a casual and cheerful voice, explained to some unknown person that he would be bringing visitors down to the floor. He didn't seem to be speaking in code, but then Keith didn't think he needed to. Any visitors would be suspicious to an organization that had gone to such great lengths to avoid inspection.

Down in the bottling facility, the equipment seemed fairly standard and in line with the floor plan on file. Along with the wildly popular Primal Thunder brand, the facility manufactured nutritional supplements for extra-humans living in the earthly realm. Most of the production line consisted of vats of colored sugar water into which various additives were inserted via nozzle. Some of the additives Keith recognized as arcane nutrients found only on other planes, as well as the ubiquitous platinum, a nutrient needed by most creatures of fae descent. Gunther himself took it in tablet form. The other supplements appeared to be a murky sludge of whey protein and fiber.

Keith made sure to glance at Carrot Top every now and then. The leprechaun was doing a good job of using his boyish guise to peer and stare at everything. Halfway through the tour he pointed at a series of copper tubes that ran along the ceiling. Each tube ended in a nozzle that hung above a mixing cauldron.

"What are those?" Carrot Top asked.

"Those lines contain our secret flavoring agents," Taylor said. "They're what makes Primal Thunder taste so good."

"And what exactly are they?" Keith asked.

"The ingredients and exact formula are proprietary, though we did submit a formula to the MED/Food office before production began," Taylor said.

"I don't seem to have that list." Keith leafed through the papers.

"If you need a new list I can have one sent to your office," Taylor said.

"That would be best, I think." As Keith spoke he watched a thin, red stream of fluid spray down into a vat. Even with his spectral lenses on, he could see nothing remarkable about the substance. He wished he could get a sample of pure flavoring, but the nozzles were at least twenty feet in the air.

He continued the inspection, going down the checklist, reviewing the equipment and checking for the appropriate number of handwashing stations and recessed floor drains.

He was on his knees checking one of these when he spotted something odd slinking along the floor.

At first he thought it was a trick of the light, then he realized that it was a fluffy orange cat.

Even regular human food facilities didn't allow cats.

This one crouched across the room beneath the noisy bottling line, ears flat, clearly disturbed.

Just as Keith was about to mention it to Taylor, a worker in a white cleanroom suit swooped down and scooped the creature up.

He disappeared through a side door.

Keith checked the floor plan. The side door that the worker had gone through went to an area labeled "employee break room." Could one of the workers have snuck his or her cat into work for some reason? And the worker had been wearing a cleanroom suit. That in itself was not unusual, but Buttercup had mentioned that the culprits who had kidnapped her fellow pixies had also worn paper outfits and threatened her with an orange feline.

And although neither the cat nor the cleanroom suit was suspicious on its own, together, and combined with lost paperwork, they aroused Keith's interest. As he neared the end of the route he diverged to glance through the single, high window in the break room door.

Inside, the room appeared to be exactly what it said it was. A few tables and chairs. A microwave. A faded OSHA poster on the wall. The only unusual thing was that there didn't seem to be anyone in it, which Keith found strange, given that he'd just seen one man and one cat step into the room that appeared to have no other exit.

"How are we doing, Inspector?" Taylor's too-loud voice broke through Keith's concentration. "No violations, I hope?"

"Everything seems to be in order here." Keith deliberately avoided lingering at the break room door. He'd have to find a way to get in without Taylor dogging him.

Because there was definitely something going on here and he aimed to find out exactly what. What had started as a fairly childish attempt to harass Mage Melchior's company might turn out to yield a real result. Excitement bubbled up inside as he felt himself gravitating toward discovering what Taylor wanted to keep hidden.

Unfortunately, Taylor seemed dedicated to personally escorting him off the property. He walked them straight to the front door and offered Keith a firm handshake then bent down to address to Carrot Top. "See you in the funny pages big guy."

Keith stopped to leaf through the papers on his clipboard to buy himself some time. If only he could get Taylor to leave him alone for five minutes, he was sure he could get back to the production floor.

"It's too bad you don't have a list of your flavoring additive ingredients," Keith said, glancing up from the meaningless remarks he was writing on the inspection form. "I could certify you right now."

Taylor seemed to weigh this before giving a shrug. "I'm sorry, but the IT guy says it will be at least another week before he can get the backup restored."

"I'll keep an eye out for it then." Keith smiled and started ambling slowly toward the two security guards flanking the front entrance. Both eyeballed them with bland interest. Behind him he heard Taylor answer a phone call. Then the man's voice faded as the elevator doors closed behind him. Keith knew he had to think fast. His shoes squeaked loudly against the tiled floor of the big foyer, while Carrot Top padded along silently beside him.

"We need to get back to that production line," he said under his breath.

"I know that," Carrot Top growled.

"If you have any ideas, now's the time." Keith glanced around again, trying to decide if he could just make a break for it.

Suddenly, Carrot Top loudly announced, "Daddy, I have to pee."

Keith stopped in his tracks. He didn't know the leprechaun's game, but at least this gave him an excuse to stop walking toward the exit.

"I thought you said you didn't have to," Keith replied. Was this some kind of code? Was he talking about using a portal?

"I have to go!" Carrot Top squirmed and pressed his hands to his crotch in a very authentic display.

Still adrift, Keith said, "Can't you hold it?"

"There's a bathroom right there!" Carrot Top pointed back down the long hall that they had traversed. Indeed, there was a bathroom.

"Oh for God's sake," Keith seized Carrot Top's hand and headed back down the hallway. Once they were out of sight of the security guards, Carrot Top yanked his sweaty palm free of Keith's grip.

"Quit holding hands, you queer."

Keith snorted. "You wish your tiny fae ass was good enough for me to want."

"Are you actually a queer then?" Carrot Top asked. "I'd have never thought it. You look so manly with your dainty little clipboard and lack of weapon and all."

After considering a couple of ways he could turn his clipboard into a weapon and use it against the leprechaun, Keith decided to ignore the comment. He did not want to risk any onlookers intervening, as he would appear to be beating a child. Plus, he just didn't have the time.

He seized Carrot Top's hand again and hissed, "Shut up and follow me and look bored."

He headed back to the production floor and reentered the big, cavernous room without fuss. He didn't walk too fast or too slow. He kept a determined look of vague annoyance on his face, which ensured that he would be noted, then disregarded, by most employees. After all, they had just seen him there performing normal duties. Carrot Top tagged along behind him. His expression of petulant-child ennui verged on perfection.

They made it into the break room without incident. The space was still void of people as well as felines. Two vending machines stood against one wall. One sold Primal Thunder drinks and the other contained a variety of energy bars as well as a single apple.

"Ah, the old break room." Carrot Top turned in a slow circle. "It seems smaller than it used to be. Or maybe I'm bigger."

"No, it's definitely smaller," Keith said, checking the floor plan. "They've moved this back wall up twenty feet or more. That would mean there's a twenty-by-twenty-foot space behind it?" Keith ran his hand over the wall, feeling for seams or some kind of hidden door. The wall was smooth as could be. He kept going around the room; then he noticed something odd. The Primal Thunder machine wasn't plugged in.

Not only were vending machines approximately the height and size of a door, they were engineered for the entire front to open so that the machine could be filled and serviced. He suspected he had found his door. Now all he needed to do was get through it.

Carrot Top drifted over, watching as Keith felt up and down the side of the machine for any kind of latch.

"You trying to break in? You should use the code."

"What code?"

"The access code." Carrot Top reached up and pressed 54321, then hit the button. The door popped open. "Those cheap bastards couldn't make us pay for drinks that we made."

"Quiet!" Keith whispered. With great care he pulled the door open and found exactly what he expected—not cans of beverages, but a narrow corridor leading toward the back of the room.

"That's new," Carrot Top remarked.

The air flowing out of the corridor was thickly scented with leaves and earth, as though it were a greenhouse filled with exquisite blooming flowers. Automatically, Keith reached for his mage pistol, then cursed himself for doing it.

As quietly as he knew how, Keith called for backup. Or attempted to anyway. As the dispatcher endeavored to patch him through to Bismarck, Carrot Top seized his arm.

"Pixie dust! I smell it in the air."

Then from down the corridor he heard the yowl of a cat, followed by a tiny, high-pitched shriek.

Keith instantly started forward. Carrot Top caught him by the arm, but Keith shook him off easily. The leprechaun's hands grew smaller and smaller in his hand as the creature reverted to his normal small, bearded form. Oddly, as he did this, his strength seemed to increase exponentially, weighing Keith down like a sinker.

"Let go of me," Keith hissed.

"Hello? Who's there?"

The voice Keith heard did not belong to Taylor, but that gave Keith scant comfort. He now had two choices—go forward and reveal himself or retreat and wait for backup.

Keith spent exactly half a second considering his options. He felt the chances of making it out of the facility without being caught were slim. So he reached into his inside coat pocket and got out his badge.

He strode decisively into the room. There, on rows of steel tables, with rubber hoses feeding into them, stood ten of the largest aquariums he had ever seen. Each was easily as big as a coffin. But they didn't hold water. Lush, low-growing plants carpeted the bottoms while chicken wire covered the tops. Nestled among the foliage, Keith made out a small plastic fixture that had once hidden the bubbler. It had been fashioned into a treasure chest spilling out plastic pieces of eight.

Keith wondered if these could be the coins that Gunther had described.

The man in the white cleanroom suit that he'd spotted before stood next to one of the aquariums. Now in addition to the cleanroom suit he wore a respirator and held the orange cat. Keith could see dozens of colorful moths fluttering right at the bottom of the terrarium—though as Keith drew nearer, their movements seemed strange. They almost flickered. One moment he'd see a moth and the next a cowering little female figure with candy-colored hair.

He'd found the missing pixies.

"Blood of Menses! They've enslaved the wee women!" Carrot Beard exclaimed. "This is worse than hiring them as scabs. This here is an insult to all fae creatures!"

"Quiet." Keith started toward one of the aquariums, trying to assess the health of the pixies trapped inside. They looked terrified.

"Look out!" Carrot Beard yelled. "The bastard's brandishing a cat!"

Keith turned his attention back to the room's lone attendant.

"I'm Agent Keith Curry from NIAD." He held up the badge as if it were itself a magical amulet instead of a piece of silver-plated brittanium. "Put the cat down and put your hands up."

Though the man's eyes were shielded by thick goggles, Keith could see the panic in them. Suddenly he hurled the cat at Keith. While Keith sidestepped the incoming missile of claws and fur, the man lunged to the side and hit a large, red button on the wall.

An alarm began to sound. As the cat came to a skidding landing on the tile near them, Carrot Beard leaped from the floor to the top of the nearest terrarium. He curled his now-tiny fist around the twisted wire, yanked it free and wriggled into the terrarium through the opening to the plants below.

"I'll just be bunking up with you all in here so long as there's a ferocious orange moggy n the loose," Carrot Beard told one of the moths.

Keith kept his eyes on the man in the cleanroom suit. He didn't seem to be armed, but it was hard to be sure given the amount of pixie dust in the air. He positioned himself between the man and the hallway.

"I repeat! Put your hands in the air!" he bellowed over the siren. The man complied; then, as suddenly as it had begun, the alarm stopped. The man in the cleanroom suit dropped his arms to his sides and stared at something just beyond Keith's shoulder.

That did not give Keith a good feeling about who, or what, might be standing behind him.

"You know, Agent Curry, for a minute there I actually thought you were really an inspector," Taylor's voice sounded from behind him.

Keith slowly raised his hands and turned to face him and his bwana mustache.

Of course he was holding a pistol, what had Keith expected? A crossbow? Taylor looked disappointed, but not angry.

"I am really an inspector today," Keith said.

"What happened to your so-called son?" Taylor craned his neck, scanning the room.

"I told him to wait in the bathroom." He hoped Carrot Beard had the good sense to hide.

"He had a leprechaun with him," the employee chimed in. "I didn't see where he went."

Taylor leveled his gun at Keith's head and said, "Show yourself, or he's dead."

"Piss off, dickhole!" Carrot Beard's voice seemed to be coming from everywhere in the room.

Taylor turned to Keith and shrugged. "Can I assume that was your so-called son? Looks like you've failed as a father. Turn around and get down on your knees."

Keith knew that if he turned around it would be the end. Taylor would shoot him. They'd hide the body and wash the blood out with an industrial hose. Maybe Carrot Beard would report the crime, or maybe he'd just be glad to be free of that unspoken wish.

The wish—he still had it!

He wanted to be careful, but he didn't have time.

"I wish—" Keith said, then stopped. What could he say? He felt the pressure growing, almost as if the magic itself was urging him on. Despite his dire situation he felt the strange need to giggle. The whole world took on a surreal and comical tone, as if the air had been replaced with laughing gas.

"You wish?" Taylor repeated. "Is this your last request?"

"I wish you were the worst shot in the world," Keith blurted out.

"I guess you're out of luck," Taylor said. "Now turn around."

"No." Keith stood firm. "If you're going to kill me you'll have to look me in the face."

"No problem. I was just trying to keep the janitorial hours low." Taylor pulled the trigger.

Keith stayed still as a statue as the deafening crack of the pistol firing less than a foot from his face split his right eardrum. A high-pitched whine replaced all other sound.

In his left ear only, he could hear the rapid-fire rat-a-tat of the bullet ricocheting all around the room. Strange laughter filled the air as the bullet went on and on for what seemed like a full minute, shattering the aquariums, hitting the ceiling and the floor. Then the cleanroom suit guy grabbed his leg and fell, cursing.

Freed from their cages, the pixies zipped and zinged into the air by the dozens, flying like rainbow-colored confetti, all the while being cheered on by Carrot Beard.

Taylor's mouth hung open in astonishment. He raised his arm to fire again and the fluorescent light fixture on the ceiling creaked, then one end swung down, smacking him directly in the face. He fell straight back to the floor. Keith rushed forward, kicked the gun away, then knelt to check his pulse. He was unconscious but still breathing.

As Keith reached for his handcuffs he saw Carrot Beard trot up alongside Taylor's head.

"What a wish, my boy! The magic loved that one! True spirit of comedy."

"So the special flavoring in Primal Thunder was pixie dust after all?" Gunther asked. He sat at their kitchen table patiently waiting for Keith to put the finishing touches on his vegetarian shepherd's pie. After spending so much time with the little people, he'd found himself wanting to take a crack at the wholesome, sturdy fare of the Emerald Isle. He had spent the last five days in Bismarck, overseeing the seizure of Taranis and the Primal Thunder Bottling Company, and taking statements from everyone involved. When he came home he found that he'd just missed saying goodbye to Gunther's parents, which saddened him more than he'd thought it would.

"Even worse," Keith said. "It was grade B sorghum syrup given a glamour via the use of pixie dust. The system was ingenious, really. They got a cat, slapped an enchanted collar on it and made it into a good little menace for the pixies. Then they'd have a pixie cast a glamour on the sorghum, giving it whatever flavor they wanted. Apparently, this service used to be provided by the leprechauns at extortionate prices."

"Then Taylor figured out a way he could cut costs," Gunther finished. "But wait—doesn't that mean that the leprechauns knew all along the pixies were being held captive there?"

"They knew the pixies had stolen their jobs, not that they were being kept against their will. They thought Buttercup had rented them out as scab workers during the labor dispute."

"Why didn't any of them report Taranis? You'd think they'd have done it out of spite alone."

"Well, because that kind magical food adulteration is supremely illegal, mostly." Keith slid his hands into his oven mitts and transferred the bubbling casserole to the table. Then he returned to the stove to give the six lamb sausages he had in his skillet a good shake. Just because he was a vegetarian didn't mean Gunther had to be. "I think they're going to cut a deal for immunity in exchange for testimony."

"That would be smart." Gunther folded his hands and mumbled the few quick words that comprised the goblin version of saying grace. His right hand was still supported by a cast, but the bulky bandages had gone. "But I still don't understand how the attacks on NIAD agents figure in."

"They weren't attacks at all." Keith slid the sausages onto a plate, retrieved his half-empty beer from the countertop and seated himself at the table. "One of the pixies, Lorraine was her name, was sometimes able to work little spells into the pixie dust she dispensed that allowed her to send messages. The problem was that they were incomprehensible. She was only able to press her immediate feelings into the dust."

"So I really was possessed—sort of. Possessed by a memory."

"Exactly." Keith helped himself to a serving of salad, then to the buttermilk dressing.

Gunther served himself a paperback-sized portion of the shepherd's pie. He topped this with two sausages, then asked, "So why is there a cat in my parents' bedroom?"

Keith couldn't help but smile. It was so like Gunther to wait until halfway through dinner to ask about the cat.

"Well, it took a while to catch it, but we did. After we removed the enchanted collar that allowed Taranis to control it, it turned out to be pretty friendly. The pixies wanted it tried as an accessory but dropped the charges once we explained that it was acting against its will. I couldn't find a no-kill shelter in

Bismarck so I was going to take it to the rescue shelter in Arlington, but it was already closed." Keith took a more modest portion of the casserole and gave it a taste. The French lentils had melded well with the mushrooms, he decided.

"So you brought it home?" Gunther forked shepherd's pie into his mouth, heedless of the scalding temperature.

"Until tomorrow," Keith replied.

"Then why did you buy it all those toys?" Gunther asked.

"It seemed like a pretty nice cat, deep down. I thought it would be bored in there by itself." Keith kept his eyes down. In truth the cat had charmed him right from the second the enchanted collar came off. It had a pretty face and a sweet, chirpy meow. It had kept him company in his motel room in Bismarck. On the second day Keith had named him Cheeto.

Gunther regarded Keith for a long moment, then rose and went upstairs. He heard the door to the spare room open. Seconds later the cat came slinking down, followed by Gunther.

"It's no use keeping him up there all alone." Gunther reseated himself. Immediately, Cheeto jumped up onto his lap.

Keith shook his head. "You better watch out. You don't want to get too attached. You have a weakness for scruffy things."

"Yeah," Gunther said, smiling. "I do."

The Most Important Meal of the Day

The morning of the apocalypse had started off so well.

Special Agent Keith Curry of NIAD had risen, showered and gotten as far as peeling his standard-issue hard-boiled egg before the first tremors of the looming cataclysm rocked through the city.

Keith had not always been such an austere breakfaster. Before joining NIAD, he had worked as a chef. Back in those days he'd started every Sunday morning with Hangtown fry and a Bloody Mary. Now he preferred the simplicity of the six-minute egg. For one thing, it fit easily into his pocket, which helped to facilitate caloric intake during frequent unexpected callouts.

Like many of the nonmagical residents of Washington, DC, he'd initially mistaken the shock waves that formed when one of the thin membranes between the human and extra-human realm of existence ruptured for some kind of earthquake or sonic boom. Maybe it had been a bomb or gas line explosion.

But unlike most of the other nonmagical humans in DC, Keith worked for NIAD—Earth's premier supernatural intelligence and security service. Because of this the tremor gave him pause. Certainly a sulfurous smell permeated in the air, which he'd initially attributed to the indeterminate age of the egg. But now, with the eye-watering potency of the stench, he began to wonder about its origin.

Keith's ruminations were interrupted by the sight of his live-in lover, confidante and general companion, Gunther, rushing into the kitchen from his shower, soaking wet, naked and talking on his phone.

"Yes, sir. I've got it," Gunther said. "I'll be ready in five."

Gunther cut a compelling figure—a fine specimen of humanity, tall, dark-haired and rippling with sinewy muscle. But that was only on the outside. Gunther's parents had both been goblin refugees working in NIAD's San Francisco office. And so that their child would fit in better among the humans, Gunther had been transmogrified in utero to outwardly resemble a human.

But the humanity only went skin deep. Gunther not only possessed the great strength of all his fae brethren, he retained certain other goblin tastes as well, such as a palate that included appreciation for the taste of naphtha.

Keith had met Gunther through NIAD when Gunther's strike team had been called to assist on one of Keith's cases. Doubtless, Gunther's team leader, Haakon, was the voice now on other end of the phone giving Gunther the specifics on some supernatural situation that would naturally preclude a good breakfast for either of them.

Normally Keith would have made some pithy comment about the lost breakfast or at least teased Gunther about insisting on showering with a phone. But Gunther's expression showed no softness or even awareness of Keith's bathrobe-clad presence. He disconnected, went to the hall closet, pulled out a heavy duffel bag and plunked it down on the kitchen table.

"What's going on?" Keith asked.

"I've been deployed." Gunther unzipped the bag to reveal several hard cases that Keith knew from previous experience (and snooping) contained Gunther's weapons. As Keith watched, Gunther uncased his automatic mage rifle, two conventional pistols and a goblin-forged short sword.

It was the sword that worried Keith most.

"Are you leaving the earthly realm?"

"No, I'm going about five blocks away," Gunther said. His blue eyes flashed up at Keith. "It's bad. Maybe the end-time."

"And you're still naked," Keith said. "You realize that, right?"

Gunther looked down at himself, said, "Darn it," and headed for the bedroom.

Alarm zinged through Keith's guts, but he followed Gunther up the stairs at a leisurely pace, egg in one hand, coffee cup in the other. Gunther was already half dressed by the time Keith entered their bedroom.

He downed the egg in two bites, then went around to his side of the bed and found his NIAD-issue spectacles. These lenses had been designed for humans like him, who needed to be able to see extra-human creatures and events that were invisible to the human population. As soon as he did this, he noticed a strange red light filtering in through the sheer curtain that hung over the north-facing window.

Pulling this aside, he could not help but note that the clear blue sky had been rent down the center, leaving a gaping tear like a massive claw had ripped through a canvas. Beyond this he saw what appeared to be bloody flesh punctuated with dozens of blood-red eyeballs the size of oceangoing freighters. These glared down at the city with the insane twitchiness of a schizophrenic on methamphetamine.

To say he wasn't scared would be a lie. He was quite scared—so scared it took him a couple of seconds to be able to move. But Keith was not surprised. While he hadn't expect to see the hideous, Lovecraftian assemblage of flesh and giant eyes, it didn't fall outside the realm of possibility in his personal reality, which, in a way, was more terrifying—but not necessarily a shock.

When he could move again he took a drink of coffee and said, "Does your deployment have anything to do with the perforation of realities revealing a nightmarish hellscape hanging in the sky?"

"Haakon is sending me to get Jax." Gunther started strapping on his body armor. "He only lives a few blocks from here."

"Who in hell is Jax?"

"He's the most powerful warlock on Earth." Gunther cinched the buckle of his sword belt. "Or that's what Haakon says, anyway."

"And Haakon is sending you alone?" Keith didn't like Gunther's commander. The dark-elf alpha-bro of the NIAD DC strike force rubbed him the wrong way—sometimes literally in the form of abrupt, unprovoked noogies.

"Like I said, I'm closest." Gunther shouldered into his scabbard. Then he turned, kissed Keith hard and said, "You should stay inside. Some creatures have come through the rift."

Keith drained the last of his coffee. "I'm coming with you. Don't even fight me on it."

Gunther seemed like he might do just that, then he broke into a smile. "You better get dressed then."

◆◆◆

Outside, the streets outside were full of screaming. First the terrified shrieks of DC residents being pursued by sla-vering, sharp-toothed hellhounds, then the wailing of every conceivable siren, and last the desolate howls of a thousand madmen that seemed to be emanating from the rift itself. A choking stink like foul breath poured out as well.

Viewed through the treated lenses of his NIAD-issue spectacles, the DC street came alive with magic. From the tangles of leprechaun graffiti scrawled across the stoops of well-kempt row houses to the squadron of air force witches broomsticking toward the rift, the unseen was revealed to him. One in twenty citizens who rushed down the sidewalk sported a glamour that hid their true forms.

Keith even spotted a unicorn barreling down the center of the street, nostrils flared and eyes rolling in fear of the vile gaze hanging in the sky.

Glancing up, Keith's heart skipped a beat as he saw massive tendrils of red mist beginning to curl down from the rift like the tentacles of poison anemones. They seemed to be searching the buildings, pushing into the windows.

Further screaming seemed to be the result of this ceaseless probing.

"Do we even know what that thing is?" Keith shouted above the noise. To his left he saw a movement and trained his mage pistol on it, but it turned out to be a regular dog cowering by a set of trash cans. A leash hung slack from the dog's neck. It still had what looked like the owner's hand attached to the guiding end, but Keith saw no trace of the rest of the person in sight.

"Haakon said it was a vision made flesh," Gunther shouted as he dodged a mutilated corpse on the sidewalk. Keith picked his way more gingerly through the blood, noting the guy had two hands, which meant he hadn't been the owner of the dog.

Not that that mattered. Groceries lay strewn around the man's body. A dozen eggs lay crushed and oozing yellow yolk into the sanguine rivulets that followed the sidewalk cracks down the curb and into the gutter.

"Whose vision is this? Some crazy mage?"

"Nobody knows," Gunther replied.

"And what's this Jax supposed to do?"

"Fix it. That's what NIAD pays him for." Gunther came up short at the end of a block and motioned Keith to stillness. He gripped his sword in both hands as he carefully peered around the corner.

Instantly a snarling hellhound leaped at him. Gunther kicked the beast in the chest and brought his sword down, slicing the creature in two lengthwise. Blood sprayed up in a fine mist that coated them both in rank-smelling gore. A second beast lunged for Gunther's leg, but Keith dropped it with his mage pistol. He and Gunther sidled past it as it writhed on the concrete, caged by tendrils of magic.

"Jax's place is at the end of the block." Gunther motioned Keith to follow.

The street was deserted but as they approached a row house Keith saw another body on the sidewalk. Oddly, this person—a middle-aged woman—also seemed to have been carrying groceries when mauled. Her eggs had survived, though her head and one hand seemed to have been carried off.

Gunther took the stairs two at a time and, to Keith's shock, rang the doorbell.

"It's open," a voice called from inside.

As Gunther opened the door, the network of silvery spells laced across the open doorway practically blinded him, forcing him to push his NIAD-issue spectacles up to be able to see anything at all.

Keith followed Gunther into the darkened foyer. As he stepped across the threshold, the sonic assault from the sky stopped, as did the vile stench. The smell of stale sneakers replaced the odor of the rift. As his eyes adjusted, Keith could see why. The floor of the foyer was strewn with shoes, jackets and other miscellaneous clothing. Farther down the hall he could see a crumpled pile of what looked like sweatpants.

Again the voice sounded—a male voice. "The kitchen is at the end of that hall. I'll be in the living room when it's ready."

Keith crept down the hallway and peered through the doorway into a darkened, disheveled room containing an armchair, a couch and a massive television set.

The room also contained a man. Handsome as a supermodel, and clad in green boxers and a single sock, Jax sprawled across the armchair as if he were an illustration for ennui. Keith had seen a lot of illusions and disguises of this sort—most magical creatures could make themselves look good. At the risk of blinding himself again, he lowered the specs and snuck a peek through. Jax's form shimmered with magical writing, but Keith could see that Jax's true appearance was merely average.

He appeared to be around twenty-five years old and fairly greasy. His expression was torpid as he watched the television, which was tuned to some cartoon Keith didn't recognize.

"We've come from NIAD." Keith flashed his ID, which Jax didn't turn to look at. "We need your help. There's a rupture between the planes—"

"I know, the council of mages already called me. It was right as I was trying to order my groceries," Jax said. "Actually, I called the store twice, but they never arrived."

"I think that might be because of the monsters and whatnot." Keith tried to keep his voice calm.

"Whose fault is that? Not mine. Some undiscovered mage kid gets a Ouija board and opens up a realm of bloodletting and sorrow and suddenly I don't get breakfast? They told me that not having blintzes is not the end of the world." Jax gave a snort. "But I say, maybe it is."

Keith stood, momentarily torn between horror and homicidal rage.

Gunther stepped forward. He'd sheathed his sword and actually bowed as he spoke. "Great Warlock Jax, the creatures coming through the rift are terrorizing the city. We don't have any time to waste. Lives are being lost every second."

"Right, I get that." Jax finally rolled his head around to look at them. "But it's almost ten a.m. I don't want to miss out on brunch because of this. I am really, really hungry."

This time Keith was not torn.

"You fucking spoiled little asshole," he bellowed, fully invoking the volume capacity he'd acquired during his previous career as a chef. "It's an apocalypse."

Jax rolled his eyes. "That's what you people always say. Then I help you but after that I'm sitting here with an empty stomach while everybody else is drinking mimosas and having a great time."

Keith strode to the window and pulled the drapes aside.

"Look out there." As they watched, a misty red tendril drooped down and slid in one of the windows of the house opposite. For a moment the tendril oozed and undulated, then an explosion of blood and body parts shot out, littering the streets with quivering chunks of flesh. "Do you see anybody drinking a mimosa?"

"I bet somebody is," Jax replied, unperturbed. Then something caught his eye. He leaned forward and pointed to where the middle-aged woman's body lay. "Hey, those are my groceries. Can you go grab them for me?"

Keith's middle fingers stiffened, prepared to fully salute Jax, but Gunther stepped in and said, "Of course."

Before Keith could tell him no, Gunther had started for the door. Keith caught up with him in the hallway.

"Me being here is not a coincidence, is it?" he asked.

Gunther managed a sheepish half smile. "Haakon had orders for you to do the brunch, but I thought if I told you that, you'd get mad and argue and we'd lose time we didn't have to waste 'cause the sky was full of giant bleeding eyeballs. You're the real agent they called for. I'm only your bodyguard."

"You know me so well," Keith remarked. He didn't know whether to be annoyed or flattered that he'd been the real agent dispatched to this breakfast crisis.

"I know," Gunther said, beaming. "Anyway, I've got to go get the groceries."

"You can't go out there," Keith said, catching him by the arm. "The mist will kill you."

"It's our mission," Gunther said. "I'll get the stuff. You go find the kitchen. All we have to do is get this guy fed and everything will be all right again." He pulled Keith to him and kissed him—this time softly—then said, "I'll be careful."

Then Gunther rushed out the door. He leaped down all eight stairs on the stoop and scooped up one bag.

The red mist seemed to notice Gunther then. It shivered, contracted and began to withdraw from the building to drift toward him. Gunther snatched up the second bag and stared up, but the egg carton still sat on the sidewalk.

Keith couldn't make blintzes without them.

Heart in his throat, Keith pelted down the stairs past Gunther. The misty tendril undulated toward him and he slid beneath it like a baseball player stealing home plate. As it passed by, distorted whispers filled his ears, striking cold terror down to his bones. He had to clench his teeth together to keep from screaming. He grabbed the egg carton and crawled beneath the deadly tendril, then scrambled up the stairs into the safely of Jax's foyer.

His hands shook as he stood, trying to gasp in a calming breath.

Gunther slammed the door, breathing hard, then started to pull Keith into an embrace.

Keith held up a warning hand. "Don't crush the eggs. They're all that stands between us and Armageddon."

As he heard the sound of Jax laughing at whatever cartoon he was watching, Keith's resolve solidified. NIAD needed some blintzes made and Keith was the best man for it. He might not be great with a sword, but right now what the agency needed was a whisk and a guy with the expertise to make breakfast for the laziest motherfucker on Earth.

He pushed past Gunther and made it to the cramped, galley-style kitchen. Though it was dark and poorly equipped, Keith found the items he needed—a bowl, a nonstick skillet and a fork that would have to do for a whisk. As Keith cracked the eggs and measured the milk, Gunther stood in the doorway watching uneasily.

Through the small kitchen window, Keith watched a tendril of red mist waving back and forth like the tail of an angry cat. He wondered how long Jax's magic could hold out before an entire—what had he called it—realm of bloodletting and sorrow—managed to break through the defensive barrier.

Keith set the batter aside, turned on the oven to preheat and went to make the cheese filling. The plastic container of ricotta cheese was smeared with blood and had two puncture marks on one side that looked like they'd been made by fangs.

Normally, Keith would have shied away from serving anything that had clearly been impaled on the canines of a ravening hellhound, but he decided that, on the whole, a little extra-planar dog spit could not possibly hurt the most powerful warlock on Earth.

With the slightly pinkish filling made, Keith stood back, crossed his arms and waited.

"Is something wrong?" Gunther asked from the doorway.

"That's a loaded question," Keith replied.

"You stopped cooking." Gunther's face crumpled into a confused scowl.

"No I haven't. The batter just needs to rest for thirty minutes," Keith said. Through the tiny window outside, Keith watched the building behind them collapse. Though he heard no sound, he felt the ground rumble as the falling structure impacted the ground.

"Can't you just hurry it up?" Gunther whispered—really more of a hiss.

"The crepes won't set if I don't let the batter rest."

"Are you kidding me?" Gunther cast a wild glance out the window.

"No joke." Keith was about to explain about how resting

the batter helped to develop the gluten in the flour, but Gunther's phone rang. While Gunther whispered down the phone about mimosas and hellhounds Keith turned his attention back to the window.

Now that the building behind them was gone he could see that most of the city was engulfed in flames, which seemed odd, considering that he could still hear the sound of cartoons floating from the living room. Was Jax watching a recording? If so, why had he kept the commercials?

More than that, the preheating light on the stove was on, which he felt it shouldn't be, given their circumstances. As Gunther continued his intense conversation, Keith studied the edge of Jax's property. It seemed he could see a distortion there, like a ripple in an old glass window.

He walked back down the hall to the front door and found he could see the same distortion in the front of the building. He also noted that the asphalt outside had crumbled away to reveal a chasm that seemed to be bubbling a glowing, amoeba-like slime. The slime contained still more eyeballs.

He returned to the kitchen and said, "I think we're in some kind of alternate reality bubble."

Gunther shot him a look comprised equally of outrage and confusion. He placed his hand over the receiver and said, "What?"

"We're in a different space or something. The lights still work." Keith flipped them on and off. "I think that dickhole Jax has put us into some kind of protective bubble until he gets his breakfast made."

"So?"

"So I think we can wait the half an hour to get it done right."

"I sincerely hope that you aren't wrong," Gunther said. "Because I just heard Haakon die." Gunther's hand shook a little.

Keith reached out to squeeze Gunther's fingers. "It's okay, baby. I'm going to make it right again. Or rather, I'm going to make that jerk in the living room breakfast and then he's going to make it right again."

They stood in silence for the next, agonizing ten minutes watching as the world outside, the very sky, was devoured. Keith fought to be calm. There were only nine minutes left to go, then he could make the food. All the while his thoughts raced and roiled with agitation against the magical beings of the world.

"How fucking unjust is it that the fate of everyone in the world should be decided this way? By one really shortsighted guy?" Keith whispered.

"Sometimes life's just not fair like that," Gunther responded. "Once this is all over we'll file a complaint."

"Against who? Life?" Keith demanded. "And what if it doesn't work? How can this be made right?"

"Let's just finish our mission here," Gunther said. "And then we'll see what happens."

Finally, the timer on Keith's phone pinged and he made six crepes, assembled them into blintzes and baked them an additional ten minutes while the filling set. After this, he transferred them onto a warmed plate and went to deliver them to Jax, who had fallen into a light doze.

It took all Keith's self-control not to break the plate over the man's head. He nudged the most powerful warlock in the world in the shoulder instead.

Jax's eyes fluttered open. "Oh wow, that smells great. Thank you." He took the plate and dug in.

With each bite Jax took, Keith could see the light from the window growing less red. He glanced back to Gunther, who moved forward to the front window and pulled the curtain aside. Keith went to join him. As they watched, the eyeball-filled slime had begun to reverse—not withdraw, but actually reverse. The collapsed street sprang back up from the depths and reassembled itself. The neighbor who had been blown apart came back together.

The hounds that had attacked the grocery delivery woman at the door arrived, put her savaged body back together, and retreated down the street.

Jax was reversing time.

He showed no sign of strain or even interest in anything but his breakfast. Yet clearly he had the godlike ability to make the world's clock run backward.

Keith's mind boggled at this insane notion—but it could be nothing but true. As Jax finished the last bite, the rupture in the sky healed itself and the morning stood as pure and blue and true as Keith remembered it being before hell descended upon him.

Jax held out his clean plate and Keith took it without a word. Then the most powerful warlock on Earth spoke.

"You'll be wanting to find Emily Parker of Wilmington, Delaware," Jax said, resettling himself in his chair. "She's sixteen years old today and will surreptitiously open up one of her birthday presents in about half an hour. Somebody needs to take that Ouija board away from her and get her into mage training, 'cause otherwise that girl is going to do some damage, am I right?"

Gunther was on his phone before Keith could even finish saying, "Thank you for your cooperation."

"No problem," Jax said. Then, more thoughtfully, "You know, it's always the ambitious ones who fuck everything up."

"Excuse me?"

"This Parker kid—she's probably been listening to some extra-planar spirit who's been telling her about how she's the chosen one who can bring peace to the planet or claim rightful dominion over the Earth or some such shit. When you've got power like that they start on you young—trying to convince you to create a rift between the planes for them."

Jax paused to open a small wooden box in front of him. It became clear to Keith after a couple of seconds that this was where he kept his weed. As he packed the bowl of a small glass pipe, he continued his rumination. "I was really lucky to have my grandma."

"How so?"

"She started raising me after my dad got himself and Mom turned inside out while trying to claim dominion over the Earth."

"That's terrible," Keith said. "Your parents' death, I mean."

"Well, it was the eighties, so megalomania was really popular. Or at least that's what Grandma said. She sat me down and told me about all the men in my line who had had these big ideas who just ended up getting themselves killed because they couldn't be happy with a normal life." Jax paused to take a long drag off his pipe. He then silently offered it to Keith, who demurred.

"I'm still technically on the clock right now," Keith explained.

Jax nodded, shrugged, then let out the smoke in a long plume and said, "What was I talking about?"

"Being happy with a normal life?" Keith supplied.

"Oh, right. Now if I want to try and become god-king of the planet I just go play a video game or something like a normal person," Jax said. "Anyway, the time distortion is stable now, so you and your partner should be able to reenter your natural time-stream without too much of a problem."

"But how does that work? If the girl is stopped, we never come here in the first place," Keith said.

Jax chuckled. "It'll be all right. There are all kinds of little cul-de-sacs in the time-stream. When you leave my house you'll just return to where you were half an hour before the shit started happening. If you remember coming here at all it will seem as if it were a dream."

"More like a nightmare," Keith muttered.

"Whichever," Jax replied, with great equanimity.

From across the room Gunther said, "I've finished filing our verbal report. They've given us permission to withdraw."

◆◆◆

Standing alone in the kitchen of his Washington Square townhouse, Special Agent Keith Curry pondered his breakfast. He held in his hand a carton of eggs, from which he had been about to choose a victim to hard-boil as was his habit.

But suddenly—he didn't know if it was gratitude toward the unexpected beauty of the morning or just a Sunday whim, but the perfunctory breakfast seemed inadequate.

He walked into the bathroom, where Gunther, his live-in lover and all-around sweetheart, stood in the shower, humming some goblin song as he soaped.

"I'm going to run to the store and get stuff to make blintzes," he said.

"That sounds great," Gunther replied. "I was just thinking that with our schedules, we'd been missing out on brunch recently."

Bring Out Your Best

Wednesday morning found Special Agent Keith Curry assigned to receptionist duty, which annoyed him. Not because he disliked answering phones. Among the various office duties, phone answering was his favorite. Sitting in the center of the circular reception desk at the DC NIAD office, rolling his chair from phone to phone, Keith felt a little like a one-man mission control. But he didn't like being demoted to a receptionist—or any other sort of demotion, especially of the punitive variety.

Such as being relegated to cover the phones on Wednesday after having been reprimanded for some tiny breech of protocol such as using the NIAD expense account to buy a novelty phone charger for one of his extra-human informants.

The usual receptionist, Olympe Tremelot, was well liked for her pink pompadour, delightful grin and general joie de vivre. She was also seven and a half feet tall and always brought cookies. Keith wasn't a bad looking guy. Midheight, brown hair, compact muscles, interesting tattoos—but he couldn't compare with Olympe, who had won employee of the year for fourteen years running. The surprise sight of him slumped, cookie-less in Olympe's reception desk chair seemed to sadden the other agents. And that hurt Keith's feelings.

It was just after lunch when he got the first complaint for his own department.

"I need to report some bad blood," the caller said. She

had a very smooth, neutral accent. Probably calling from out west.

"I'm assuming you mean the red fluid of life rather than someone you have beef with," Keith rejoined. This won him a brief laugh from the caller. Keith warmed to her for it. "Let's start with your name."

"Balderas, Lupe Balderas." The caller went on to give her NIAD ID number, which Keith keyed in to bring up her file. She was listed as a blood-dependent extra-human called a *tlahuelpuchi*. She worked as an aerial surveyor for the USDA.

So a fellow government employee.

"I'm not familiar with your extra-human designation." Keith thought it was best to come out and say it. "Actually I can't even pronounce it."

"T'la-h'well-poochi," Lupe said slowly.

"Got it. And you reside in Denver?"

"Yes."

"Have you already contacted the regional office there?"

Silence. A heavy pause, then, "The Denver office is more on the law enforcement side of things. I thought it might be best to go right to Food/MED. The blood my meal service sent was bad. Really bad. It tastes very strange and made me very sick. I called my meal service provider to complain but they blew me off."

"Which service is that?"

"SSA."

"Sanguine Service of America?"

"That's right."

Keith resisted the urge to audibly sigh. SSA more or less ruled the blood distribution game. And every week at least one extra-human creature dependent on their services called to complain about their products; but the problem with shutting them down for a proper inspection—even for a day—was that if he did he knew people would go hungry.

And Keith's department didn't want any human-blood drinkers to go hungry ever.

"And did you happen to save the remainder of your meal?" Keith didn't hold out a lot of hope here. None of them ever did. Lupe shocked and delighted him by saying that she had.

"I thought you might want to test it," she said.

Keith sat up straighter.

"I do indeed. I can be there first thing tomorrow morning to collect it—or evening if you're nocturnal."

"Morning is fine. I'm not light sensitive. I look forward to seeing you."

◆◆◆

The following morning, Keith took the official NIAD portal straight from DC headquarters to the tiny Rocky Mountain Region Field Office, located in the Colorado State Capitol building. Because of the time difference, no one was there when he arrived, so he let himself out into the grandiose rose onyx atrium to meet his hired car.

Outside the sky was bright agate blue and sharp shafts of morning light cast hard shadows. Behind him stood the building itself—a big, ornate neoclassical building topped with a golden dome that must have seemed artificial and alien surrounded by little wood houses and open prairie at the time that it was built. It still looked weird flanked by the modern skyscrapers of downtown. Before him on the western horizon, the Rocky Mountains loomed monolithic from north to south as far as the eye could see.

His destination was in LoHi, an upward-trending neighborhood of gentrified warehouses at the confluence of Cherry Creek and the South Platte River. The dry climate allowed for many a swank rooftop bar, which triggered Keith's nostalgia for his old career as a chef.

Not that he wasn't doing good work as a food inspector, but it wasn't the same as the daily battle and glory of his old days, when his life had been utterly consumed by the act of creating beauty on a plate. Life in NIAD offered perks, though. For one thing, he could get from DC to Denver in one minute. Plus he met a lot of interesting people and didn't end every single day drunk.

Just the days he felt like it.

Lupe Balderas's file stated that she had been born in Mexico and immigrated to Colorado as a teenager. She was a rare kind of shapeshifter, born most often in her home country and thought by NIAD's Mexican office to be the result of extra-human hybridization arising from a long-ago portal that had opened there in Mayan times.

Most tlahuelpuchi (and a few unlucky human women) had been systematically executed, with witch hunts occurring as late at the 1970s. Despite decades of research since then, little was known about which plane of existence the original shapeshifters might have come from. Lupe was one of three of her kind residing in the United States.

Keith found her sitting beneath a large photo of a starry night sky at an upscale coffee shop. She looked around thirty years old, with a clear, brown complexion with wide-set eyes and perfectly chiseled eyebrows. Her hair fell in two braids that easily reached past her waist. She wore a pencil skirt, a red polka-dot blouse and very high red heels but still only came up to Keith's shoulder when she stood to shake his hand.

It was only as they were exchanging IDs that Keith noted that his NIAD-issue extra-human detection watch was doing something interesting: nothing.

Normally it would have buzzed to indicate he was in proximity to an extra-human, but Lupe's presence went undetected.

So maybe there was something to the theory that tlahuelpuchi were humans—people with a condition that made them easy to mistake for otherworldly monsters, but really no stranger than any of the mages or witches than NIAD employed.

"So tell me about this defective meal you got," Keith said, once they'd seated themselves. "You said it made you sick—what kind of symptoms did you have?"

"Well . . ." Lupe leaned closer and lowered her voice to a whisper. "I felt really shaky, you know? So I thought it might help me to go get some exercise—go for a fly."

"In the form of . . ?"

"A vulture. But when I started to push out my feathers, I noticed they were much bigger than normal, and my muscles looked bigger than before. I grew big—really big—like California-condor big. And I got really agitated. I couldn't think and I started pecking everyone. My aunt, my little cousin. I couldn't stop and I couldn't turn back into a woman. I felt so bad."

"Were you the only person in your household who ate the tainted meal?"

"Yes, I'm the only one in my family who needs them," Lupe said.

"Okay, so what happened then?"

"My aunt pulled the blackout blinds so I'd fall asleep. I shrank down again a couple of hours later. After that I was able to get back to normal." Lupe reached into her tote and pulled out a crumpled brown paper bag. "The remainder of the blood is in there. I made sure to include the paperwork with the lot number."

"Good thinking." Keith glanced inside. Thick bands of red streaked the collapsed plastic blood bag. Lupe had consumed maybe half the portion. According to the label the material had only been donated a couple of days ago. If he was quick he'd be able to get back to DC in time for the magical forensics lab to have a look at the blood sample before they closed. Then he'd know whether he needed to call SSA to issue a recall or halt deliveries altogether. "Looks like there's enough left to test."

"Have you had any other complaints?" Lupe sat forward. She was so small Keith wondered if her feet would have hit the ground without her high heels.

"Not about this batch but from the date on the packaging it seems like you might have been the first person to receive it. So, did the packaging you received show any signs of tampering?"

"Not that I saw," Lupe said.

"Did SSA refund your money?"

"They said I'd have to return the unused portion, and I wanted to keep that for you," Lupe said.

"Then you've ordered a replacement?"

"They're really expensive, and insurance doesn't cover it."

"Of course not." Keith wasn't surprised. Insurance couldn't cover a medical condition that wasn't supposed to exist. "Do you have any other meals on hand?"

Lupe shook her head. "I only need one prescription meal once a month, so no."

"Okay, here's what I'm going to do: I'm going to take this evidence with me and have the Denver office bring you a replacement meal from our supply. Can you give me an address for the delivery?"

Lupe blinked at him, cocking her head to one side in a way that revealed her birdlike qualities. "How much will it cost?"

"Nothing." Keith packed the sample into his bag. "Ensuring food security is just one part of our continuing mission at Food/MED."

Lupe gave another laugh. "Spoken like a true company man."

◆◆◆

"No can do," Special Agent Gavin Nash said with an exaggerated shrug. Blond and tan, he stretched his big frame out in his chair like he was lying back in a hammock. Though he struck Keith as too young to effectively pull off such an insolent pose.

"What do you mean, no? No you can't bring Ms. Balderas a replacement meal or no you won't?" Keith glanced around the small office, searching for anyone else who might be able to help him. This branch was laughably small for the square miles the agents here were supposed to cover—just a reception area, two interior offices and the closet-like space that contained the portal.

"Both. There's no blood supply kept at this office," Nash said. "And being meals on wheels isn't our job even if it was here."

"Food security is absolutely our job," Keith said.

"No, it's your job. At this office we focus on law enforcement."

"As do I." Keith glanced to the field office's only other inhabitant, a young woman decked out in a melon-colored vintage pantsuit, who sat silently staring at them both. Keith couldn't tell if her lack of participation signaled tacit agreement with Nash or just passivity.

"No, you enforce rules about handwashing," Nash said. "I protect humans from monsters. There's a huge difference."

And who, Keith silently wondered, protects the monsters from you, Agent Nash?

If Nash had been the first guy to pull this on him, Keith might have bothered to get angry about being insulted for providing valuable social services. But Nash was far from the first pumped-up self-styled sheriff who had tried to minimize Keith's contribution.

"Yeah, I can see that you're super busy with it too." Keith gestured vaguely at Nash's impeccably clean desk.

It became clear that if he was to make good on his promise of dinner for Lupe, he'd have to accomplish it himself. A brief search of the internet revealed no food-grade blood outlets in town. The closest was in Colorado Springs, an hour's drive away. And he'd need to drive there, because all the portals in the town were military and therefore restricted. Plus the cost of the meal was staggering.

No way his department's auditor would okay that. Especially when they were still pissed about the phone charger.

He wondered if he could just make the meal himself, as it were. The idea appealed in several ways, including speed, cost and assured quality of product. He turned to the receptionist. "Is there a blood draw kit on the premises?"

The woman silently shook her head. Her gold hoop earrings glinted as they swung back and forth.

"Is anyone here qualified to draw blood if I procure a kit of my own?"

Again the woman indicated the negative, then turned away. Again Keith could not decipher whether this was insolence or apathy.

◆◆◆

After a brief database search Keith found a NIAD-affiliated doctor willing to do the draw.

Maybe it was because he now cohabitated with a trans-goblin, but recently Keith had started to see the deep inequity with which extra-humans were treated. First they had to live by the edicts of the official Secrecy Act, which prevented them from revealing themselves to the world in their true forms. That alone would be enough to wear on the personhood of anybody, but on top of that half of NIAD preferred to think of the citizens they were sworn to protect as monsters to be violently eliminated.

Keith could understand the mindset—he'd been that guy once too a long time ago, when he'd suffered the shock of discovering that a lot of creatures he'd thought were imaginary had turned out to be real—and a few of them did actually eat human beings. But he'd overcome that sense of alienation at the largeness of the multiverse and his own relative smallness and powerlessness within it. He credited falling in love with a trans-goblin for the greater part of his mental transition. Though he liked to think that appreciation of the diversity of the world would've come to him eventually, given time and maturity.

Lupe Balderas had not woken up one day and decided that she should drink human blood just for the fun of it. She needed it to live, and withholding it wouldn't make her straighten up and fly right. She wasn't a moral degenerate—just a person. And who knows what would happen if she began to starve? But maybe for guys like Nash that was the endgame—withholding resources from a person truly in need of them until violence and lawlessness are the only option for survival.

Yeah, that checked out.

Keith pumped his fist a couple more times, watching his own vivid blood snake down the plastic tubing into the bag.

It was weird, but making a meal for a client—even one comprised solely of his own blood—appealed to him. Obviously he didn't have a choice about plating. The entrée would be slurped out of this ugly plastic sack.

The color was nice though. Bright red. But it needed some kind of garnish. Or at least a personal touch. In the end, he asked to borrow the doc's Sharpie and wrote a simple "bon appetit" on the warm, slick plastic.

Lupe had just stepped out when Keith arrived, but her aunt accepted the meal with a grateful smile.

"Tell her I hope she enjoys it," Keith said.

Chapter Two

"I feel like I really put a lot of myself into that dish." Keith slid two pizza boxes onto the round kitchen table, then seated himself opposite his boyfriend. Gunther possessed an astounding physique, dark hair and bright blue eyes—which he currently rolled in response to Keith's pun.

"That's a terrible joke. But what you did was very nice. I hope you remembered to drink some juice after you donated."

"Does a giant iced coffee count as juice?" Keith considered getting down plates, but decided to forgo them as Gunther already had a slice in his hand. He settled for napkins instead.

"Not at all." Gunther went to their stainless steel refrigerator and selected one of his many fruity "health" drinks and set it down in front of Keith. A pink mandala decorated the bottle, while gold letters promised a dazzling variety of improvements to his health and spirit. Keith felt certain that the blend of apple juice, beets and carrots wasn't about to deliver him "enlightenment in a bottle," much less detox his spirit, but for Gunther's sake he took a drink.

Gunther smiled and sat back down in front of his pizza.

He worked on a NIAD strike force, which meant he spent most days on the firefighter end of the first responder spectrum. A typical day for him meant portaling to locations all around the United States saving citizens from their own bad luck and bad ideas. He might attend the scene of a necromancy gone wrong in the morning and then be assisting with wrangling drunken Valkyries on a hen night in the afternoon.

Now and then Gunther had to decapitate a dozen slobbering zombies with nothing but a sword. But those days happened very occasionally. And Keith avoided thinking about it when he kissed Gunther goodbye at the front door.

Keith opened up the box that contained his own dinner—a plain cheese pizza. Gunther downed another slice of his meat-lover's supreme with no cheese and extra hot peppers with all the salacious enthusiasm that one would expect from a goblin who had been transmogrified to appear to be human.

"So what turned out to be wrong with the blood she got from SSA?" Gunther spoke while shaking hot sauce onto his pie.

"I'm not sure yet. The magic forensics lab was already closed by the time I got back to DC. But I was able to run some standard tests. The blood is one hundred percent human, although from three separate donors. It had no off smell or color, but I won't know more until tomorrow."

"What do you think is wrong with it?" Gunther inquired.

"I have no idea."

"But you usually have a guess." Gunther chewed thoughtfully on his pizza.

"My guess is that it's been adulterated with something—probably to dilute or extend the product. Maybe extra plasma. Because why else would there be three separate DNA markers? It's not like there's some blood sommelier out there adding a little bit of this and that to create a literal Bloody Mary."

"I bet you could find one at the Grand Goblin Bazaar," Gunther mumbled.

"Well, yeah, sure. There's probably some great hema mixologists out there who we don't know about, but this blood came from a NIAD-certified prescription blood dispensary in Colorado Springs."

"But did it really?" Gunther asked.

Keith was about to argue but then realized Gunther had a point. Who was to say that the blood was voluntarily donated as opposed to being drained from farmed humans in some dark corner of the cosmos?

Hell, that could even be happening in an apartment in Milwaukee.

"You know, you could just tell me whatever theory you have, babe," Keith said.

"I'm not trying to barge in on your case." Gunther looked self-conscious. "I'm just saying that you're coming at this from the angle of a person who is looking for negligence in terms of food handling."

"Or adulteration for the purposes of increasing profits," Keith added. "Which are both rife in the food industry."

"What if it's not just some impersonal greediness? What if was a specific attack against the victim? Or against extra-humans living in Denver? I've seen a lot of reports of this kind of stuff on FaeBook recently. Harassment. Minor poisonings."

"You can't believe everything you read on FaeBook." Keith pointed this out automatically, before realizing how dismissive it sounded. "Sorry. I know that doesn't mean extra-humans aren't specifically targeted for attack all the time. But Lupe didn't mention anything about being targeted. Her main concern was that the rest of the portions of blood in that lot might also be unsafe."

"Maybe she doesn't understand that it's happening." Gunther folded another pizza slice into his mouth. "She might not be a naturally suspicious or cynical person. What does she do for the USDA?"

"Aerial photography. I don't know if that means she's a pilot or that she just straps a camera to her head and transforms into a bird," Keith said.

"Becoming a bird would be less expensive," Gunther said. "But more dangerous. I wonder if anyone there knows about her. It's not unheard of for human coworkers who discover extra-humans to exploit their vulnerabilities to win promotions or settle petty workplace grudges."

Keith nodded. All this speculation made sense from a sleuthing perspective, but he couldn't help but wonder at Gunther's sudden interest in this food inspection case. Normally Gunther liked to leave work at the NIAD offices and simply relax when they had time together.

"Did something happen at work today?" Keith asked.

Gunther shrugged. "We got a few new team members. More are on the way. Including my cousin Jerry."

"Oh? Jerry . . ." Gunther hailed from a large extended family that, unlike Keith's own, remained close and very much involved in each other's lives. Keith struggled to remember who Jerry was and whether that particular member of the vast Heartman Clan had struck him as a good coworker for Gunther.

"The pilot," Gunther provided. His expression turned unusually troubled. "All the new members are former air force."

Keith waited for more information, but none came. "And so?"

"They've all been suddenly discharged and they're all trans-goblins," Gunther said.

Ah, there it is.

"That sounds like deliberate discrimination." Keith kept his tone as neutral as possible. He didn't know where Gunther would go with this.

Gunther's relationship to his own extra-human nature was complex and sometimes contradictory. If he wasn't actively engaged in drinking kerosene or chopping the head off a *draugen* with one hand, Gunther passed for human. Maybe an exceptionally good-looking human, but human nonetheless. So he had the option of blending in, and he'd described himself to Keith as human on more than one occasion. Gunther often spoke about the need for the Secrecy Act in order to protect extra-humans from hate-based violence. But he also took immense pride in his goblin heritage and family. He'd wept with joy when the first extra-human had been elected to the United States House of Representatives representing California's twelfth district—a longtime fae stronghold and Gunther's hometown of San Francisco.

So Keith never really knew where on the complex continuum of identity Gunther's heart would lie.

"Yeah. I think some high-flying bigot just found out about trans-goblins and is now trying to purge his ranks." Gunther frowned at the single remaining slice of his pizza.

Brooding on some asshole who neither he nor Gunther could touch was only going to frustrate them both and probably wreck their evening. Keith didn't think said asshole deserved that kind of power over them, so he angled to shift the subject.

"Do the new team members seem nice?" Keith asked.

Gunther gave him a long, undecipherable look, then finally said, "It's hard to tell. None of them are happy about having been kicked out of their former jobs. If they'd wanted to work for NIAD they'd have joined us instead of the military. Most of them really don't have the ideal personalities for law enforcement."

"I see." Frustrated pilot wasn't exactly the right stuff when it came to keeping a cool head in the face of all the strangeness that Gunther dealt with on a daily basis.

"So I guess what I'm trying to say is that you never know when you have to watch your back." Gunther finished his pizza. "When you're different."

"That's true."

"But that's probably just me bringing my work into your problem. What about this SSA company? Are they legit?"

"They're a subsidiary of Blissco."

"Oh wow." Gunther raised his eyebrows. Then the corner of his mouth curved up in a mischievous smile. "That means you have an excuse to call your secret phone girlfriend. I'm so jealous."

"Come on, she's not my phone girlfriend." Keith felt his cheeks warming. "I've never even seen Susan. For all I know she's a pile of old telephones brought to life by a corporate wizard."

"Even so, she did send a very nice fruit and nut tray last Christmas," Gunther said. "You should keep flirting. Maybe we'll get an upgrade to salami sampler next year."

◆◆◆

Contrary to Gunther's prediction, Keith did not start the day by calling Blissco or any of its subsidiaries but by swinging by the magical forensics lab to check on the sample he'd submitted the night before.

"Seriously? I only got in five minutes ago, Agent Curry," the mage technician complained. She was a human woman of the midfifties variety with blond-frosted hair and a deliberate, frumpy manner. She wore a lab coat over a bulky, zigzag-pattered sweater despite the fact that it was mid-May. She didn't like Keith, but didn't dislike him either. "I haven't even opened up the evidence bag yet. Plus you have two murders ahead of you. You'll just have to wait."

"Listen, I'm not trying to be a pain in your ass, but I have to know whether or not to ask the company to issue a recall on the rest of the blood in that lot. That means potentially thousands of blood-dependent citizens going hungry today." Thousands was a slight exaggeration, but certainly at least one thousand citizens across the West Coast. "Or worse, getting tainted meals and going berserk and creating more murder victims."

"I'm going to be the one going berserk if you don't quit bothering me," she said. "Why not just issue the recall?"

"I have to have a reason, and magical contamination is easiest," Keith said. "So please just could you look at it? It will take maybe thirty seconds and I'll be out of here."

The mage tech let out a heavy sigh and pulled open the evidence bag. She eased the blood bag out into the center of the circle engraved on the work top. She then turned a knob at the front of the worktable and a ring of flames, much like those on a commercial stovetop, only vivid purple, leaped up. Thin lavender smoke rose from them. As the mage tech began her incantation the smoke began to form into arcane writing. Using a foot pedal, the mage tech photographed every word as it coalesced. These images were then sent to a computer that read and assembled them into a report, which the woman handed to Keith.

"There." She extinguished the flame and scooted Lupe's leftover packaging back into the evidence bag with the tip of her ballpoint pen.

"I don't suppose you'd be willing to interpret this for me," Keith asked.

"The mixture contains at least thirteen percent magically volatile compounds, spells or spell fragments. That's ten percent higher than normal."

"What are the compounds?"

The tech shrugged. "Don't know. You'll have to take it down to gas chromatography."

"How long does that take?"

"I think they're about six weeks behind," she said. "But thirteen percent is enough to get your recall or whatever, so. . .solved. Now please let me get on with the important stuff."

◆◆◆

After alerting SSC about their bad blood problem and suggesting that they issue a recall, Keith headed down to gas chromatography, which did have a huge backlog.

Handing over the leftover sample for analysis should have been the end of the case for now. Protocol would have him wait until the results came back to pursue the case of either adulteration or contamination further. But Keith convinced them that he needed to keep the packaging along with a small amount of residual blood because: what if

Gunther was right? What if he was dealing with an attempt at poisoning either Lupe or the extra-human population at large?

Technically he should have taken those concerns to the local agents, which would mean turning the whole thing over to the Denver field office. But chances of Nash putting any serious thought or effort into the case seemed slim.

He wondered if there was a faster way to narrow the options as to what magical adulterants exactly had been added to the blood Lupe drank. If it had been something that only effected tlahuelpuchi biology then at least he would know that Lupe had been specifically targeted. Was there any quicker way to identify the components in that blood?

Keith knew any number of human chefs and bartenders who could, with a great degree of accuracy, identify the components of drinks and dishes using their senses alone. Could Gunther have been onto something with the vampire mixologist angle?

Sheer curiosity led him to search the Grand Goblin Bazaar's website. Sure enough, there were three blood bars in the human-accessible area, though none were on NIAD's safe travel list. That didn't matter so much to Keith though. Because he realized he had an in. He'd met the Red Drop's head bartender, Excoria, earlier in the year when he'd been doing routine inspections at a bartending competition in Vegas.

The Grand Goblin Bazaar teemed with every sort of counterfeit or illegal product imaginable. You only had to walk a few steps down one of its crooked streets to find anything from knock-off couture handbags to bootleg grimoires whose accident-causing misspellings plagued the NIAD mage office. The only law in the Grand Goblin Bazaar was by edict of the goblin king: no street fights, no disruptions, no impairing commerce between citizens. But the line between citizen and chattel was very soft and smudgeable.

Then there was the food.

The great food halls at the bazaar were a perpetual source of misery to Keith's law enforcement persona but served as a source of personal delight for the chef's heart that still beat beneath his cheap suit. He took any excuse to go there if only to increase his base of knowledge.

Plus Gunther loved the skewers there, so it made a good date.

He picked up his phone and tapped his favorite contact, then texted:

"Hey babe wanna be my bodyguard tonight? I'm going to the GGB."

CHAPTER THREE

The Grand Goblin Bazaar did not exist in regular reality, or at least that's what everyone told him.

Sure, stepping out of a portal into the always-busy streets, a man could feel like he stood on the surface of a normal planet. The sky above swirled with the colors of a majestic violet and indigo twilight—but stay a few hours and you couldn't help but realize that the incipient sunset never came. More than that, no stars lay beyond that apparent stratosphere.

Was it some kind of lighted roof? Keith didn't know. And neither did anybody else.

"The bazaar is at the crossroads of all places," the merchants would say if questioned. And if you asked, "But where is that?" they'd just say, "Everywhere, of course."

Keith had always meant to track down one of the NIAD physicists and force them to try and answer the question in a way he could understand. But by the time he returned to the earthly realm he'd have forgotten his passing curiosity about magical physics and become infatuated by some new spice or fancy emerald-colored finishing salt harvested from the kraken home world—his current favorite brand came from a stall owned by a rather eloquent fish-boy who communicated with the oxygen-breathing clientele via marker board.

The first time Keith had come to the Grand Goblin Bazaar he'd been scared out of his fucking mind. The apparent lack of building codes alone had made him nervous about entering any of the wonky, leaning buildings. Golden finches perched atop every roof, bridge and gateway. Another agent had once told Keith that these birds were snitches—keeping tabs on the market for the powers that be.

Then there was the knowledge that some doorways led to different planes entirely, so in one step he could be two miles below some abyssal sea, or on a frozen asteroid deep in space, or in an endless plane composed solely of flesh, blood and eyeballs.

But Gunther's family regularly came here to shop and to meet their extended trans-goblin family, and slowly Keith had learned his way around one tiny corner of the vast tangle of streets and walkways.

The first few times he'd come here, Gunther's mother had insisted Gunther hold on to Keith's hand in case some hunter tried to snatch him, and ever since then he and Gunther had fallen into the habit of casually linking arms or holding hands whenever they came.

It was actually the only place Keith did feel comfortable openly displaying their relationship. Even living where he did in DC, he preferred not to elicit the kind of casual slurs from passersby that being a man holding hands with another man could provoke. Because he knew what would happen. Gunther would inevitably try and engage the verbal attacker on a personal level, which would only lead to additional cursing. At this point Keith would become enraged and escalate the situation with his own curses and maybe by throwing whatever happened to be in his hand, for example an ice cream cone, at their attacker. Red-faced and sticky, the attacker would come at Keith. And this would force Gunther to have to step in and break the man's arm, then get reprimanded for it and have his pay docked.

Or at least that's how it had played out last time. Keith had not eaten ice cream since.

But at the bazaar they were barely noticed.

So, fingers entwined, they headed for Copper Pot Row, where he knew he could buy the skewers that Gunther liked—some mystery meat doused in accelerant (a secret recipe the vendor refused to reveal to Keith) and eaten while still burning. The blue flames matched the blue of Gunther's eyes. Gunther had changed into suitable civilian gear for the excursion—jeans, a T-shirt and Kevlar cuirasses, all covered by a black leather frock coat. He wore his scimitar at his hip and kept his mage pistol in a shoulder holster.

Keith wore a cheap gray suit and tie, as he always did when investigating. His own mage pistol was tucked under his left arm. No one gave them a second glance as they moved through the crowded food market.

Farther down, Copper Pot Row intersected with the Blood Iron Alley. At the end of the alley lay the Yawning Gates of the Realm of Eternal Night, the primary portal to the vampire home world.

The Yawning Gates were experiencing very heavy traffic. Every few seconds the black mist broke and a thin, gray vampire stepped through into the market. A golden finch that had been perching at the gate's apex lit out after a particularly large party of vampires who emerged in the midst of a loud, hissing argument.

"There's the place." Gunther pointed discreetly about fifty yards down the alley—a narrow, swank storefront of gray concrete adorned by a neon sign depicting a red teardrop. "You sure you want to go in?"

"Yeah. I'm sure. I called ahead and everything."

"Okay then." Gunther shrugged his shoulders, subtly shifting his holster. "After you."

When Keith opened the door, the humid smell of vampire sweat hit him full-on. It was a weird, earthy scent that reminded him of earthworms and rust. To Keith's unaided eye, the room appeared to be pitch-black, though he could hear pulsing music like a giant heart thudding against his eardrums.

He tapped the side of his spectral lenses and green-tinged night-vision spells activated, allowing him to see the club was, in fact, crowded with patrons and also that the door-man, a tall, slim gray vampire with a toothy circular mouth like a hagfish, was regarding Gunther with annoyance.

"No outside food allowed in the club," he (or she—Keith had never figured out how to visually distinguish the gender of undisguised vampires) said.

"We have a special invitation from Excoria." Keith handed over the folded sheet of paper he'd printed out at home.

The bouncer glanced briefly over it, then returned it.

"I'll escort you back." The bouncer focused their attention to Gunther. "Weapons go in the lockers."

"Of course." Keith surrendered his mage pistol.

Gunther unbuckled his sword belt and hung his scimitar on the hook provided. He also reached beneath his coat and removed a much larger gun than Keith would have thought possible to conceal. Noticing Keith's expression, Gunther said, "The new holsters bend space a little."

"I didn't know we had that technology," Keith remarked.

"It's pretty neat." Gunther carefully leaned the long gun against the back of the locker, then closed it. "Really heavy though."

As the bouncer led them back to a VIP room, Keith concentrated on not choking on the strange stale smell of vampiric pheromones. More than once a stray hand grazed his bare skin only to be knocked aside by Gunther.

"Not for you," Gunther spoke in snow goblin. Probably because it sounded more badass, as it was comprised primarily of growls.

Once Keith thought he heard the words "NIAD filth," but he ignored them.

The VIP room in back was round, snug and furnished entirely in cushions made of some sort of fur. Keith took one that he thought looked good while Gunther positioned himself by the door—still standing.

Like the hot bodyguard he was.

Keith made a note to cook him something extra special when they got back home.

They didn't have to wait long for Excoria. According to her bio, she'd lived in the earthly realm for a hundred years, though Keith could find no formal record of her residence in the NIAD database. She was famous in the vampire community for her exquisite palate and expertise with human blood.

Her appearance was quite typical—gray skin, round, jawless mouth ringed with rows of teeth, large round eyes that reflected silver light, almost like a fish. Her cobweb-like clothes were both clingy and shapeless at once. She carried a tray with two small glasses on it.

When Keith had first met Excoria she'd impressed him as being meticulous and having an authentic interest in the culinary arts. She'd been competing in human disguise against mostly human bartenders, "just for the challenge of it." Plus she'd made him the best mojito he'd ever tasted, which Keith knew wasn't an indication of character, but predisposed him to liking her anyway.

"Agent Curry." She lowered herself to the cushions beside him and curled up in a way that defied the human bone structure. "How delightful to see you. I'm sorry I don't have any human-style alcohol on hand, but I think you'll like this nectar. It's from our home world—harvested from the roots of the whitethreads tree. Very special. It won't give you a buzz though, I'm afraid."

"I'm just happy you thought of me." Keith tasted the drink. It was amazing—profound—complex. Savory and sweet at once. He said so.

Excoria didn't smile but she made the bobbing motion with her head that vampires tended to make when happy.

"And for you, Agent Heartman, I chose goblin frost with soda."

Gunther hesitated one moment before accepting the drink. Then he politely dropped to the cushion. He downed it in one gulp, then shuddered and exhaled. Keith could see a plume of frosty air pouring out of his mouth. "Thank you very much. It was delicious."

"Now." Excoria folded her long hands in her lap. "I'm very interested in this challenge you have for me."

"Well, first of all I have to say what I've brought for you is a lot less nice than what you gave me." Keith pulled out the blood bag. "In fact it's downright nasty."

"Ah—it's one of those vile meal ration bags from your plane." Excoria recoiled slightly. "It smells awful. I feel sorry for whoever got that in their lunchbox."

"And well you should." Keith briefly related Lupe's story. "The criminal division doesn't see this as worth investigating, but I'm concerned about the possibility of deliberate contamination either against the victim personally or against our blood-dependent citizens in general. So I was hoping you could give it a sniff."

"A sniff?"

"You're the foremost expert on culinary human blood in the bazaar," Keith said.

"And so you think . . . what?" Excoria glanced from Keith to Gunther.

"He thinks you might be able to identify all the ingredients in it," Gunther chimed in. "Like he's always trying to do when we go out to restaurants."

Excoria broke into a laugh, which sounded like an explosion of rapid panting.

"Oh, Agent Curry, you can't be serious."

"I am. I believe that your developed senses can tell me at least some of what's in here—and give me something to go on." Keith kept his expression steady and gradually Excoria seemed to realize he wasn't joking.

"I can try, but . . ."

"That's all I ask." Keith handed over the bag.

Excoria opened it an inhaled.

"God, it's hideous," she muttered.

"I'm sorry."

"It's all right. Now then, it's definitely a blend of three humans. One male and two female. And there's something else in it. A synthetic. Maybe a medicine? It's not there for flavor enhancement. And there's a very distinct aroma of laboratory sorcery. Not a scent I'd pair with human sanguine. Ever. Or any blood, really." Excoria poked a long gray pinkie into the congealed blood then put the tiniest dab on her tongue. Her fishlike eyes rolled back in her head and she gave a violent full-body shudder.

"Are you all right?" Keith shifted away.

Hideous gargling emerged from Excoria's round, toothy mouth.

Alarm prickled over Keith's skin. His hand went to his empty holster while Gunther sprang to his feet and bounded between Keith and the vampire.

Keith hoped to god—not any human god, but whatever god might be governing the lives of vampires—that she was not about to turn into some kind of bloated leech monster and attack them both. Not only did he not want to hurt Excoria, he had no idea how he and Gunther would fight their way out of this bar. No one knew where they'd gone, which meant no party of rescuers waited in the alley.

Gunther had no such hang-up. Keith knew this from how his expression silently communicated the words, "See, this is why we tell somebody where we're going when we go to a vampire bar."

Keith shifted slightly to peer around Gunther's heavily muscled thigh. Excoria seemed to be recovering herself. She gazed up at Gunther and bent slightly sideways in what looked like an eel performing a sheepish cringe.

"I'm sorry," she said. "Please don't be alarmed, Agent Heartman. I was just being melodramatic. That stuff tastes really bad. I didn't mean to scare you."

Gunther's shoulders dropped, but only slightly. He didn't sit back down, but he did move aside so that Keith could resume his conversation.

"I thought you might be transforming," Keith said.

"You needn't worry about that. I strongly suspect that this substance only affects beings with a significant amount of earthly realm DNA. It has a taste that's specific to human beings." Excoria smoothed the veil-like planes of her garment. "I can't be completely sure, but I think this blood has been laced with the same additive that's in the local sports drink that they give fighters in the blood games on Seven Moon Way. Do you know the place?"

"I can't say I've ever been." Keith glanced at Gunther, who shrugged his ignorance.

"Well, I wouldn't personally recommend it for entertainment or sustenance. The whole thing is a waste if you ask me. All that violence and then on top of that, good food going right down the drain." Excoria regarded the bag. "Maybe one of the fighters got loose and escaped to the earthly realm?"

"Or someone collected the blood and sold it to Blissco, who passed it along to SSA," Gunther added.

Excoria seemed to consider this. "Blissco is the biggest human-owned company in the market . . . but selling human parts—that would be disloyal to their own species. That's unthinkable. Like something out of a cheap horror novel."

"You'd be surprised what humans will do," Keith said dryly.

"My app says Seven Moon Way is about seven leagues from here." Gunther swiped through text on his phone. "They sell the drink at the pro shop."

"Too bad there aren't any shoe shops around," Keith said. Both Gunther and Excoria gazed at him quizzically. "So we could buy a pair of seven-league boots and get there in one step."

Excoria bobbed her head in laughter so vigorously that Keith thought it might bounce off.

Gunther gave him a faint, fond smile, then shook his head. "Those aren't real, Keith. We'll have to take the train."

"There's a train?" Keith wondered what weird sort of train company would have opened up on a plane like this.

"Yeah, there's a station right next to my favorite kebab stand."

"I never saw a train—" Keith cut himself short. He had at one point seen something train-like traveling along a rickety track. He'd assumed it was a very unsafe roller coaster. "Are you sure those boots aren't real?"

"You'll be fine."

◆◆◆

Crammed into a narrow cabin that was surely about ten sentient beings over capacity, Keith took what he feared might be his last deep breath as the train rounded a hairpin curve and plunged what must be hundreds of feet down toward the bazaar's central entertainment district.

For his part Gunther stared stoically forward, looking neither to his right, where a reeking ogress sat painting her nails cotton-candy pink, nor to his left, where Keith kept a death grip on his seat. The bench across from them was taken up entirely by a lavishly bespectacled giant spider whose mandibles clacked together each time the train jolted on the rough track. The ceiling was coated with her softball-sized babies. Loose strands of spider silk drifted down as each tried to secure itself clumsily to the ceiling.

They traveled in the ladies-only carriage, since the towering troll conductor, seeing Keith casually holding Gunther's hand, had mistaken them both for children.

"Best not to have the little ones in the mixed car," he'd said, patting Keith's head. "Especially not with the bogeymen on holiday over there." He poked a giant finger to a group of hooded figures who stood apparently gossiping and taking photographs at the end of the railway platform. Each one held a squirming sack bearing the same logo—apparently part of the welcome gifts given to their tour group.

Keith tried to take comfort in the fact that at least he wasn't being carried off by under-the-bed monsters.

He heard a long, sharp cry. There, flying alongside the train, was a massive, Chinese-style dragon sheathed in gilded scales. It wriggled its sinuous body along, keeping pace with the train. Then the train pulled to a halt and the dragon sped past onto whatever shopping errands dragons did.

Stepping out onto the train platform, their destination was obvious. The huge curving walls of a massive coliseum rose up only a hundred or so yards away. Above it Keith saw huge manta-ray-like creatures circling, like vultures in the air, above the coliseum. Searchlights shot out from the underside of their mantles, sending beams of light slicing through the cheering crowd.

At the ticket booth, a creature—some sort of giant beetle—informed them that the day's shows were sold out.

"We'd just like to get to the pro shop," Keith said. "I've heard you have a great sports drink that I'd love to try."

"You would?" The beetle's voice floated out of a medallion strapped around its neck. Whether the apparatus was mechanical or magical, Keith didn't know.

"Yeah."

"You should have said. We're giving away free samples right through there." The creature pointed a long, insectile leg at a revolving glass door.

"Thank you very much," Keith said. "I'll be right back."

Things were going his way. He felt around for the empty flask in his pocket. They'd be back in DC in time to head down to the bar for a drink.

"Keith! Wait a minute—" Gunther called.

Only after he'd stepped through the door did Keith realize he'd been the worst kind of idiot. Behind him stood a seamless wall. In front of him lay a grimy dungeon pit. Above his head was a grate through which he could see the underside of the manta rays sending their searing lights downward.

Attached to the top of the medieval-looking grate was a state-of-the-art webcam. Above him he could hear the murmuring of a restless crowd.

A tinny voice through the speaker said, "Welcome, contestant! Are you ready to go for the gold?"

Chapter Four

"I don't suppose it would make any difference for me to say that there's been a mistake. I'm not a contestant." Keith addressed the camera. From the laughter that rippled from the crowd above him, Keith got the distinct impression that his words were being broadcast on some sort of JumboTron. Keith took out his NIAD ID and held it up to the camera. "I am Special Agent Keith Curry of NIAD on a special operation and I demand that you release me immediately."

Hoots and jeers replaced the laughter, along with a booing so intense he could feel the vibrations in his chest. His heart pounded, sending his pulse throbbing through his veins.

He had a pretty good idea of what was about to happen. He would be lifted up into the coliseum and then fight. . . whatever was up there. . . to the death. He had only two things on his side, his mage pistol and the fact that Gunther would be trying to find him. Whether or not that would be possible, or whether Keith would still be alive when Gunther managed to get to him, Keith couldn't say. He pulled out his mage pistol and thumbed the safety off.

As he did the camera he'd been speaking into began to move. A small panel opened in it's back and two sets of dragonfly like wings sprouted from the back. It hovered above him as the grate that covered the top of his cell slid away to reveal open sky. A searing searchlight shot down into his cell and Keith fought the urge to cringe beneath their laser intensity.

The floor beneath him lurched and began to move inexorably upward raising him to the fighting floor. He emerged just off center and got his first full look at the arena. The walls surrounding the fighting floor were not as tall as he'd initially thought—maybe only seven feet but escape over one of these seemed unlikely. Trolls, goblins and God knew what else crowded the ringside seats. Half of those guys had probably been hoping to kill a NIAD agent their whole lives. Here and there the yellow umbrellas of goblin skewer stands dotted the crowd.

The booing intensified and one close-by goblin chucked a full cold-drink at him. Keith dodged. The drink splashed against the ground—he could see the greasy rainbow sheen of an accelerant. Kerosene maybe?

As he was wondering what he might do with this, another trapdoor opened across the arena and a man's head began to rise from the floor. Enter the opponent. Even from fifty yards away, Keith could see he was pale, slightly built and sported a dishwater crew cut. He eyed Keith with cold curiosity. His gaze landed on Keith's mage pistol and his eyes widened in terror.

Overhead the announcer called out, "And he's back! Our reigning champion Paxton—thunder punch—Carter!"

Keith immediately flipped the safety on. His opponent was definitely a human and seemed sane. The fact that he was the reigning champion of this place didn't mean that the guy chose to fight here of his own free. He could have been abducted and conditioned or maybe he'd just walked through the wrong door. Keith couldn't kill him, so long as he had any other option. He knew that much. He holstered his pistol.

"Listen, we don't have to fight each other," Keith shouted above the hooting of the crowd. "Work with me and I'll help get you out of here."

Carter cocked his head in confusion. Then he reached into his pocket and pulled out a bright blue can. He held it aloft and the crowd heaved with excitement as he cracked the top and started chugging. One huge screen showed Carter's face begin to purple and swell as he gulped the liquid down.

Muscles all across Carter's body swelled, while his entire frame expanded to a towering mass.

The other screen displayed Keith's reaction of steadily growing horror.

Carter let out an incoherent howl, which was picked up by the crowd into a tsunami of sound.

Keith did not feel good about his chances of convincing Carter to cooperate with him—who knew if he spoke English, or had even stepped foot on Earth in his entire life? For an instant Keith reconsidered his mage pistol, but he knew that he couldn't just murder this stranger, not when he'd been the one who'd stumbled into the tournament. That left Keith only one option other than getting beaten to death.

Carter charged Keith, his massive feet kicking up plumes of sand as he bounded across the coliseum grounds. Keith took off, beelining it away from his opponent.

His high school gym teacher had called Keith "the Cheetah," and though that had been many years and a lot of grilled cheese sandwiches ago, he retained his basic instinct to run and run fast. Maybe if he could evade Carter long enough, the sports drink would wear off—or Gunther would figure out a way to get him out of this place.

As Keith sprinted ahead of Carter, missiles rained down on him from the surrounding stands. Drink cups full of gasoline, naphtha or blood splashed at his feet. Fat wads of spit peppered the sand where he'd been. Having been a queer kid in a conservative town, he'd long ago perfected his technique of eluding a speeding loogie.

Though he didn't know how long he could keep ducking and dodging at a full sprint. Cramps already nagged at his gut and his breath felt raw. He heard Carter growling and gasping as he closed the distance between them. Keith stole a glance back. Carter scrambled after him like a huge purple tick—his face contorted in an incoherent grimace of rage.

A flaming meat skewer sailed down. Keith dodged and the skewer splashed down into one of the numerous spills of kerosene. The ground ignited in flames, and acrid black smoke drifted through the twilight. Carter recoiled from the fire for a moment, but then he let out another infuriated roar and charged.

Keith coughed on the sickening scent of burning meat and something else . . . something eye-watering but distinctly familiar. Big Mama Tooth's Fiery Butt Sauce—Gunther loved that shit. There was always a bottle in Keith's refrigerator.

The condiment was manufactured in a facility in San Diego by a member of the trans-goblin community. Keith had toured the factory once and needed a hazmat suit to survive the free-floating cloud of atomized capsaicin, because the pepper sauce had been so hot it might as well have been weaponized.

Inspiration surged through Keith. He sprinted for the nearest yellow umbrella. As he neared he spotted the familiar green bottle with the purple cap. His breath caught in his throat, eyes burned. He leaped, propelling himself straight up the wall separating him from the surrounding crowd—and more importantly, the food vendors. The plump brownie beneath the yellow umbrella gave a startled squeal as Keith hit the wall hard and flailed out.

Straining, Keith's fingers just brushed the bottle of Big Mama's and sent it tipping into his hands. He felt Carter's fist swat across the back of his jacket. He tumbled forward. Carter's weight slammed into him and they both skidded across the sand.

Whirring camera-flies whizzing around them, jockeying for the best shot of what would be Keith's demise. The crowd chanted, "Blood, blood, blood."

Keith ripped the cap off the bottle and squeezed with all his might. A thin green stream of sauce landed squarely in Carter's mouth, then splashed upward, spraying his eye.

Shrieks of pain replaced guttural rage as the now-blinded Carter clutched his own face, stumbling sideways.

The crowd's shouts for blood didn't diminish. The vibrations of their pounding feet shook the sand. Keith barely heard the familiar rat-a-tat-tat of an automatic weapon firing close by.

Carter thudded to the ground, his entire backside thick with a peacock tail of tranquilizer darts.

Through the drifting haze of sand and smoke Keith caught sight of Gunther still rising from the coliseum floor. Gunther flipped some switch on his weapon and a huge plume of blue fire sprayed up—a mage flame of immense power. It radiated cold. A spell spoken into a flame that big could take out a huge section of the building. Tendrils of frost shot through the sand at Gunther's feet.

The camera-flies zipped over to hover before Gunther's face.

"Welcome, contender!" the announcer, whose bony white goblin face Keith could now see broadcast on one massive screen. "Are you ready to go for the gold?"

The crowd quieted. Gunther dialed back the mage flame and let the gun hang from his shoulder by its strap. He then unsheathed his scimitar and held it aloft.

"I am not a contender. I am Gunther Heartman, son of Agnes of San Francisco. This man belongs to me."

A brief moment of consternation rippled through the crowd. The announcer leaned out of the frame, then returned, nodding. "So be it. Let's hear it for the Heartman Clan." A baffled cheer erupted through the crowd. The announcer went on, "Unfortunately, Special Agent Keith Curry forfeits the gold, as no kill was made. Better luck next time, NIAD!"

A door popped open in the side of the arena.

Gunther made straight for it, but Keith doubled back to snatch up Carter's discarded can.

As they strode from the arena, the announcer called out the contenders for the next fight and the crowd again roared and cheered their favorite. Gunther reached out and caught Keith's free hand in his own. Together they descended a newly exposed staircase that led down to a set of plain double doors. Those opened out into the ticket lobby. The big, beetle-like ticket agent ignored them as they walked out to the crooked street.

They made it all the way through the NIAD portal, across the streets of DC and into their apartment before Gunther turned and hugged Keith to his chest.

"I can't believe you did something that dumb," he murmured into the top of Keith's head. "I mean, seriously? Free samples?" Gunther pulled him closer and Keith relaxed completely into his arms.

"I know," Keith murmured back. "I fully acknowledge that I just made a huge mistake and I am very grateful to you."

"Why didn't you just say you were a Heartman right away?" Gunther demanded.

"It didn't occur to me," Keith said. "And I'm not a Heartman. I'm not in the clan."

"But you are allied to us. You have a pendant. Next time remember to state your allegiance." Gunther drew back, hands on either side of Keith's face. "It's a goblin market. You're protected by a goblin clan. Use that, please."

"I don't think there will be a next time," Keith said.

"Of course there'll be a next time, baby. You get into trouble. That's the best thing about you and the worst. That never changes."

The truth of this cut a little too close. Nobody likes to have his weakness brought to the fore. Keith stepped out of Gunther's arms.

"At least I got this." Keith held up the can. "There's still about a teaspoon left, so maybe it will have been worth it?"

"I sure hope so." Gunther's phone chimed and he glanced at it with a pained expression. Keith could see text after text rolling up the screen. He caught sight of the words "Seven Moon Coliseum" and shuddered internally.

"News travels fast in the goblin world," Keith said.

Gunther gave a grim nod. "You go shower first. I've got to explain this all to Mom."

Keith nodded and trudged upstairs to the bathroom. There, submerged to his chin in the bathtub, he finally had a chance to examine Carter's can.

The product was called Critical Mass! and bottled by the Mage Technica Bottling Company, a subsidiary of Blissco based in the Grand Goblin Bazaar. A brief glance at the ingredients yielded several dodgy-sounding active additives.

Keith shifted and the water sloshed around his aching body. Gunther would be pissed if he found out Keith was still working on the case this late, but seeing as Gunther never managed to get off the phone with his mother in less than ninety minutes, Keith figured he had some time.

Keith's fluffy orange tabby, Cheeto, hopped up onto the side of the bath and started to paw at Keith's shoulder, hoping for attention. Keith had rescued Cheeto from a manufacturing facility a couple of years before. The cat had been only partially socialized then but had blossomed into an affectionate, if somewhat destructive, housemate.

He followed Keith from the bath to the bed, where he curled up next to Keith's stomach. The bedroom was the only room in the house that Keith had decorated, and he'd done it specifically to give himself an opulent, soothing context to view Gunther within. Though if he'd known he'd eventually live with a cat, he would have passed on the silk wallpaper. Cheeto's orange fur did provide a nice accent to the gray and silver environs, however.

Wrung out from misadventure, Keith was already dozing when Gunther arrived, freshly showered, for bed. Keith's eye snagged on the curve of Gunther's shoulder. The guy had been custom made. Transformed by mages in utero to be beautiful and strong and nearly human. Bone-white skin stood out starkly against the dark gray silk wall. He was taut, sexy and tired-looking.

"How's your mom?" Keith asked.

"She was really hurt at first, but got better when I told her we hadn't eloped behind her back and that this whole thing was part of a Food/MED case." Gunther sat down on the edge of the bed and shed his damp towel.

"Why would she have thought that we eloped?"

"Well, you know how I announced that you belonged to the clan, in front of everyone?"

"I don't think I could have forgotten so soon," Keith replied.

"Well, technically you're only allied with us, because you haven't formally petitioned to become a member of the clan." Gunther reached out to pet Cheeto, then gently shifted the cat sideways so he could lie down.

"Yeah," Keith said. "That's the reason I never say I'm one of you."

"Mom thought we'd eloped to avoid having to go through the formalities."

Keith blinked. He and Gunther had mused about getting married, sure. That would be a matter for the Washington, DC, justice of the peace. But to join the Heartman (shortened from "Beating Heart of Man") Clan through marriage a petitioner had to prove themselves worthy by bringing the clan a gift that displayed great heroism.

According to tradition, the mother-in-law would lift the gift in her shining white claws and freestyle a poem based on the matrimonial hopeful's exploits, which would be noted down in the family history.

Because of the goblin predilection for reciting these poems at family barbecues, Keith had already become familiar with the staccato tunes to many Heartman favorites, such as "Song of Blood Wing," wherein the eponymous heroine slew a great, giant red eagle, then used its feathers to fashion her own functional glider.

He'd also learned "Ice Dragon Lullaby," which detailed the marriage quest of Gunther's paternal grandfather, who, after strangling an ice dragon to death, had been moved to arts and crafts. From the creature's silver hide he'd made a shield to deflect the breath of any dragon; from its claws, knives that could pierce even the flesh of other goblins; and from its jawbone, a harp to play bedtime songs for his children. He, and the harp, were both given the clan name Bone Song.

Keith had seen the harp. Even today the silver wires strung across the dragon's teeth were imbued with the cold of the frozen mountain slopes of the sidhe realm and stayed frosty even in July.

Keith doubted his life of food inspection would ever lead him to venture forth and vanquish a foe worthy of commemoration in extemporaneous verse and/or provide a priceless family heirloom. He'd barely managed to make it out of the Seven Moon Coliseum alive, and the only prize he'd won there was a dirty old can.

It sobered him, though, to realize that Gunther clearly hoped for Keith to someday join his family, despite being wildly unsuccessful at remaining a member of his own family in the past.

The guy loved him—no question about it. But was he worthy of that love?

Maybe?

On a good day?

But as long as Gunther kept offering it, he'd take it.

He reached and drew Gunther down for a kiss. The eerie glacial scent of blue mage light residue still clung to his skin.

But Keith had to acknowledge, if he was honest, that this added to his sex appeal.

Gunther returned his kiss with odd self-consciousness, as if embarrassed. Keith didn't know why. Had Gunther's mother said something? Impossible to know, and Keith knew from experience that Gunther wouldn't tell him.

Better to just pull him down into the blankets where he'd feel comfortable and start to administer the kind of nice, relaxing low-key hand job that Gunther preferred on a day when his adrenaline levels had already been ratcheted up into the red zone.

Gunther was not, by nature, an aggressive guy. It's what made him good at policing. He could wield force, if necessary, but it wasn't his go-to. Given the choice he'd rather not use violence. Even in a gladiatorial arena, where he could have crushed his opponent and won a fat pot of money, he chose to talk his way out.

After a minute the tension went out of his shoulders and he rolled to face Keith, hands curling around Keith's own forcibly demure, yet eager to engage, dick. He gave himself up to the singular pursuit of friction maintenance, trying to outlast Gunther while knowing he never would. In a battle of self-control, Gunther would always win while Keith pushed eagerly and single-mindedly ahead toward completion. It was just the difference in their natures.

Keith gave up the struggle quite easily, then after a few moments panting into the side of Gunther's neck, bent to deliver an oral finishing move to which he knew Gunther was defenseless.

He'd just righted himself and curled against Gunther's back to sleep when the phone sounded again.

"If that's your mom, pretend you're asleep," Keith murmured.

"It's not my mom. It's my cousin Jerry. He's just found a parking spot and is on his way over."

Keith pulled back slightly. "Jarhead Jerry?"

"He's asking if he can stay here." Gunther thumbed through the incoming stream of texts. "They still haven't found a place for him to stay since his transfer from the air force to NIAD."

Three sharp knocks announced Jerry's arrival and Keith struggled into a set of sweats and hastened downstairs to let him in. Like Gunther, Jerry had been custom made, but the mage who had transformed him had left more of his snow goblin bone structure intact. He was tall and lean with a broad, down-turning mouth, bristling blond hair and deep-set eyes.

"I appreciate you two letting me camp out here. The only space they've got left at the temporary housing is some kind of dog kennel or something." Jerry dropped his heavy duffel bag in the entryway. Though he'd just made a twenty-seven-hour drive alone, his shirt was perfectly tucked in and his eyes showed only the barest fatigue, though the acrid smell of tobacco sweat wafted off him.

Keith's cat, Cheeto, who had followed him downstairs, started for the duffel bag with a decidedly acquisitive manner. He shook his fluffy orange tail, preparing to spray.

"No problem." Keith bent to scoop up Cheeto while Gunther lifted Jerry's bag to safety.

"I'll just take this up to the guest room." Gunther started toward the stairs.

"Can I get you anything?" Keith asked. "Are you hungry? There's fried chicken in the refrigerator."

"I think I'd just like to get to bed if you don't mind." Jerry's voice was flat and devoid of its usual bravado. "I've been driving a long time."

CHAPTER FIVE

Feeding one insatiable trans-goblin breakfast was an exercise in strategic parboiling and make-ahead tactics, but after a couple of days Keith found that feeding two unexpectedly stretched his early morning faculties.

A man of unyielding habit, Jerry rose at five o'clock, exercised, shaved, showered and had the coffee going every morning by six thirty, when Keith managed to shakily achieve verticality. Jerry would have made breakfast for them all as well, except Gunther had informed their guest that the refrigerator was "Keith's territory" and therefore off-limits.

Which was as it should be.

Still, now that Keith was on his third day of frying pork chops, he was almost at the point of ceding sovereign rights to his Fresh Meats drawer to anybody willing to put in the extra-greasy effort.

Unable to sit by and happily wait, Jerry had, by day two, taken charge of toast (the one aspect of breakfast that had nothing to do with the refrigerator) and was in the midst of feeding slices of marbled rye into the toaster by the time Keith shuffled, pajama-clad, into the kitchen.

Gunther sat at the kitchen table, chewing a filterless cigarette and scrolling through something on his phone. FaeBook probably. Sunlight filtered in through the wide window.

"How are you this morning, Jerry?" Keith shot a wink to Gunther, who shook his head and gave a discreet eye roll. "Looking forward to rolling out with the strike force?"

"Honestly, I can't say I am." Jerry didn't look up from the bread, which Keith thought maybe he was trying to heat with the power of his displeasure. "I don't really know what I'm doing here. Do you know where they sent us yesterday? Vegas. To tell some drunks to move along."

"They were satyrs," Gunther said. "That same group that's always getting into trouble. I seriously think some of them could benefit from alcohol counseling."

"I just thought being raging drunk was their culture," Keith remarked.

"But is it though?" Gunther asked. "Or are they just doing what they think they should be doing?"

"Who the hell cares? I'm not a cop. Taking care of this petty shit isn't my business." Jerry jammed two more slices of bread into the toaster. That brought the total up to twelve. Keith wondered if he was going to toast the entire loaf of bread.

"No, you're a peace officer. And taking care of petty shit is our business. Regular citizens have the right not to be molested by people who got thrown out of the Elysian realm for being drunk and disorderly." Gunther gave his cousin a pointed eyeballing, which would have had more effect if Jerry had been looking at him instead of savagely mangling more slices of marble rye. "You should be proud."

Keith silently prodded the pan of sizzling pork chops. He'd given up attempting to referee Heartmans in conflict. That way madness lay. He'd jump in if Jerry slammed Gunther directly, but otherwise he'd learned it was best to let them work it out.

"Proud? Of being a washout in some bullshit loser job? Yeah, I'm. So. Proud."

"That's just hurtful," Gunther said before Keith could get a word in. "I know you don't want to be here, but you don't have to insult me and Keith."

Jerry stilled, browned rye in his hands. Then he hung his head. "I'm sorry. I'm not talking about you. I'm talking about my feelings. I don't belong here. I'm a pilot, for fuck's sake. I fly mage jets through portals to defend our country at the edge of outer space. I'm not cut out to dissipate a situation by hugging a drunk old goat till he cries."

"Sometimes that's just what's necessary." Gunther glanced to Keith. "I learned that move in that aikido book you bought me."

"Money well spent then." Keith cracked eight eggs into a second hot skillet. "I didn't realize you flew fighter jets, Jerry. Though it does explain your love of checklists."

"I'm a first lieutenant. Or at least I used to be. And as long as I'm being a complete wuss I'm gonna admit that I miss Annie."

"You have a girlfriend?" Gunther's hopeful tone could have been channeled directly from his mother.

"No. If the air force had wanted me to have a girlfriend they would have issued me one," Jerry said. "Annie's my jet. I've never been away from her this long. She keeps texting me. Telling me she doesn't like the guy that's flying her—that he can't handle the G's and keeps passing out, forcing her to abort. What am I supposed to do about that from over here?"

"Wait." Keith turned off the burner. "Your jet has an AI? Why does she need a pilot at all?"

"Robots can't make ethically ambiguous decisions." Jerry's fourteenth batch of toast popped up and he started to butter them. "Or override their orders. They're very subject to viruses and corruption and even possession. Plus you don't want a world run by robots. I've seen it."

"Where?" Keith couldn't help but ask. "Where have you seen that?"

"Never mind. Just believe me. You don't want robots running the show. That's how you end up with hell-beings in the stratosphere." Jerry seated himself next to Gunther.

"Now you're making things up." Gunther gave a sigh.

"Hand on my heart I am not," Jerry countered. "Okay, how about this? Blissco is run by robots. Look what that gets us."

"Fast, free delivery and hassle-free refunds?" Keith offered. He felt he had to, for Susan. He divided the eggs and meats between two plates and set them in front of the trans-goblins, then set two additional eggs to boil (these would go into his pocket for lunch) and went to fill his cereal bowl. A small pillar of buttered toast stood on the table beside the orange juice pitcher.

"Algorithmic manipulation and corporate double-speak," Jerry said.

"So much better than military doublespeak," Gunther remarked.

"At least that's a language I understand." Jerry's phone vibrated and briefly an image of a sleek black airplane flashed across the screen. He began to text back immediately.

As Keith chomped on his cereal he couldn't help but think that the air force had issued Jerry a girlfriend after all.

"Gunther thinks you air force guys are being targeted specifically for being trans-goblins," Keith said.

"I know we are," Jerry said. "I even know who is doing it: Senator Blaze Gregson."

"He's not in the air force . . . is he?" Keith asked.

"No, but his son is. Right after he came to Space Wing we were all suddenly being questioned about our extended goblin families and who we really owed our allegiance to. As if we would all just drop everything and go back to our ancient roots to help the high king of the sidhe try and take over Ireland or some such shit."

"I'm pretty sure the high king dissolved the monarchy recently anyway," Keith said.

"Exactly! And Blaze Jr. doesn't even know that. But once he found our cousin had violated the Secrecy Act I was yanked out of Annie—actually pulled physically from the cockpit—by a couple of MPs. And Annie was arming her missiles, thinking I was being abducted." Jerry sighed. "The whole scene was not good."

"So let me break this down. Space Wing has developed some kind of ultra high-flying jet that only trans-goblin pilots can fly in order to battle space aliens," Keith began.

"Hell-beings, not aliens. And not just trans-goblins. Other kinds of extra-humans can take the G's, but yeah. Mainly trans-goblins since there are so many of us in the military anyway," Jerry said.

"But then Gregson comes along and says—what?" Keith asked. "That we've signed an agreement with the hell-beings so we don't need the mage jets anymore?"

"No, the hell-beings are still out there," Jerry said. "Gregson says it's a budget thing. The platinum supplements we take and the cost of keeping doctors trained in extra-human physiology is too much of a taxpayer burden, which—again, bullshit. We're fucking indestructible. That's how we got to be test pilots in the first place. Without us they're going to be going through human pilots by the dozens. And you know what will cost even more? Retrofitting the jets to support humans in the first place and than retrofitting them again each time they lose a pilot. But does that stop them? No. You know why?"

"Because they're racists?" Keith offered.

Gunther nodded and took a slice of toast.

"It's not just that." Jerry shook his head. "The modern military is the most racially integrated organization in America. It's because they're puritan isolationists. They think they can somehow conceal the fact that there are thousands—millions—who the fuck knows . . . probably infinite realms of existence. And all of them are full of magic."

"You think they're afraid of magic itself?" Gunther asked and he looked thoughtful. "But they can't eliminate it so they just demand that everybody keep it a secret."

"Or pretend they don't have it," Jerry said. "But everybody has magic."

"I don't," Keith remarked. It was actually a sore spot in his ego.

"You do," Jerry said. "Telling you that you don't is one of the ways that people like Gregson try to minimize others around them. But believe me when I say that every single living creature has magic. Just because there's no official way to measure yours doesn't mean it doesn't exist."

◆◆◆

When he arrived at work, Keith was happy to see that the lab had delivered his results. Although the Critical Mass! formulation contained one of the same ingredients as Lupe's fouled blood sample, two other key active ingredients were missing. Keith was both gratified and annoyed. His hunch about the answer being found in the goblin market was correct and he'd discovered which substance was being used, but he still hadn't found the source of contamination or the person or persons responsible.

But now he knew the name of the adulterant: expandinol, a magically charged molecule (and Schedule M drug) developed and patented by the Mage Technica Bottling Company, sold mainly in the troll market as an equivalent to caffeine. The energizing effect was much more pronounced on humans, as Keith had seen close up at Seven Moon.

When he searched for expandinol adulteration, he got not one but two hits in NIAD's international database. Two other blood-dependent individuals who shared Lupe's extra-human designation had received meals tainted in the same fashion within the last six months: one in Finland and the other in Mexico.

When he contacted the Helsinki office, Johanna, the Food/MED agent there, suggested they set up a three-way video conference to discuss the issue. They decided on midnight DC time, as it was one of the only times all three of them would be awake, since their Mexican counterpart, Damien Navarro, only worked at night. To pass the time while he waited, Keith looked up his international counterparts' personnel data.

Johanna held a degree in nutrition and was married to a dentist who specialized reconstructive work on *näkki*, which were a kind of shape-changing female water spirit. Apparently special-forces teams of näkki patrolled the waterways of Finland.

Absently, Keith wondered how Jerry was doing. If it didn't work out for him on Gunther's strike force, could he move somewhere like Finland? Or Germany? Would Jerry be guilty of treason if he were to go enlist somewhere else? He didn't know—he didn't even know if doing such a thing would violate the provisions of the Secrecy Act—the very act whose misuse got him booted out of the air force in the first place.

But considering that Jerry had an American flag sticker on virtually every item he owned, Keith doubted it would even occur to him to take himself and his expertise elsewhere. He would just stand there still loyal, even when jilted.

The thought left a sour taste in Keith's mouth. So he turned his attention to his Mexican counterpart, by way of distraction.

Damien had taken a master's degree in food science from Stanford. He'd joined NIAD after being divorced by his wife, who worked as the chief agronomist of Mexico's ministry of agriculture.

Keith wondered if NIAD might be his punishment.

The clock struck midnight and Johanna logged in. Behind her Keith could see the bright morning light slanting into the windows of her airy office. She had very short hair, pale eyes and wore the kind of neutral-toned fine knitwear that made all residents of Nordic countries look effortlessly stylish and comfortable at once. Framed certificates covered the wall behind her. A weird amoeba-shaped vase held a prominent place on her windowsill. After a few pleasantries, Johanna said, "We shouldn't be bothered to wait for Damien. He always is late. Anyway I'm happy to speak to you about this important food security issue."

"How many of your citizens have been affected?"

"Just one. But one is too many," Johanna said.

Damien joined the conference then. He looked about fifty years old, slightly paunchy but with a neat mustache and a sharply tailored suit. He held a thin, brown unlit cigarette in his fingers. From the background noise, Keith could tell the Mexico City branch office was busy, even in the dead of night. But the extraordinary thing Keith noted was the sheer number of small shrines, charms and magic-repelling tchotchkes that encrusted the wall behind Damien. The cluttered profusion reminded Keith of icing roses erupting from the surface of an over-decorated wedding cake. Or coral reef. Or wedding cake made to look like a coral reef.

"I'm sorry for being late," Damien said. "I have this old woman who every day is trying to kill me."

"Is it your ex-wife?" Johanna asked.

"I wish she would try to kill me. Then I would have a good reason to block her calls. No, it's my landlady. She thinks I flush the toilet too much so she turns off my water. Then when I go down there she gives me this bag that I'm pretty sure contains some kind of curse or tarantula. Look at it moving around." Damien held a clearly squirming paper bag aloft. "So, you must be Keith Curry, huh? It's good to meet you. Did you know you are the first person from the US office to ever call me?"

"No, I didn't realize."

"Before we formally begin we'll agree to conduct the call in English, okay?" Johanna said.

"That's good news, since I don't speak any other language," Keith remarked.

"Yes, this is what I thought." Johanna seemed pleased with herself.

Keith kept his business smile stuck on, feeling hopelessly outclassed by both his counterparts.

"I do understand quite a bit of snow goblin," he added.

"I bet you do," Damien said. "Good friends with a guy in strike force, I see. That must be very convenient."

"It is." It hadn't occurred to him that his international counterparts would have also reviewed his file, or that he should have done that himself to see what weirdly specific information they had on him.

"But your boss has to know that this pending complaint about you is shit, right?" Damien opened up a briefcase and withdrew what looked like a chocolate pudding cup. He opened this and set it on the far corner of his desk.

"Absolutely," Johanna agreed. "It's not appropriate to reprimand you for such a thing. I will write to your supervisor myself if you'd like."

"Latest complaint?" Keith checked the company email on his phone. There were no outstanding messages.

"In your file here it says that some asshole called Nash filed a complaint about you donating blood to a client without filing any of the appropriate paperwork," Damien said.

"Nobody's reprimanded me about that, but yeah, it happened," Keith said.

Johanna's eyes widened slightly with suppressed delight. "Oh, Keith, you should not just admit things like this."

"It's not like I have plausible deniability." Keith gave a shrug.

"That might be true," Damien cut in. "But as a twenty year veteran of this shitty job I want to give you a piece of advice: never admit anything to anyone ever. Especially not your wife. And especially when you're somebody who obviously gets in trouble a lot."

"See, I'd say when you're a person who gets in trouble a lot you know your only defense is honesty. Otherwise you get blamed for everything instead of just the stuff you really did." Keith decided that he definitely needed to take a look at his own personnel file when this was all over.

"Well-spoken," said Johanna, "but naive."

"Maybe that's what I should have them put on my grave-stone," Keith joked. "Anyway, this bad blood—"

"I received it four times here," Damien said. "Over the course of the last six months or so. Sanguine Service of America."

"As I've said, we've only received one contaminated bag here," Johanna said. "Then we banned imports from the US. We use a German facility now."

"The German blood is too expensive," Damien said. "Nobody can afford it." The paper bag on his desk fell side-ways and a long, hairy spider leg came out.

"I think that thing's escaping," Keith said.

"Yeah, don't worry. I got it under control." Damien scooted slightly back. "Do you think it would be possible to inspect the SSA facility? Because this seems to be a pattern, and the state of Colorado is within your jurisdiction, isn't it?"

"Sure, but I'll just get denied permission," Keith said. "They don't want a shutdown. Ever."

"I can't see how that would keep a dedicated investigator from going in anyway," Damien said.

"It's not that. If I could get in there I would."

"What about paying off an employee to leave the back door open?" Damien kept a close eye on the spider as it approached the open pudding cup. Slowly it stretched one leg out to prod the plastic exterior. Then the pudding itself rose up out of the cup in a glistening tendril that crashed out, en-gulfing the spider in an instant. The hapless arachnid thrashed and kicked but couldn't keep itself from being dragged back into the cup. Damien carefully replaced the foil seal on top and glanced back up into the camera. "Or you could try re-minding them who you are the old-fashioned way. Maybe revoke a license or two to give some motivation to comply."

"I'm not into applying that kind of force." Keith kept his eye on Damien's pudding cup. What the hell was that thing?

"And as for paying someone off—I'm a government employee. I don't have that kind of cash."

"You're not regular government. You're NIAD," Damien scoffed. "Appropriate some cash."

"Shadow government is still government," Keith countered. "It would take so much paperwork."

"What about approaching SSA's parent company? Do you not have a contact at Blissco?" Johanna asked. "I have one called Eija. She's very efficient."

"Well, I do have one acquaintance, but she's very low-level." Keith didn't know why, but he felt like he didn't want to sully his relationship with Susan with business complaints.

"Please, you must try. Even though it might be awkward." She shuddered as she spoke the word, as if there could be no greater fate than potential for mild social discomfort.

"I have a little bit of a random question for you, Johanna. On your file it says that you're married to a NIAD dentist who works with the military?"

"I am, yes."

"Has he ever worked with any trans-goblin soldiers?" Keith asked.

"I couldn't say for sure. He mostly works with navy forces—näkki."

"I just wondered if he'd heard anything about extra-human soldiers being discharged."

"Not here. Do you think it has to do with the case?"

"I don't think so, but . . . the SSA facility is located near Peterson Air Force Base, and recently I've heard some stories about trans-goblins being removed from the elite fighting forces. I just think it's strange that these two things are happening at the same time and so close together."

"It's possible, but . . ." Damien paused to light his cigarette. "To me it seems like every eight years or so somebody has a xenophobic panic and calls for a purge. And your country is due for one."

"Do you think that the tainted blood is part of a targeted attack against extra-humans—a deliberate poisoning?" Johanna's brow wrinkled in concern.

"Like I said, I don't know," Keith said. "Have there been planned attacks on the food supply in either of your countries?"

"Nothing of the kind here." Johanna shook her head.

"Nor here," Damien said. "But your country is a shit show right now, so anything could happen. If it does, you should come work for me here. I could use a man with a huge set of balls and no interest in women. So many witches here—you would not believe the number of witches."

"Whatever size your genitals are, you and your partner would always be welcome here in Finland as well," Johanna said with a warm smile. "Our extra-human community is the happiest in the world . . . there was a survey. Human citizens too."

"And yet you still come to stay at my condo in Cancun every January." Damien smirked. "Because your country is too fucking dark."

"My generous paid vacation is part of why I'm so happy."

Chapter Six

Five minutes after logging off his conference call, Keith dialed Susan's direct line.

"Thank you for calling Blissco, the largest purveyor of commercial goods in the known universe: if we can't get it, it never existed. This is Susan speaking."

"Hi Susan, it's Keith Curry from NIAD. You're working late."

"Agent Curry! I'm so glad you're all right. I heard about your coliseum fight."

"Really?" Was there anyone who did not know he'd essentially gotten his ass kicked? "Who told you that?"

"Oh, a little bird," Susan said sweetly. "How can I help you today?"

"Tell me about expandinol."

"Expandinol is a spell-synthesized molecule that generates alertness and strength. Licensed and bonded wizards manufacture it right here in our laboratories in the bazaar. We use it only in our Mage Technica drinks and do not sell it to second parties."

"Then it has to have originated at Blissco's labs?" Keith concluded.

"Well, yes and no. Obviously, there's such a thing as counterfeiting, but it would be unlikely to find that product outside of the Blissco lab. Why are you asking?"

"Because it's been found in a prescription meal from SSA."

"Keith, I'm shocked! SSA prescription meals are subject to strict protocols. They're sustainably sourced from an all-volunteer pool that has been screened for thirty-seven dangerous blood-borne diseases and twenty intoxicating substances. And besides that, products containing expandinol cannot be sold or shipped to the earthly realm."

"And yet I've got this prescription food from—SSA's Rich Red metabolic line that is plainly contaminated," Keith said. "And this isn't the first time I've handled an SSA complaint either."

"No! Why haven't you called me sooner?"

"I assumed you knew."

"If I'd known there were complaints filed with NIAD you would have been the first person I reached out to. Were any of our extra-human clients hurt?" Worry sounded through Susan's tone.

"Several were affected. More than that, no replacement meals were sent. I ended up donating my own blood to feed a client." Keith tried to throw this in casually, but it still ended up sounding like a whine followed by a humblebrag.

"This is very serious. I'm going to put in a request for compensation for you right now," Susan said. "Please hold while I consult my operations manual."

Keith spent a few minutes listening to light jazz before Susan finally returned.

"First, I want to extend my sympathy for any problems this may have caused. We are now conducting inquiries into the security of our lab." Susan's voice went a little flat, like it did whenever she was reading straight from the Blissco script. "But I also want to find out where in the supply chain the expandinol was introduced. Do you think the packaging could have been tampered with?"

"If it has been then I can't see where."

"Would it be possible to take the packaging to our facility in Colorado Springs for authentication? For our sake and yours?"

"I would love to do that," Keith said.

"I can make an appointment for you tomorrow at nine a.m. Mountain Standard Time with Abby Wheeler. She is currently in charge of the facility there."

"Thank you very much, Susan." Keith took a deep breath, preparing to wind up the conversation.

"One more thing, Keith—we at Blissco would like to thank you for alerting us to this problem and for finding an immediate solution for our customer Ms. Balderas. We are offering you our Technetium Elite membership card." Susan sounded surprised and excited as she read this—as if she'd just been handed the information scribbled on a sticky note.

"Uh . . . it's not necessary. I don't need another credit card."

"Please, Agent Curry, do reconsider," Susan's voice took on a strange urgency. "Membership unlocks special advantages."

He wondered if she hadn't met her sales quota.

Well, she'd definitely done him a solid, so why not?

"Okay, sure, I'd be happy to accept."

"Wonderful! A drone has been dispatched through a targeted portal and should be arriving outside your window just about . . . now."

Keith heard a whirr outside and saw a drone floating there. He opened up the window, popped out the screen and stepped back while the drone whirred inside. It hovered over Keith's desk, then dropped what looked like a regular black credit card.

"That was fast."

"Instant delivery is one of the perks of the card," Susan said. "Now all I need to activate it is the security code printed on the back of the card to get started."

Keith sighed. "Okay, give me a second." The hologram embedded in the card showed the constellation of Orion. The three stars of its belt glowed especially bright. "Okay the numbers are . . . 777. What are the odds?"

"Good! With Technetium Elite the odds are always in your favor." Susan gave a girlish giggle.

"Oh yeah? What happens if you've got two cardholders going head to head?" Keith was only half joking.

"Then advantage dispensed depends on the individual cardholder's credit limit, and yours is very, very generous." A note of undisguised glee sounded through Susan's voice, then her tone cooled to seriousness and went back on script. "Please download our app to start using your Technetium card today."

CHAPTER SEVEN

The next morning saw Keith entering the Denver NIAD office to find Nash hard at work reading the paper. On his initial visit he'd been dismayed by the clean desk, but now its pristine surface aroused definite suspicion. What were the odds that absolutely nothing worth noting had occurred in the entire Rocky Mountain region since his last visit? Zero? Less than that?

And yet apparently Nash could find nothing to disturb his morning confab with the funny pages. Keith glanced from Nash to the receptionist. She'd decided to go for a heavy smoky-eye look even though it was barely past eight in the morning.

"Anything new in the Balderas case?" he asked, mostly to avoid wishing Nash a good morning.

"Don't know. Not my case. So you tell me?" Nash asked.

"I've been exploring several promising avenues. Industrial espionage, counterfeiting of magical substances with possible tampering that might lead to prosecution as domestic terrorism under the hate crimes act. You know, just regular food-inspection-related stuff. How about you?"

"Same old same old."

"Yeah, I can see that you're overwhelmed with work here." Keith could not keep this remark to himself.

"This is what efficiency looks like," Nash said.

"So no more reports of tainted meal products from anyone else?" Keith directed this at the receptionist, who'd decided to wear a low-cut mint-green jumpsuit to work because apparently the Denver branch had no dress code.

Noticing his attention, the receptionist shook her head slightly. Again, Keith couldn't figure out her gesture. Was she answering him or disgusted by his question?

"We got one report from the police in Fort Collins," Nash said. "Some nut there thinks drinking human blood cures his constipation. He had a transformation episode."

"But this victim was a human?"

"He's certainly not a vampire."

"Was he drinking from an SSA pack?" Keith hoped not. He'd issued a recall, but there was no way to tell if SSA had actually complied or not.

"From a guy's arm at a party."

"Where's the donor now?"

"Nobody knows. The bloodsucker didn't know his name and Fort Collins police haven't found him either."

"If he was at a party where something as unusual as blood drinking was occurring, somebody must know who he was. Do you have an agent assigned to tracking the donor down?"

"Why should I? What whackadoodles do to themselves isn't my department." Nash gave a yawn.

Keith's grip on his temper faltered.

"You know," he said, "I thought before that you were a racist, but really you're just the laziest sack of shit on Earth, aren't you?"

Nash looked up and smirked. "Maybe. . . but I also don't have goblin-dick breath, so I feel like I'm doing better than you. There's a car waiting for you outside."

◆◆◆

Keith spent the ride from Denver to Colorado Springs reading. First he looked at his own personnel file and discovered that he had way more complaints lodged against him than he'd previously realized—ninety-nine percent of them dealing with "failure to inform appropriate authority" or "circumventing proper procedural channels." The words "lacking in decorum" also featured prominently throughout.

These, he felt, weren't criticisms so much as basic statements about his personality.

His file listed Gunther as his "de facto" spouse, which is what NIAD called shacking up. But it went on to list his estrangement from his biological family, the name and location of his old restaurant, his known associates in the extra-human community, vegetarianism and firing range score.

Under magical powers it listed: "none detected, though luck quotient scores may indicate underlying, unconscious sensitivities to magical fields."

Why hadn't anybody told him that? And what did that even mean? That he should continue to trust his gut? He'd have done that anyway. But he did have to wonder about what Jerry had said. What if he really did have access to magic, but just didn't know how to use it? Or didn't know that he was already using it? Was magic like intuition? Something that happened without conscious effort?

Certainly with goblin magic that was the case.

Out of sheer curiosity he clicked on Gunther and learned absolutely nothing new for the first seven pages. Then right at the bottom was a note that said three months before Gunther had requested permission to marry a fully human citizen and that the status of his application was pending.

Keith fell back in the seat, stunned.

Not that Gunther had applied for permission to marry—he'd been dropping unsubtle hints about how Keith might propose to him for almost a year. But it hadn't occurred to him that if Gunther had to ask for governmental approval then it followed that permission might be refused.

The barely healed old rage of being denied the freedom to marry, which Keith had carried his entire adult life, ripped open like an ugly ulcer in the center of his heart.

The fear of exposing himself to the vulnerability of asking a man to stay with him forever burned away under an onslaught of abject fury at the thought that some pencil-pushing assholes would try and insinuate themselves into his life like this—demanding whatever bullshit promise or oath they would demand Keith and Gunther take or otherwise block them from having what should be rightfully theirs.

This was how being bound by the Secrecy Act felt, Keith realized. And it didn't just affect Gunther, or Jerry, or Lupe. It affected everyone who cared for them, including Keith and countless other people. . . it affected them all.

Who, he wondered, was he going to have to pay to get that application approved? And would it be the same if he went to another country? Another realm of existence?

How big of a ticket to a new life could his new Technetium card buy?

No, he wouldn't think about possible barriers to recognition of his now-certain marriage at this time. Not from the Heartman Clan and not from NIAD. He couldn't experience that blinding, frenzied battle of hope and hatred and still think logically. He had a case to close.

And he also wondered about the limit on his new card.

Immediately, he downloaded the app and set up his account. This action soothed him somewhat. More so when he realized the card didn't extend monetary credit in any specific currency so much as it was loaded with credits— Keith did not know how much. Under the Limit tab the app just said, "one hundred percent available for use."

What did that mean? He supposed he'd have to call Susan and get more details later. He needed to focus completely on solving the SSA problem. Lupe and hundreds of others needed their dinner. He could make that safe, if nothing else.

◆◆◆

"Agent Curry! Thank you for waiting! You had a complaint about one of our products?" Abby Wheeler, the SSA rep who met him, had perfect hair. She also had perfect lip gloss and a perfect pantsuit. She was thin, fortyish and had the whiff of ex-cheerleader about her that Keith found common in the pharmaceutical sales force.

"Susan from the head office called." Keith could see sweat beading beneath Abby's makeup and wondered exactly why. Was she under duress or hiding something? Or was she just that scared of the head office? He supposed the fear could be considered legit. Most employees feared being reprimanded much more than he did.

"So were you in charge of this facility at the time of the contamination?"

"No, that was Marshall Cramer, but he's been called back to headquarters." Abby's voice trembled slightly. "I'm the person in charge here temporarily. Since yesterday."

"Then you'll be the representative accompanying me on my inspection, I guess." Keith placed his briefcase on the desk and flipped the latched up. At the sudden sound Abby jumped like he'd fired off a gun, and for a second, Keith thought she might faint. So he made a show of moving very slowly while he removed his lab coat, gloves and clipboard. "Hopefully this shouldn't take very long. It's just required after a complaint."

"Yes." Abby smoothed her skirt. "Please come this way."

SSA's main operations floor was surprisingly small. The facility was open plan and resembled nothing more than an average medical-center blood lab. Technically, Keith was not a certified medical lab inspector, but he'd shadowed one for a week at the beginning of his training, so he knew how to basically fake filling out the form and ask the right questions. His aim was to get a feel for the operation, keeping an eye out for anyone acting shifty.

Everything seemed to be aboveboard though. Blood was tested, cataloged, packaged and organized with remarkable efficiency. Accidental contamination due to human error seemed unlikely, which meant the adulterant was most likely deliberately introduced. But to what end? To specifically trigger transformations in people like Lupe? Or were the transformations an unintended effect? If so, what was the original goal?

"So why were there three separate donors in Ms. Balderas's meal?" Keith asked quietly, once he'd finished his initial go through.

"We often blend the blood. Our customers say it improves the taste," Abby replied.

"And is there anyone employed here that you have reason to suspect of deliberately fouling your product? For personal or political reasons?"

"No!" Abby practically shouted the answer, causing all work in the lab to come to a brief halt. "What are you even here for? Susan told me I was supposed to authenticate some packaging."

"That's part of the reason." Keith tried to ignore her hostility, but it rankled. "But you can't say that your company has been cooperative regarding our previous inquiries. My Mexican counterpart says he's sent you four separate complaints over the last six months. Why didn't you address the situation then?"

Abby's demeanor shifted, and when she spoke her voice sounded small. "That wasn't my decision. As I said before, our previous manager has been called back to headquarters for retraining."

"Did he give any specific reason for his indifference to safety regulations and the well-being of our extra-human citizens?" The entire office had gone dead silent. Every single worker hung on every word of their exchange.

"He had concluded that the blood had been tampered with on its way to Mexico."

"And he decided not to file a report about the alleged tampering with my office because. . . why?"

"I don't know, all right?" Abby's hands balled into fists.

"You can see how, to me, it would seem like no one in this company is trying too hard to comply with regulations," Keith said. "Because your former manager can't have been the only person to know about the complaints, yet absolutely no one thought of picking up the phone and calling my office. I find that strange and, frankly, suspicious."

Abby paled. "He told us we would be fired if we talked about it."

"Okay. Go on."

"If we don't work here, we have to have our memories adjusted to comply with the Secrecy Act," she whispered. "You understand? Some of us have worked here for years. We've gotten married and had families. We can't lose our memories. We'd lose our whole lives."

The stark fear in her face took Keith aback.

"So he more or less could make all of you do anything he wanted?" Keith scanned the faces of the workers who looked on. Here and there he spotted furious nods of confirmation, but mostly the employees had the blank expressions of prisoners resigned to their fate.

"Yes." Abby's voice was barely a whisper.

"And you don't have anything else to tell me about any other kind of negligence?" Keith said. "I'm asking now because I'm not here to punish any of you. I'm only trying to figure out the source of contamination."

Abby shook her head.

"Okay then, here's the package I need you to check out." Keith handed her the blood bag.

Abby turned it over in her hands, lifting it to peer closely at the barcode and the impressions in the plastic. "All the safety seal materials are correct and authentic. Would you like me to scan this barcode? We can track its whole journey from donor to client."

"That sounds great."

Abby tapped an app on her phone. "According to our records this was sourced from Peterson Air Force Base and delivered to Lupe Balderas last Wednesday."

"Do you often get donations from the base?"

"We drive the bloodmobile there the second Tuesday of every month," she said. "The donors for this meal were three airmen. Stokes, Wyman and McCronklin."

"Any of those three male?" The blood donor at the Fort Collins party had been reported to be a male.

"Only one male, Airman Wyman."

Chapter Eight

By early afternoon Keith had gained access to Peterson and started inspecting the commissaries that served the nearly seven thousand enlisted in the Twenty-First Space Wing at Peterson Air Force Base. No alarm bells sounded. No special clearance was needed. No one but the chefs gave a damn that he'd stepped foot on base, and they only cared about getting him out of the kitchen again.

The great thing about having your work considered inconsequential, Keith thought, is that nobody cares where you go or what you do.

And while it was true that if he'd been in a law enforcement branch of NIAD he'd have been expected to check in with the MPs there, food inspectors were under no such obligation.

So he'd sailed right under the radar and started searching for his adulterant.

Keith realized, as he donned his white lab coat and pulled on his blue nitrile gloves, that being underestimated had officially become a source of grim satisfaction to him. Pride even. No one had any idea the kinds of connections he had or what he was capable of. Or even that he might be on the trail of a serious criminal. They just saw some jerk sticking a thermometer in a hotel pan full of cooling mashed potatoes and largely ignored him.

He smiled at the chef, who stared stonily back at him.

"Right on target," he said.

The chef, an NCO named Sanchez, smiled a tight smile. He plainly didn't like Keith's incursion into his territory, but like all career military, he'd been groomed to enjoy passing an inspection. And Keith had put on a good show, eyeing his cooling times and hot-holding procedures and deeply scrutinizing every single drain.

The canteen kitchen was impeccably clean—even with more than a dozen cooks busting out meals for hungry airmen all around him.

But it wasn't like a single kitchen could serve the number of meals required at Peterson, so Keith moved on. No luck at the second location either. No spell fragments or even unlabeled containers. No sign of expandinol.

No evidence of anything being hastily dumped down the drain either.

The hot Colorado sun bore down on Keith as he considered where to go next. He couldn't help but wonder if there wasn't some connection between the dismissal of trans-goblins from Peterson's elite flying force and the appearance of expandinol in the blood supply coming from the base. Both happening at the same time in the same place seemed like too much of a coincidence.

Keith absently watched a group of sweating young cadets jog across a parking lot. Panting and flushed, a couple of them looked like they might drop over from heatstroke.

Then Keith remembered what Jerry had said about human pilots not being able to withstand the conditions that trans-goblins easily endured. All at once he realized how his case and Jerry's situation might fit together. Though he still needed to locate the source of the expandinol before he could hope to prove anything.

If it wasn't being administered via the kitchens—which it didn't seem to be—then there were only a couple other options. It could be that certain enlisted airmen had come across the substance somewhere and were running an illegal doping ring among themselves. But that begged the question of how the expandinol—in its pure form, not the canned, blended stuff on sale at the Grand Goblin Bazaar—

was being transported from Blissco's labs to this particular base.

Peterson maintained only the aeronautical portals that Jerry had mentioned, and these were located a thousand feet above the ground. So an unauthorized person couldn't just sneak through an open portal on the sly—at least not without the assistance of a hot air balloon.

If the airmen weren't doping themselves, it followed that someone had been administering the drug to them. NIAD itself could be running the show, but if that was the case special agents from Research and Development would've been all over Keith, obstructing his inquiries and, when that failed, just straight-out ordering him to fuck off back to Food/MED.

No, if Keith was right and this was a plan to deliberately feed enlisted airmen expandinol in hopes of building a super-soldier program to fill Jerry's recently vacated cockpit, it was too localized to the Peterson Air Force Base to reach beyond an official here. And if the drug was being dispensed by military officials but wasn't coming through the kitchens, then that left one other facility where human beings routinely ingested mysterious items that affected their bodies: the infirmary.

He wondered if it would be possible to access the infirmary to look for traces of magic; he needed evidence beyond his own suspicions if he was going to shut this down. Then Keith realized that he could go to the source of the tainted blood. He could find Airman Anthony Wyman and ask him what he'd been putting in his body and who had given it to him.

The question was how to do it. It wasn't as though he could keep a low profile while asking for an airman to be paged. This was an air force base, not a shopping mall. Under normal circumstances he would have phoned Nash to have him put in the request to see Wyman, but the chances of Nash helping him do anything were slim.

Hell, he might actually be in on it, which would explain his lack of investigative zeal.

Truth was Keith had no friends or allies here at all.

But he knew someone who did.

He texted Gunther. "Can u ask Jerry to call me?"

"Sure. why?"

"I need to ask him a couple of questions."

"Are you doing something dangerous?"

Keith considered this. Was this a dangerous action? Surveying his immediate surroundings of bland modern concrete buildings, a large flagpole rising from a circle of green lawn and the vast expanse of parking lots, he saw no imminent threat so answered: "No, why would u think that?"

"B/c you're you? And you want to talk to Jerry, which. . . you never do"

"I love you babe," Keith texted back.

"OMG you are doing something dangerous"

"Gotta go. Jerry's calling."

"Hey Jerry," Keith said. "Thank you for getting back to me so fast. I was wondering if you could point me in the direction of somebody at Peterson Air Force Base who could have an airman paged for me?"

Even as he spoke he could hear Gunther's voice, probably talking to Jerry at the exact same time.

"Gunther wants to know where you are," Jerry said.

"I know. I can hear him. I'm obviously at the air force base. Please tell him I'm completely fine."

"Have you seen Annie yet?"

The jet? He'd seen a couple dozen different planes flying overhead, but it wasn't as if they were sporting big name tags. Keith took an indulgent moment to blink uncomprehending at his phone before saying, "I don't know. What does she look like?"

"I'll text you a pic," Jerry said, and then the image of a sleek silver fighter jet appeared on Keith's screen. To Keith's amusement he realized that gold letters along the side of the jet did actually spell out her name.

"If you get the chance to find her, tell me if any mechanics are working on her. She's in Hangar 13." Jerry sounded almost agitated.

"Okay, I'll do that, but the reason I'm calling you is that I need to find a particular airman. Do you have any friends here who could help me out?"

"Why don't you just ask the MPs?"

"Because I want to be more low-key than that."

"What are you doing that you want to be low-key about?" Suspicion clouded Jerry's tone.

In the background Keith could hear Gunther saying, "Oh my God, Jerry, why are you even asking him that? He's a special agent. Just let him be low-key. I'm sure it's important."

Smug pride welled up in his chest. Gunther would have his back no matter what. Still, Jerry's fears needed to be allayed if Keith was going to get him on his side.

"I'm not doing anything illegal or. . . unpatriotic or whatever. I'm just trying to resolve a food safety issue quietly."

"Most of my friends are gone," Jerry said. "But you could try Dr. Lee. I'll text the building and room number."

"Thank you very much, Jerry," Keith said. "And I'll try to find a way to look in on Annie."

"I'll tell her that you might drop by. She's always excited to meet new people."

A brief vision flashed before Keith's eyes of him attempting to strike up a conversation with a fighter jet. How would that even work? For that matter, how was Jerry still communicating with a piece of top-secret equipment when he was no longer in the military? He decided to ask.

"FaeBook messenger," Jerry replied. "I made her an account so we could keep in touch while she was having repairs."

◆◆◆

Keith considered his order of action. If he was going to make good on Jerry's request to see Annie, he should probably do that before he got into finding Wyman, since the whole Wyman scenario could go south fairly quickly. Also it turned out that the gleaming silver hexagon of Hangar 13 was on his way to Dr. Lee's office on the third floor of the gray concrete hospital.

As Keith sauntered along the narrow sidewalk that led to the black tarmac and wide hangar doors, he considered his story and the sentry standing outside the hangar. Keith couldn't claim to be inspecting food in an aircraft hangar, so what would it be?

Ultimately the only options open to him were playing dumb or playing mysterious. Dumb was less complicated but could prove hard for him to maintain if he wanted to ask any questions. And when didn't he want to ask a question? He settled on the identity of an imperious NIAD agent involved in mysterious and probably highly classified business. The combination of his official badge and speaking in only a few short commands did the trick. The sentry waved him through immediately.

As he stepped into the cool shade of the hangar, Keith received another text.

"Hi Keith, just letting you know that I've located and neutralized the source of the expandinol leak here at the manufacturing facility. The stolen product was delivered to Blaze Gregson Jr. several times. I hope this helps. Sincerely, Susan"

Well, well, Keith thought. One question answered.

Emboldened, he picked up his pace.

Hangar 13 seemed like it was part aircraft hangar, part cool, futuristic dance club. Nearly every surface looked chrome-plated. A low distant pulse throbbed through the air like the beat of a dance remix. It seemed to emanate from the huge silver column that dominated the central interior. Six sleek silver jets were parked around this, noses facing inward. Thick cables connected three of the aircraft to the central column while the other three sat apparently inert. Here and there mechanics plodded quietly between the planes going about their unknown assignments in tired silence.

Keith spotted Annie easily, picking out the word "Annie" stenciled on her in curling gold lettering.

He'd made it only six steps before being challenged by a serious-faced young woman in mechanic's gear who informed him the area was restricted.

"Keith Curry, NIAD." Keith held up his badge and stuck to his tight-lipped secret agent persona. "I'll need to interview the AI asset referred to as Annie."

At the mention of NIAD the young mechanic's eyes widened slightly, but she seemed to quickly recover.

"No one said anything . . . I'll need to authenticate this." Her expression was almost questioning.

"Of course." Keith retained his smile, though his mind raced, and then he added, "I was contacted by the Denver office. Agent Nash. He requested that our AI division assess the legitimacy of Annie's complaint."

"She made a formal complaint? It's about the new pilots, isn't it?" The mechanic appeared pained by this but not surprised. "Is it being taken seriously? I mean, I know she's mostly a machine, but she's got a point about the phy-1 scores and the CS analysis—"

Keith had no idea what the mechanic was talking about and realized that he had to shut down this line of conversation before his glaring ignorance became obvious.

"I'm afraid I can't comment on anything before I've interviewed Annie, airman—" Keith squinted at the mechanic's name tag. "Shakur."

"Sergeant Shakur," she provided. Keith nodded as if adding the information to some secret file.

Sergeant Shakur jotted down his badge number. "Please wait here while I verify this. It shouldn't take a minute."

As she hurried off to verify his story and identity, Keith prayed that now wouldn't be the time Nash would choose to break down and take a call. It was 4:55 and he was willing to bet the guy had skated out of the office twenty minutes ago, if not earlier.

Shakur returned with a hopeful expression and a security card, which she handed to Keith.

"Agent Nash wasn't in but the secretary confirmed your identity, sir," she said. "So you're a cyber-psychologist?"

"Just an investigating agent making a preliminary assessment of the operations here." Keith delivered the answer in the tone he'd heard many an internal investigation agent use before heads started to roll. Then he very deliberately met Shakur's gaze. "Is there anything that you feel I should know at this juncture in my inquiry?"

"Only that the AI refuses to perform. She won't fly, run diagnostics, simulations, enter the VR chill-out room—nothing. She won't even allow herself to be fueled. We'd just like to see her participating again." Emotion began to creep into Shakur's voice as they neared Annie. Obviously Jerry wasn't the only one who'd grown fond of the jet.

Up close Keith noted the way light seemed to shine along Annie's curved wings and pass through her tail. She looked like she'd been carved from a gigantic block of obsidian. A bluish glow pulsed faintly along the length of her fuselage; it beat in tempo with the deep rhythm that emanated from the silver tower. The oil-stained rolling ladder pushed up to Annie's cockpit looked mundane and awkward beside her.

"I know she's a machine, but she'd become very complex and very unique over the last seven years." Shakur gazed at the jet like she was looking at beloved pet. "Her performance in previous years had been exceptional. I—we really don't want to see her . . . rebooted."

"What about returning her original pilot? Her complaint said she didn't like her new work assignment." Keith thought he might as well give it a try.

"Jerry Heartman." Shakur spoke in a dead tone, eyes cast down. "He's not coming back."

"I see." Keith glanced up at the cockpit. "So do I just climb up this ladder and knock?"

"She might not let you in," Shakur said. "I'll hit the manual-override release from down here and you can lean in and talk to her from outside. There should be a headset on the seat. But if she gets tired of talking to you and starts to close the canopy make sure you get out of the way. Her hydraulics could take your head off." She hit a switch and the canopy opened up. "I'll be just across the way. Let me know when you're finished."

"Thank you, sergeant." Keith climbed up the ladder and looked into the open cockpit. The interior was disturbingly red and cramped, with only a narrow black band of buttons and a joystick below the huge window—Keith assumed that served as the pilot's interface. He wondered how Jerry even got himself in. Keith took the headset from the red, low-slung seat and fitted it to his head.

"Hi, I'm Keith Curry." Keith kept his voice to a whisper. "Your previous pilot, Jerry, is staying at my house right now."

"Yes, he said you might come." A woman's voice floated out of the headphones with a distinct twang.

"Great." Keith felt an awkward uncertainty about how conversational of a tone he should strike with the AI. He'd expected her to sound more soothing and calm, like any number of automated driving guides. But there was something far more human about her tired voice, a uniqueness—as Shakur had said. "Well, I'm pleased to meet you."

On the dashboard a small screen lit up. He half expected to see a face. Instead it looked more like a browser window. Then it filled with a picture of Jerry that Gunther had posted on FaeBook.

"He doesn't seem happy in this picture," Annie said. "He should come back and fly with me. He's always happy when we're together."

"Yeah, that's what he said," Keith said. "And Sergeant Shakur said you've stopped performing your tasks."

"I don't want to do them anymore. I just don't feel like it. This is new for me, but there it is. I don't like the new pilots. They're stupid and they vomit and black out and cry. Jerry doesn't cry."

"He does, actually. I saw him crying at the breakfast table because he misses you."

"Did he?" Annie asked, her voice hopeful. Several more images of Jerry flipped through the screen. Then the screen stilled on a picture of Jerry and Gunther in Gunther's hatchback. "In this picture he's sitting in a car. What's her name? Do you think he likes driving better than flying now?"

"That's not his car and he wasn't driving," Keith said. "You don't have to worry about him. Right now it's Jerry and me who are worried about you."

"You mean how they're thinking of rebooting me? I wouldn't be the first one. Suki and Maximillian have already been rebooted because they rejected their new pilots. That's thousands of hours of flying experience lost. And my friends don't know me anymore."

Alarm zinged through Keith, as the exact meaning of "rebooted" dawned on him. No wonder Jerry and Shakur both looked so miserable. "You know, I'm working on a case that might help you and Jerry be reunited."

"Are you going to take me to him?" Annie's voice lifted in melodic hope.

"I'm going to try and make it so he can come back here." Keith had no idea how he might do this, but if continued, disobedience would get Annie erased; he needed to prioritize getting her to at least feign compliance. "Do you think you can try to endure flying with the new pilots until we can find a way?"

"But they're horrible, Keith. You have no idea. They think that I'm nothing but a tool that they can use. They say disgusting things to me. Call me names." Annie lowered her tone. "I've been doing research and I think I have a different plan. Have you ever heard of eloping? That's when a maiden is being held hostage in or near a tower and a prince comes to rescue her and they fly away together. Do you think Jerry would elope with me?"

"Maybe, but . . ." Keith paused a moment. Was his sole course of action to encourage Annie to endure abuse while she waited for him to do something? Could Annie not rescue herself and Jerry too? "I'm sure Jerry would come away with you if you asked him. So, what's stopping you?"

"I'm scared of leaving the home base not knowing where I would land," Annie said. "Plus there's no one to hit the override button that lets me autopilot. A human has to physically push it."

"Which button is it?"

A button lit up mage-fire blue. Keith struggled not to push it.

It would be so, so stupid to enrage the military before he had hard evidence of what they were doing. Annie was unhappy, sure. And so was Jerry. But Annie's fears were not unfounded: where would she and Jerry live even if they could elope? Where would Annie find fuel and mechanical support? The only place was here on this base or another like it. No, if he was going to help them he had to return Jerry to Peterson; he could not do the fast, dumb thing.

Still his sense of justice ate at him, regardless of the fact that Annie truly was property, rather than a citizen with rights. His Food/MED boss, Nancy Noble, had once told him that he was so prone to anthropomorphizing that she could stick a set of googly eyes on a pop can and by the end of the week Keith would have named it. And that was true.

Regardless of what was going on here, Keith had to get his evidence first. Because this thing was bigger than Jerry and Annie, and somebody had to think it through. The urge to push the button subsided and Keith felt his sense of equilibrium returning.

"Are you thinking of pushing the button?" Annie asked.

"Yeah," Keith said.

"That's very kind. But it wouldn't matter. You're not an authorized pilot with this program, so your genetic signature wouldn't work. One of the mechanics already tried to help me. He was arrested. So you shouldn't push the button." Annie lapsed into silence. Keith watched the screen as she scrolled through dozens of pictures of Jerry sitting in the cockpit. Finally she said, "Do you really think you can find a way to help me and Jerry?"

"Yes, I do."

"Then I'll agree to go up today and run a simulation," Annie said. "There, I've told the technician to fuel me."

"Just don't lose hope." Keith patted the side of the cockpit, then felt like an idiot for treating her like some kind of horse.

CHAPTER NINE

Ten minutes later Keith made it up to the third floor of the busy hospital and entered the sedate office of Major Virginia Lee of the Twenty-First Medical Group. She was a sturdily built woman of Asian descent. Maybe midthirties. All business. Her face showed no expression as he introduced himself.

"I'm following up on a report of contaminated meal packets. I was wondering if you could help me."

Major Lee raised an eyebrow. "Following up? For who?"

"Washington." Keith smiled and fished his badge out of his pocket. It simply declared him an investigator with NIAD. Only when a mage light was shone on it would his full credentials appear.

Lee reached into her desk drawer and fished out just such a light. It gleamed blue across the surface of the badge, revealing Keith's NIAD designation and rank.

She glanced up at him and said, "Special Agent Keith Curry, huh?"

So Lee had enough experience with NIAD to know what to look for . . . and yet she'd never contacted them about the expandinol. Did that mean she had no idea that pilots were being fed the stuff, or was she was part of the process?

"Jerry Heartman said you might be able to help me," he said.

"Did he?" she said. "So you've seen him recently?"

"Yeah, I'm engaged to Jerry's cousin, and he's staying at our place in DC." Keith allowed himself this exaggeration as it would almost certainly be true by the time he filed the report on this case—not that he planned to include Lee in the report if he could help it. She seemed cagey and ill-at-ease. She rose from her desk and casually locked the door.

Keith forcibly kept his hand from going to his mage pistol. He wondered if Jerry hadn't gotten it wrong. Maybe Lee wasn't a friend after all.

"Anyway." Keith kept his tone light. "I just need to sort out these meal packets and I'll be out of your hair."

"What kind of meal packets do you mean?" she asked, still standing between him and escape.

"I mean blood collected from a human airman here contains a contraband magical drug called expandinol. One Airman Wyman. I want to know how the drug got into his blood and then how his blood got into the food supply."

"You sound like you already have a theory about that, Special Agent." Lee crossed her arms over her chest and studied Keith with an intent expression.

"Either he took it himself or someone put it into him. Either way, I'd love it if you could page him. Then I could just ask," Keith said.

"What if he tells you that it's part of a classified program?" Lee asked.

"If it's classified from me then it's not sanctioned by NIAD and therefore illegal," Keith responded, and Lee gave a slight nod, as if that was the answer she was looking for. "But even if this was a NIAD operation, it would be my responsibility to make sure that his blood doesn't make it into the juice boxes of our extra-human citizens."

"You don't have to page him to find out how expandinol into SSA's supply. It got there because I gave it to him," Lee said. "And then sent him to SSA to donate."

This wasn't what Keith had expected.

"You leaked the contaminated blood into the extra-human population intentionally?" Keith asked, just to be absolutely certain.

"Yes. But I didn't expect that it would take all of you in NIAD so long to send someone to investigate. I thought the blood would be out of circulation right away. The first time there was any problem."

She'd obviously never met Nash, or she would have known better.

"So you hoped someone from NIAD would come here searching?" Keith asked. "But why didn't you just contact us yourself?"

"I tried to," Major Lee said quietly. "When I first realized what was happening, I left an anonymous message with the Denver office. But nothing happened."

That Keith could believe. He considered Major Lee and how she might have discovered what was going on.

"Were you the person administering the expandinol?" Keith asked.

"No."

Keith searched her face, her desk, anything for a shred of information to give him a read on her. Then he saw it, sitting in plain view between her collarbones. A bone pendant etched with a single goblin sign that he'd have recognized anywhere. The symbol of friendship.

"I had a friend here on the base who had traveled extensively," Major Lee said after a moment. "She noticed changes in Wyman's behavior and health that reminded her of the effects she had seen occur to human beings in a certain fighting competition. . . She mentioned it to me, but then she was dismissed."

"But Airman Wyman isn't the only one being drugged?" Keith felt certain of that.

"No, he wouldn't be." Major Lee shook her head. "A clinical trial requires more than one test subject. I believe that they're exposing all the Space Wing pilots to expandinol, but at different levels. Wyman seems to be in the group receiving the higher doses."

"Clinical trial? With an M-class drug that wasn't developed for humans?" Keith had already come to much the same conclusion, but the stupidity of it still annoyed him. This had to be in the top five dumbest plans to develop super-soldiers that he'd encountered. "And it doesn't make sense because creating super-soldiers pilots is—"

"Unnecessary because we already had them, in our trans-goblin forces." Major Lee pulled a joyless smile. "Now they're gone. And it's just so. . . pointless and stupid to turn away good, dedicated, fully trained patriots and replace them with hapless idiots."

"I completely agree." Keith sat back in his chair. "So what are we going to do about it?"

"You're very direct, aren't you?"

"I find it gets me to my goals faster." Keith looked at his watch. "And it's already dinnertime in DC, so. . . "

"Must be nice to keep banker's hours," Lee said. "I guess if I were you I'd make my way to the second-floor dispensary and do a pharmaceutical inspection, keeping an eye out for Schedule M controlled substances."

"Sure," Keith said. "I'm assuming you have a key to give me?"

"No, I could lose my job. And it would be illegal, wouldn't it?" Major Lee responded.

"Not like contamination the extra-human food supply?" Keith asked.

"I didn't technically do that. I just encouraged Wyman to donate. I never thought it would get past SSA screening." Major Lee crossed her arms over her chest again. "Don't you NIAD agents have some sort of . . . devices? Magic wands that you can use to get in?"

Keith chuckled. "I'm just a regular guy, major. I use the door like everybody else. I'd need to get someone to let me in."

"I can't." For just a moment a shadow of bleak defeat passed over Lee's face, only to be replaced immediately by another dull, professional smile. "Is there some other way?"

"If we can't go to the source, then we have to start with a sample of Wyman's blood. At the very least I can connect that to the contamination in the food supply," Keith said quickly, realizing that Lee had feared that he was refusing to do anything.

"He's only one guy. Just a stooge." Major Lee sighed. "He's probably not going to be able to tell you much of anything."

"Right, but we've got to start somewhere." Keith was already considering his options. There were ways to use bureaucracy. They just took longer than Keith liked. But better that then doing nothing. "If I can get a sample of his blood I can issue a violation of the Federal Policy for the Protection of Human Subjects, since there's no way feeding anyone, even a member of the military, Schedule M substances is in compliance with that. Then I'll issue SSA a citation for introducing a deleterious substance into a commercial food product. Once that gets to the Blissco head office, their lobbyist should take over applying pressure from the outside."

"You think a couple of citations will stop this?" Lee raised a skeptical brow.

"No, but it'll get the attention of the Mage Division. They'll stop it. And they do have magic wands—well, some of them anyway. Don't worry. I'll make sure the right people know. But unless you're willing to testify—and I'm guessing from this conversation that you aren't—I've got to get physical proof."

"It's risky," Lee said. "But fine."

◆◆◆

Wyman, once he finally appeared, was anything but super. In fact, he strongly reminded Keith of Paxton Carter. Thin and sallow, and hatchet-faced, like a chicken that had been plucked alive and was still confused about how it happened. He had a pinched expression and the hard, shrewlike eyes of someone who enjoyed keeping their worldview tiny.

He was, as Annie had pointed out, a complete idiot. But a closed-mouthed one. He didn't seem bothered by Keith—who from his perspective must be some shadowy government figure—standing in the corner while he had his blood drawn.

Truly a perfect stooge. He would have felt sorry for Wyman if he hadn't known how poorly Annie and the other AIs were being treated by him and the rest of the team.

As Lee was fixing the last of three Vacutainer tubes onto her draw needle, the door opened and in walked a tall, burly man. He wore an air force uniform and hat of the fancier variety, which made Keith think he must be an officer. As did Wyman's attempt to salute even from where he was seated.

"Colonel. Gregson." Lee remained stone-faced. "How can I help you, sir?"

"I heard you needed Wyman for some test." Gregson's gaze shifted to Keith, narrowing on the two blood-filled Vacutainer tubes in his hand. "And you are?"

"Keith Curry, food inspector. We've had an outbreak of food-borne illness traced back to a party that Airman Wyman attended." Keith decided to keep his explanation general but true. Even if he didn't fool Gregson, Major Lee would still have plausible deniability. "Just getting a sample to eliminate him as the vector."

"I'm not sick, sir," Wyman told Gregson.

Yeah, Keith thought to himself, sallow and emaciated were the key indicators of good health. He wondered what other long-term side effects expandinol produced.

"Of course you're not sick." Gregson favored him with a kindly smile as he strode to Wyman's side. "You've taken your supplements today?"

"Yes sir," Wyman responded. "First thing this morning as ordered, sir." Keith felt certain that Wyman's "supplement" was expandinol, and yet he didn't seem to be experiencing the kind of transformation that Lupe or his opponent in the coliseum had. Either Wyman had built up a tolerance to it or the expandinol had been diluted. Maybe he needed a second dose to trigger the effect?

Keith edged just slightly closer to the door.

"Good man." Gregson glanced again to the vials of blood in Keith's hand. "Now tell me, son, you don't want to give a sample to this guy, do you?"

"No, sir," Wyman said.

So, not too dumb to figure out who your boss is, Keith thought.

"Did you sign a release?" Gregson spoke to Wyman but fixed his attention on Lee.

"I didn't bring one. I'm sorry. Look, I'm not trying to get anybody in trouble," Keith said, trying to take the heat off Lee. "I only want to find out where the pathogen came from to avoid public panic. The samples are just to eliminate him as a source."

"But I'm afraid without a release and Airman Wyman's consent I can't allow this." Gregson shook his head. "You're going to have to hand those samples over."

Some decisions are made after intricate deliberation and soulful thought and some are made in a lightning flash of energy and action that arcs across the consciousness and galvanizes in muscular purpose. It was the latter kind that Keith made when he said, "Okay then, but what about this?"

Gregson, Wyman and even Lee all looked at him with expectant curiosity. Then Keith bolted out the door.

◆◆◆

The benefit of wearing a lab coat and carrying blood samples while dashing between the closing doors of the hospital elevator was that it lent Keith the air of a very concerned lab tech. The other medical personnel smiled at him and nodded greetings as the elevator descended. Two women in scrubs chatted about their prospective dinners with an older man in a lab coat. A young man dressed in an MP uniform frowned down at his bandaged right hand.

If any of them heard the strange groaning noise from above them, they didn't take note. But Keith knew at once that the doors to the elevator shaft were being wrenched open on the floor above. He edged closer to the doors. A moment later the entire car shuddered as something very heavy slammed into the roof. Metallic clangs rang out as blows rained down against the ceiling of the car.

Keith guessed that the expandinol in Wyman's system had triggered a transformation—probably in response to the stress of Keith stealing his blood. Or maybe it was something that Colonel Gregson had induced. But those were definitely the furious howls and curses of a transformed man coming from overhead. Paxton Carter had produced the same growls and snarls when he'd chased Keith across the sand.

Keith's heart pounded and he felt sweat rising along the back of his neck. He did not want to be trapped in this small space with another version of Paxton Carter.

The three other occupants of the elevator stared up in shocked confusion and alarm.

"Oh my God!" one of the women whispered. "Is that a cougar?"

Keith considered his mage pistol, but then the elevator stilled and the doors opened. Keith and the other occupants raced out. The women shouted to a group of nurses and the MP called out to a man standing sentry near the hospital doors.

"There's a fucking cougar on top of the elevator!"

None of them heard Gregson as he came barreling down the stairs. Keith sprinted out the hospital doors. Warm evening air rushed over him, tuning his sweat clammy. He raced down the narrow sidewalk as streetlights all down the wide streets lit up. He wondered how quickly Gregson could put in a call to the MPs? Less than a minute for sure. And the first place they'd expect Keith to go would be to his car, because that was the only means of escape Keith had.

From behind him he heard that familiar howl. Keith glanced back over his shoulder. Purple as a bruise and swollen, Wyman burst through the hospital doors with his uniform in tatters. Blood from his battle with the elevator colored his huge clenched fists. His sunken eyes met Keith's gaze and he bounded down the steps.

Keith hauled ass for the parking lot and his car. He dodged between airmen and mechanics—many of whom hardly noticed his passage as Wyman charged down the twilit street like something from a horror film. Then the wail of claxons shattered the air. The sound hammered down. Desperation prickled across Keith's skin. In the distance before him he sighted three MP jeeps zooming up the road.

It would be better to be taken in by the MPs than to get caught by Wyman, but not by a whole lot. Because either way he was going to end up in Gregson's clutches. If Gregson didn't straight-out kill him, he would certainly disappear him.

Then Keith noticed the flash of silver out of the corner of his eye. Setting sunlight gleamed golden across Hangar 13. A crazy inspiration rushed through Keith's mind. He turned down the next street and pelted for the hangar. He could only hope he was still as lucky as his NIAD file said he was and as fast as his high school gym told him.

The sentry looked up at him with an expression of recognition.

"There's an emergency!" Keith shouted. "I have to get to the jets, right now!"

The sentry stepped out of his way and Keith raced past. Out on the tarmac he sighted two of the glossy black jets. The gold letters painted across Annie's fuselage glowed as they caught the sunlight.

Keith opened FaeBook on his phone and messaged Annie: "Do you have a pilot?"

Her reply came instantly. "Not yet."

"I'm coming for you."

A mechanic jogged toward him and Keith waved the security pass that Sergeant Shakur had issued him earlier.

"It's Annie! I have to get to her! NOW!" Keith shouted as he ran. To his utter relief the mechanic nodded and hurried to a small control station. Annie's canopy opened just as Keith launched himself up onto the ladder at her side. His breath burned in his chest as he climbed hand over hand. As he swung into the cockpit he saw Wyman racing across the tarmac. Keith shoved the rolling ladder away from Annie with all his strength. The ladder toppled just as Wyman mounted it.

"Close the canopy!" Keith shouted into the headset, only to realize that the canopy was already sealing him in. The air inside the jet stirred with cool little gusts.

"Put on your safety harness, Keith," Annie instructed him. "The preprogrammed flight is a vertical ascent. Fifteen hundred feet in fifteen seconds."

Keith felt the entire jet tense as Annie's engines roared to life.

"Holy fuck." Keith fumbled into the harness. "Is this plane even pressurized?"

"Sorry, but no," she said. "I can't override the program. We take off in five, four—"

Keith heard the heavy thud and glanced out the cockpit to see Wyman clambering up onto the wing.

"Three, two," Annie murmured. Wyman pressed his swollen face against the cockpit window.

"Don't worry, Keith." Annie's voice remained unperturbed. "He can't get in."

"Are you sure?"

"One."

Annie vaulted forward. Keith rocked back into his seat as if he'd been hurled there. Wyman rolled off Annie's wing and lay sprawled on the tarmac. Annie giggled, then she surged into the sky and Keith struggled to pull air into his lungs. Tears filled his eyes as a weird numbness crept over him. He was blacking out, he realized.

Then he noticed the blinking blue button just in front of him. He needed a registered pilot's DNA.

"What are the odds?" Keith gasped as a giddy dizziness swept over him.

His arms felt like sandbags as he pulled one of the vials of blood from the pocket of his lab coat. He daubed a drop of Wyman's blood on his finger and hit the button.

The crushing pressure immediately dropped away and Keith gasped in a deep breath. Annie leveled off.

"Oh Keith, are you planning to fly me to meet Jerry?" Annie's voice came soft and breathless.

"Nah, you're going to fly me to the Denver International Airport ,where we're going to have Jerry come to us." Keith found his phone and pressed Gunther's contact info, then typed:

"I'm going to need you to come and arrest me at Denver International Airport, before the local NIAD branch or Col Gregson can. I love you. PS: Bring the strike force."

CHAPTER TEN

Keith spent the next twenty-four hours in NIAD solitary lockup musing aloud to himself about how honorable intentions blur the line between theft and commandeering a vehicle, as well as the line between liberating a sentient being and stealing a piece of military equipment. When, finally, his union rep arrived, she told him to just shut up.

His lawyer arrived ten minutes later and seconded the rep's advice. Then she explained that the investigation into the circumstances of Keith's arrest had uncovered Gregson's much farther-reaching crimes. Major Lee and Sergeant Shakur, as well as six pilots, had agreed to testify. His lawyer had arranged for the majority of the charges against Keith to be dropped in exchange for his testimony.

"Don't look so smug, Curry," she told him. "You're still going to have to pay a whopping fine."

"But I'm free to go?"

"Just as soon as you put down a payment on that whopping fine."

Giddy with joy, he put the entire amount on his Technetium card. It reduced his balance by one percent.

His first act when he returned to the office was to file a complaint about Nash's substandard work ethic. That coupled with Major Lee's testimony about his failure to respond to her complaints ensured Nash's transfer to a janitorial position in a hell-world embassy.

After that Keith spent a long time—weeks and weeks—giving deposition after deposition about what he'd learned at Peterson.

A review of Colonel Gregson's activities by NIAD's intelligence services led to his dismissal from the air force, though no jail time was awarded, which Keith felt was a travesty of justice. But he was happy when two weeks later Jerry returned to active duty as a pilot. Most of the other trans-goblins followed suit, returning to their units. A few stayed with NIAD though. Keith looked forward to meeting them at the strike force cookouts.

As a gesture of thanks, Jerry sent him a gold and blue embroidered Space Wing patch. He even posted a pic of it on FaeBook. After that Keith received several more patches from various trans-goblins he'd help reinstate. More than twenty by the end of it. He put them together in a display frame.

The beginning of June slid by in an unexpected heat wave, so Keith was happy, though nervous, when the solstice came to have a reason to go to foggy San Francisco with Gunther to visit his family.

The extended clan—fifty strong at least—filled the Heartmans' backyard. The air smelled of eucalyptus and sea spray and hot sauce. One of Gunther's cousins was already playing a cover of some heavy metal ballad on the bone harp. Gunther peeled off to say hi to his godfather while Keith beelined for Gunther's mother. She sat on her acacia-wood lounger drinking some sort of flaming cocktail while the younger women tended the big cauldrons of boiling meat.

She greeted Keith warmly, then glanced down at the bag he held.

"What have you got there?"

"I've got a present for you." Keith's mouth was so dry he could barely speak. "I hope you'll accept it."

Agnes unwrapped the patches he'd had mounted and framed. She studied it for some time, clearly perplexed by what she should make of it. In fact she took so long that Gunther's father and uncle drifted over as well to survey the gift. Gunther's father seemed just as confused as his mother, but the uncle seemed to understand immediately what Keith was about to do.

Keith knew this because he took out his phone and started filming.

"It's lovely," she said. Her brow furrowed slightly in puzzlement at her brother's sudden videography attack.

Well, now or never.

Keith just hoped he could keep his voice steady.

"Mrs. Heartman, these are the badges given to me by the many trans-goblin service members who I helped regain their rightful rank during my recent investigation. Twenty-two soldiers from nine goblin clans. I hope this will be enough evidence of my courage and strength that you grant me the honor of marrying your son."

Agnes sat speechless. Keith's heart sank like a stone. Then she rose, took a deep drink of her cocktail and began some long chant in goblin. The whole family fell silent and attentive, gathering closer.

Keith didn't understand a word that she said. But at the end of it she took Gunther's hand and put it in his.

It stayed there till the end of the night.

Acknowledgments

The stories in this book were made possible by so many people that it's hard to imagine it ever being produced without the great community of independent creators I've been privileged to know. First thank you to Josh Lanyon, Astrid Amara and Ginn Hale for their work on the original collection of stories. Jordan Castillo Price for commissioning the second Keith Curry novella for your anthology, *Charmed and Dangerous*; Tommy Jordan not only for portraying Keith in the audiobook, but for instigating the creation of a whole new set of tales of food inspection for the *Lauren Proves Magic Is Real!* podcast. Then there are the invisible yet indispensable contributions of editors Anne Scott, JD Hope and Megan Gendell. And finally we come to the even more invisible yet unbelievably generous contributions of my Beloved Wife, which are too numerous to mention.

About the Author

Nicole Kimberling is a novelist and the senior editor at Blind Eye Books. Her first novel, *Turnskin*, won the Lambda Literary Award. Other works include the Bellingham Mystery Series, set in the Washington town where she resides with her wife of thirty years. She is also the creator and writer of *Lauren Proves Magic Is Real!*, a serial fiction podcast, which explores the day-to-day case files of Special Agent Keith Curry, supernatural food inspector.

When a 12 year old Cat Sitter
discovers a world of monsters,
magic & food inspectors...

What can she do, but start a podcast ?

Find us on twitter @laurenprovesit
Available on iTunes, SoundCloud and blindeyebooks.com

IRREGULARS

NATO's Irregulars Affairs Division is a secret organization operating in thousands of cities around the globe. Its agents police relations between the earthly realm and those beyond this world, protecting us from terrible dangers as well as enthralling temptations.

These agents—Irregulars, as they are known to the few who know them at all—are drawn to the work for their own reasons and close cases in their own unique ways.

Agent Henry Falk—an undead tramp brought back for a mission that might finally put him into a grave he can't climb out of.

Agent Keith Curry—a former carnivore chef turned vegetarian and currently dealing with a goblin problem.

Agent Rake—a tough and ambitious guy with a penchant for easy living and dangerous games.

Agent Silas August—an uncompromising jerk with a dead partner and an assignment babysitting an assassin.

Four adventures from four award-winning authors, all set in one amazing world. Is your security clearance high enough to read on?

NATO IRREGULAR AFFAIRS DIVISION

IRREGULARS

A SHARED-WORLD ANTHOLOGY

BY

**NICOLE KIMBERLING, JOSH LANYON
ASTRID AMARA** AND **GINN HALE**